MERCY FORSAKEN

MEREDETH CONNELLY MIND HUNT THRILLERS
BOOK ONE

E.H. Vick

DARK TRIAD PUBLISHING
NEW YORK

Dark Triad Publishing
769 Broadway #1060
Manhattan, NY 10003

Publisher's Note: This is a work of fiction. Names, characters, places, and incidents are a product of the author's imagination. Locales and public names are sometimes used for atmospheric purposes. Any resemblance to actual people, living or dead, or to businesses, companies, events, institutions, or locales is completely coincidental.

Mercy Forsaken/ E.H. Vick. -- 1st ED.
ISBN 978-1-951509-28-6

TABLE OF CONTENTS

DEDICATION

For my great uncle, Special Agent C. Edwin Glass, who loved to tell me funny stories about the Federal Bureau of Investigation.

I hope you enjoy *Mercy Forsaken*. If so, please consider joining my online community—details can be found at the end of the last chapter.

CHAPTER 1

THE FIFTH KILL

Hanable's Valley, NY

MEREDETH CONNELLY GRIMACED as she stepped into the young boy's room. Her gaze drifted around the room—a sailboat in a storm-tossed sea—from the open closet over-stuffed with cheap toys and little else to the battered dresser with its hanging, open drawers, then across the threadbare carpet and up to the bed and away. Each time the bed and its blood-soaked pillow swam through her awareness her frown deepened. The coroner had already taken the remains, which was about the only thing Meredeth could count as a positive in the whole stinking trailer.Brushing her auburn hair behind her ear and biting her lower lip, Meredeth closed her eyes—squeezed them shut, as though that might change the scene before her—and drew in a deep breath, then instantly regretted it. The smell of the blood, the wastes released by the two people who had died in the sweltering little mobile home, the mold, and everything else invaded her sinuses like an evil red tide.Unbidden, a scene invaded her mind. Humid air that stank of mold and earth and sweat swam around her head, while wooden beams creaked and thudded above her. But rather than pleasant sounds—not the relaxing tune of a hammock swung by the wind, nor the bump of a wave-kissed fishing boat rubbing against a well-loved dock—the staccato rattle-thump of a brawl overhead pounded out the rhythm for the sorrowful lament of a hangman's rope rubbing against the gallows pole as a corpse swung in the afternoon breeze.

Meredeth shook her head, then darted a glance over her shoulder—careful to keep her expression neutral, cold. The local policeman stood behind Bobby Van Zandt, hovering, going up on his tiptoes to see the famous FBI agent do her magic, grunting a little like a school kid wanting his teacher to call on him. Bobby knew what she wanted without anything as prosaic as her saying it aloud. He knew she wanted the local cops kept out of her way until she was ready to talk, and he was good at running quiet, if chucklesome interference. She fought a sigh and won, though it was a close thing.

She steeled herself, then turned her cold, assessing gaze on the bloodstained bed and the noisome narrative she could read from it. She noted the way the blood had pooled—not splattered, pooled—on and beneath the pillow. Her gaze crawled to the walls that the bed touched on two sides. Nothing. No secondary splatter, no gray matter, nothing.

Taking a single step deeper into the cloud of odors, Meredeth grimaced at the olfactory assault—a safe expression, since no one could see her face anyway. A black-ringed hole penetrated the pillow, and gray matter coated the bullet's path as well as the surface of the pillowcase. The tendons in her jaw creaked, and she forced it to relax, only then realizing how much her molars and jaw ached.

"Got him in his sleep, right?" asked the officer.

Meredeth didn't answer, and after a heartbeat, she heard Bobby turning and dropping one tanned, manicured hand on the cop's shoulder. "Come on," said Bobby. "Let's see if we can round up some coffee."

"But—"

"Only take a minute," said Bobby, and Meredeth could hear his wide, shit-eating grin in his voice.

"Well..."

"Come on, I think better with a little black-gold in my bloodstream."

As their footsteps retreated, her mouth dropped open, and she exhaled in a silent wail. The victim would have turned seven in two months. She pinched the bridge of her nose, feeling the maelstrom coming, and hoping the headache this scene induced would leave her a modicum of dignity, that it wouldn't lay her out. Once again, she closed the gruesome scene out by squeezing her eyes shut.

Her vision flashed—red, blue, red—and the memory of the creaking scene came crawling back to the front of her mind, bringing with it the scent of copper and butcher-shop and the heat, always the heat. A door slammed, and she started, fear blossoming in her belly like a spring flower. She snapped her eyes open and turned away from the bed, looking into the closet instead, sending her gaze somewhere *safe*. Whatever the brain bubble was, she didn't recognize the memory as her own, and she sent it on its merry way.

Shaking her head, she spun and walked back into the hall as silent as a burglar, turning away from the living room and Bobby's yuck-yuck-yuck patter, her gaze frozen on the darkened maw of the so-called master suite, which, except for its closet-sized bathroom, wouldn't be much bigger than the other bedrooms. As she passed the communal bath, she glanced inside, cataloging the mess, the mold, and the cheap toilet paper as she did.

The master was in the same messy state—and whoever had processed the scene hadn't helped that one bit. Her gaze rested on the bedclothes, which lay on the floor as if tossed aside in a valiant—yet doomed—attempt to protect the little boy down the hall. The woman had taken the first .40 caliber round high in the chest on her left side, just above her collarbone—as if she hadn't stayed where the killer had expected her to stay.

Did you make it to him? she wondered. *Did he make noise, wake you up? Is the murdering bastard's skin under your nails?* Her eyes stung momentarily—even after twenty-three years investigating wanton acts of violence and terror, acts of maternal heroism still got to her. She knew this poor woman thought she had a chance. *But you didn't, momma. The .40 Caliber Killer always kills the littlest kid first. Always. You're still a hero, sweety, because you went after the son of a bitch, anyway.*

Blood splattered the wall above the bed—flung there by that first assassin's round. The second slug had gone where he'd wanted it...or close enough. It hadn't drilled through her left eye, like the slug the unsub had put into the boy, but from what the coroner had told her on the phone as they raced down from Buffalo, he hadn't missed by more than an eighth of an inch. *Pretty impressive shooting. Hit her in the torso to straighten her up? Maybe spin her a little? Delay her long enough to set up the headshot?* She shook her head. That kind of shooting, the cold assessment and snap decisions required, spoke to advanced training and long experience. *More experience than just the four previous murders we tagged him with.*

The coroner had also told her about a series of post-mortem gunshot wounds that peppered Debra Besson's chest. *Why'd you do that? Why did you shoot her five more times? What did she do that required Momma Besson to take a little more punishment?*

Her practiced gaze swept the room, noting that nothing appeared to be missing, that the brief fight hadn't disturbed the knickknacks, hairbrushes, and cheap perfume on the dresser. She saw no additional blood splatter—only the wall above the bed from the first shot, and the mess half on and half off the fitted sheet. *Hope you hurt him, hon. I really do.* Her breath hitched in her throat. *God speed.* After another silent, jaw-stretching wail, she pushed her emotions away, feeding that demon deep inside her, the one that caused the headaches... What other choice did she have?

One last look, then she composed her face in the flat calm everyone expected—as though her brain was solid-state, and her blood could chill ice—and headed out to the front of the trailer. As she entered the living room, the policeman's face lit up with that puppy-dog excitement she detested.

Still, she didn't hold it against him—not really. He was young, and the excitement overrode his horror. At least for the moment. *He probably doesn't know he looks like a ghoul.* She nodded to him, then turned her gaze on Bobby. "Coffee?"

"You got it, boss," he said with a wink at the local officer. He strode to the counter separating the kitchen from the living area and grabbed a Styrofoam cup with a lid on it.

Officer Carlsbad or Carson or Carlton—*whatever*, she thought—leaned forward, light dancing in his eyes. She nodded at Bobby and took the offered cup, taking a long sip to forestall the eager cop as long as possible.

"Seen enough?" he asked.

"Too much," grumbled Meredeth.

He gave her the expression, then—the one all the young local cops gave her when she said something like that—a little confused, a little unbelieving. "Did you...get anything?" He waved his Styrofoam coffee cup at the hallway. "Back in there?"

"Garson, I told you," said Bobby, "it's not ESP. It's science."

"Yeah," said Officer Garson with a frenetic bob of the head. "I mean, I know it's not ESP, but she's a profiler"—he snatched his gaze from Bobby to Meredeth—"you are a profiler, right? From that Behavior Analysis Unit?"

She swallowed the coffee and nodded. "Behavioral Analysis Unit, but yeah."

"Right, right. I always get that wrong." Garson did his best not to leer at her like a goon.

"I assume he picked the lock?" she asked.

Garson nodded. "We think so. There are some scratches on the knob outside."

Meredeth nodded, then cut her gaze to Bobby. "And there's something new this time? Besides..." She waved toward the master bedroom with her free hand.

Garson glanced down the hall, then brightened. "Oh! Right! C'mon, I'll show you." He turned and fast-walked to the door, then pushed out through it.

With a one-sided grin, Bobby waved her on, falling into step behind Meredeth as she walked out into the brisk spring morning, putting on his ridiculous, black-tinted aviator glasses as though his eyes couldn't stand even a hint of direct sunlight.

Garson was already down the small deck's steps, heading around the end of the trailer. "We found her out back."

"Want me to shoot him?" asked Bobby sotto voce, then smiled his perfect smile, his perfect white teeth standing out against his perfectly tanned cheeks.

"Too much paperwork," she said with the best she could do for a smile. From Bobby's expression, she hadn't done all that well. "Keep him off me as best you can."

"You know it, Mere. I always do."

She nodded once, then followed the patrolman through the dew and mud, grimacing at the state of her sensible, yet dressy new shoes as she squelched through the grass.

Around the back of the trailer, Garson stood looking at the muddy ground beneath an open window. He waved his coffee cup at the swath of mud, the long skid, the body-shaped depression. "She fell," he said. "See that dent that looks like she landed on her hip?"

"Her name?"

"Katrin," said Garson. "The daughter. Fourteen or fifteen." He whirled around, slopping coffee over his wrist and not seeming to notice. "He got her over there. She almost made it."

"Where did he hit her?"

The officer's expression flickered, almost a grimace. "Two shots. Neck and head."

Meredeth raised her eyebrows and nodded, walking toward the rectangle staked out in the well-kept "yard" of the next trailer. Garson was right—she'd almost made it around the corner. *Smart girl,* she thought. *If you'd been two steps faster...if you hadn't slipped in that damn mud...* She turned and looked back at the Besson's poor excuse for a trailer, at the green algae blooming on its sides, at the missing piece of lattice under the trailer beneath the window. "He fired from inside?"

"As best as I can figure it." Officer Garson waved a hand at the mud. "No sign but hers."

"What did the CSI team say?"

Garson laughed. "We got three cars, Agent Connelly. We don't have a CSI team."

She frowned, her gaze flicking to Bobby. "Tell me the scene has been processed."

Bobby shrugged. "The chief of police did it."

"The chief..." She closed her eyes.

"He used to be a statie," said Garson. "He was BCI with the state police. Murders. Kidnappings. All that."

"Maybe we can have the State Police CSI team come in to process the scene?" said Bobby as if the thought had just struck him. He really was exceptional at the bonhomie routine.

Garson frowned. "The chief—"

"Oh, I know, I know," said Bobby, striding toward the man and putting a brotherly arm around his shoulders. "But the state's paying all those CSI guys, right? They need something to do. Let's go give them a call. What do you say?"

Garson looked at him uncertainly. "Well... I'll have to clear it with the chief."

Bobby nodded as if that had been his plan all along. "Of course! Let's head back to your car and call him, get this road on the show." Back in Quantico, the running joke was that Bobby could sell shoes to a snake, and watching him handle the locals, Meredeth believed it.

Garson sipped his coffee, squinting a suddenly shrewd gaze at Meredeth. "Uh. Sure, okay." His gaze said, *What do you think you know about me*? *Think you're better than me, Ms. FBI agent*? After a brief, probing look, he turned and started back toward his car.

She'd seen it at least a thousand times before and knew from experience that part of his budding hostility came from her demeanor—that cold, calculated FBI profiler expression she'd picked up somewhere along the line. She rubbed her eyes with her thumb and forefinger, already feeling the spikes behind her left eye, the pounding in her brow, the throbbing at the base of her neck. "This damn headache," she said, loud enough for Garson to hear it across the yard. "Bobby, bring me my aspirin when you come back, would you?" A bitter scowl threatened as she said it, knowing the aspirin would help about as much as a bullet to the brain. It was a prop—that bottle of aspirin—no matter how much she wished otherwise. "Maybe after that kicks in, Officer Garson, I'll be a little less FBI, a little less imposing." She flashed a brief grin, letting her professional expression slip a little, and he nodded once—slowly. "I grew up in a town a little smaller than this. I know how important it is to make do with what you've got, but we need the extra help, and not just in Hanable's Valley."

Garson's face relaxed—not quite into a smile but close. He nodded once more, then turned back toward his car. Bobby caught her eye and gave her that little wink that said he approved as if he were the senior special agent with two decades of experience, and she was only seven years out of the Academy and a canonical example of a blue-flamer—the half-admiring, half-dismissive term for overeager agents whose dedication to the FBI leaves them no room for a life outside of it.

She gave him as much of a smile as she could manage before she turned back to examining the yard. The chief had probably not screwed anything up—not if he really had been an investigator for the New York State Police Bureau of Criminal Investigation. He'd likely measured the distance between the taped-off rectangle marking where the poor girl's life had drained into the rich black soil and the trailer she'd lived in. *Marked it down in his report, no doubt.*

With a shrug, Meredeth paced it off anyway. At just under five foot ten inches tall, her stride was an even twenty-eight inches, and it took fourteen of them to reach the budding mud-pit underneath the window. Almost thirty-three feet. She turned and held up her right hand, mimicking holding her pistol. An eleven-yard headshot, in the dark, and with a running target. You only missed once, and even that stray round hit your target? If that were true, it would mean he was either extremely lucky or a godlike hand with a gun. She squinted at the exposed wall of the neighboring trailer, then her gaze darted up to the window, expecting either the unapologetic stare of a lookie-loo or rustling window coverings. Instead, she saw nothing but blinds that hung in perfect, funeral parlor stillness.

Meredeth walked around the staked-out rectangle, studying the vinyl sheeting, but the damn headache had brought a friend—an ocular migraine in her left eye—making her distance vision less than stellar. *I don't have time for this. Not today, not this week, not this month.* Of course, chastising herself did nothing to relieve her symptoms and probably made them worse.

In the pocket of her jacket, her phone beeped and jangled, and a lightning bolt of pain shot through her left eye. She knew the snippet of the song all too well—it was a custom notification for the cyberstalker Bobby referred to as her "secret admirer," the man that had been sending her taunting emails for about a year. In other words, for any email in which she was both the sender and the receiver. She silenced the phone without taking it out of her pocket. *Sorry, bucko. No time for idle chitchat today.*

She didn't see it until she was five steps away—and had closed her left eye—but it was there. A tiny, slightly smaller than a half-inch diameter hole punched through the siding. She turned back and looked. It was a laser-straight line through that taped-off rectangle and the window of the Besson trailer. She stepped up to it and squinted her right eye to peer into the hole, hoping for an easy round to extract, something they hadn't managed to find in the other five scenes. Meredeth frowned at the hole, stepping back. The slug had punched all the way through.

Her gaze snapped to the window, to the still horizontal blinds behind the glass. She stood stock-still for a heartbeat, thinking hard, and then she was running. "Van Zandt! Garson!" she shouted. She didn't know if they could hear her, if they were already ensconced in the Hanable's Valley Police Department Crown Vic, but she didn't slow a whit, didn't stray from her path toward the trailer's front stoop.

She pounded up the four wooden steps, her head pounding in time with the rhythm of her footfalls, threw a glance over her shoulder, and shouted for the two men again, this time raising her volume to a skull-splitting level that made her vision pulse in her left eye. She slid to a stop in front of the door and pounded on the flimsy thing, rattling it in its frame, rattling the frame in the wall, then froze as an errant memory flooded her mind: footsteps thudding up other wooden steps, another fist pounding on a different light door, and a horrible foreboding filled her in the present. After a moment, she took control of her emotions and thrust them down deep, thrust the unrecognizable thoughts (*memories*?) away.

After a quick glance behind her, she pounded on the door again, this time holding her breath, straining her ears, listening for any sign of life from within. She heard the quiet mid-morning sounds of trailer parks everywhere but nothing from inside the trailer. She lifted her hand and hammered the door again, then turned and crossed the gray deck to the side closest to the Besson trailer. "Van Zandt!" she cried, then squeezed her eyes shut and held onto the rail as the world swayed, and the dancing sick in her guts made a try for fresh air and the freedom to splatter her pants and shoes.

She blinked her eyes open, taking the world, the damn spring sunlight, the annoying bright green of nature reasserting herself, in brief, bite-sized chunks. It was enough to know Bobby had finally heard her. He was coming with his pistol drawn—of course—concern for her splashed all over his chiseled face. Garson, to give him his proper due, was half a step behind. His pistol still hung in his holster, but his eyes were bright, and his gaze was fixed on her face.

"What?" shouted Bobby, and she winced.

"He missed. At least once. Through-and-through." She waved her hand toward the vinyl-covered wall. "No movement inside. Couldn't rouse anyone." The sick swirling in her belly lunged up her throat, and she slammed her teeth together.

"Maybe she's at the grocery store," muttered Garson, worry etching the words into something sharp and ragged. "Mildred Constantine's place. She teaches second grade. Used to, anyway. She helped me get the hang of reading."

Meredeth waved at the locked door. "I don't see signs of a break-in. Maybe we should contact her next-of-kin and get—"

Garson glanced at her, brow knotted, a certain wildness in his eye, then turned and bashed the door in with his shoulder. His momentum carried him inside, and he yelled, "Mrs. Constantine? It's Richie! Richie Garson!"

Bobby followed Garson into the trailer's dark interior. Meredeth took a step to follow, her head spinning, her gaze locked on the dark rectangle. Fear tickled her belly, but not for the present, not for anything in Mildred Constantine's trailer at all.

"Mrs. Constantine? Are you here?" Bobby shouted. "It's the police, ma'am."

Meredeth followed the men inside, not bothering to sing out. She knew what awaited them down the hall, knew it in her gut. Garson had gone toward the back of the trailer, and Bobby stood in the living room, glancing back at her. She jerked her head toward the hall, then turned—the picture of savage weariness—and followed Garson toward the back of the trailer.

Garson knocked softly on the master bedroom door, then glanced back at her, his eyes a study in anxiety.

Meredeth wanted to say something, to say anything that would help, but nothing ever could. She nodded him onward, encouraging him to investigate the bedroom—which was twenty feet past the bullet hole in the exterior wall.

Garson closed his eyes for a heartbeat, then said, "Mrs. Constantine, I'm coming in." He hesitated, his hand hovering over the knob. "Please be dressed," he muttered before turning the knob and disappearing inside.

Meredeth stopped at the bathroom door and opened it softly. She looked inside and shook her head, just as Richie Garson stepped back into the hall.

"She's not here," he said, then his gaze flicked to the bathroom door and then on to hers. "Is she..."

"Yes, Officer Garson. Richie. She's in here." As she swung the door closed again, an almost overwhelming sadness assaulted her. Despair born from yet another senseless death in a career full of them. Her head hurt. Her brain felt loose, her skull so much crushed calcium.

Garson swallowed hard and squeezed his eyes shut.

"You go on outside, Richie," said Meredeth in her best motherly tone. "Let me take care of her."

His eyes opened, and he shook his head. "No, I should—"

"Richie, let me do this. You don't need to see her this way. Don't *want* to see her this way."

His eyes slid shut once again, and once again, his Adam's apple bobbed as he swallowed convulsively.

Meredeth shot Bobby a glare, and he started, then said, "Come on, Richie. Let's allow Meredeth to make her ready for the people who'll be coming. We need to call it in, anyway."

With a slow nod, Richie stepped past Meredeth, his gaze averted, then hesitated. "Not even twenty-one hundred people live in Hanable's Valley," he said in a harsh whisper. "In the last twelve hours—in ten minutes of terror—four of them died."

Meredeth opened her mouth but then closed it without speaking. *FBI platitudes won't help. Statistics won't help. Nothing will help what this man feels right now. Not one iota.* She watched as Bobby shepherded the man outside, then walked into the bathroom, passed the blood and brains sprayed across the vanity, and arranged Mildred Constantine's clothing, giving her a bit of dignity. Her emotions felt close, feral, and her head pounded and pounded and pounded.

CHAPTER 2

NO SENSE OF DECENCY

Hanable's Valley, NY

CHIEF KEVIN SAUNDERS took a deep breath, his gaze burning down at the steering wheel of his ten-year-old cruiser. He blew out a breath, puffing his cheeks. "Collateral damage?"

Though Meredeth could hear the derision in his voice, she nodded and said, "That's right. Wrong place, wrong time."

Saunders nodded once, still not looking at her, his anger an almost palpable force crashing against her. "Calling in the NYSP CSI team was overkill. There's nothing at the scene. It's a complete waste of time."

Meredeth raised her chin. "Maybe, maybe not. We won't know until the time is spent looking, right?"

Saunders scoffed, and though his eyes twitched in her direction, his gaze didn't reach her. "I know right now. That's why I didn't call them. You're not the only one with a lifetime of homicide experience, FBI. Anyhow, this guy doesn't leave evidence...not if what my friends in BCI said is true." He turned and looked her in the eye, one eyebrow arched.

"It is," she said with a sigh. "But still. He'll make mistakes. They all make mistakes, sooner or later."

Another scoff. "Sooner or later. Meantime, I've got four dead, Agent Connelly." His blue eyes blazed, but again, not at her—this time he directed his thousand-yard glare out the windshield.

"I know, Chief," she said. "I know how much stress this lays on your department. On you. I grew up in a town about this size—one traffic light, two patrol cars, and one old jail cell they used for a drunk tank."

For the first time, his expression softened from his grim, disapproving frown. "Yeah? Where?"

"You won't know it. It's down south. Georgia. But I'll bet there's more in common between the two than population and the size of the police department."

The chief sighed and shook his head. "But I bet they don't have an active serial killer in town."

"No," said Meredeth quietly. "Then again, the chances of the unsub being from Hanable's Valley are so remote we should consider it an impossibility."

"Yeah, I know that." The chief cut his gaze away from infinity and glanced at where Richie Garson and Bobby Van Zandt sat, Bobby's hand on Richie's shoulder. "He's known Mildred Constantine for over twenty years. She taught him in school. This is going to bust him up but good."

Meredeth nodded absently. "He's young, yet."

Saunders snapped his gaze around, blues eyes blazing once again, his gaze on her profile. "Richie Garson is a good cop, FBI."

"Yes. I think so, too. And a good man." She turned to look him full in the face. "But that's not what I meant."

"No?" His tone was challenging, but some of the hellfire had left his eyes.

"No. I meant that Richie doesn't have the benefit of the calluses you and I have developed to tragedies like this. He doesn't have that lifetime of homicide experience. He doesn't have the benefit of being as jaded as we've become—and let's hope he never does."

"Oh." Saunders returned his gaze to his officer. "Yeah, I suppose you're right."

"I almost rattled off some tired FBI garbage when we found her. Statistics. Probabilities." Meredeth shook her head and frowned. "But that wouldn't help him."

"No, it wouldn't," said Saunders. "I'm glad you resisted the urge."

Meredeth drew a deep breath into her lungs, then exhaled through a perfect O formed by her lips. She squeezed her eyes shut and pressed her fingers against her eyes until she saw stars.

"Headache?"

"Yeah. A real bastard."

Saunders grunted. "That's why I left BCI. You need to think about another job, Agent Connelly."

"It's Meredeth, and what else could I possibly do after a lifetime of Bureau politics? After over twenty years of going from town to town, looking at atrocities, at body after body, looking into the eyes of good men like Richie? Like you? What good would I be at anything else?"

"You could head back to that small town down south. Become the police chief. Or the librarian, for that matter. I'm sure they'd love to have you."

"Maybe I'll do that," said Meredeth, "but not before I help you catch the .40 Caliber Killer."

"I'm going to hold you to that," Saunders said.

Meredeth smiled and wagged her head to the side. "You and every other police chief in Southern Tier." For a moment, Kevin smiled back. *It's a nice smile,* she thought.

"Tell me your impressions."

Smile fading, Meredeth couldn't stop herself from glancing at the Besson's trailer. "The Press's nickname is apt. He's a lot like Berkowitz in many ways. He's more of an assassin personality type than a true serial killer. I expect that when we find him, we'll find a bookcase full of journals going back to his teens. They'll be full of examples of how he was 'mistreated' by teachers, his parents, or bullies. Someone, anyway. He's probably got a few beefs on his record—minor arson, maybe stalking or assault.

"His approach is interesting—" When Saunders grunted, Meredeth nodded, and her shoulders moved up and down a tiny bit. "Interesting in a clinical sense. He always targets a family barely making ends meet. Always multiple children, a mother. If there is a man in the picture, he's no more than a boyfriend and usually not worth much. The unsub kills the youngest child in the house first, then the adults, then the older child." She jerked her chin at the trailer. "All of the murders have taken place in a trailer park, which tells me that he grew up in a place like this. A trailer like this." Again, her shoulders twitched in an almost-shrug. "His kill order tells me he's probably the oldest or middle child. Definitely not the baby of the family."

Kevin's brows drew together. "Why?"

"He kills the baby first, without waking the child, without pain. If that child represented him in the family dynamic, it would be metaphorical suicide, and that's not what he's about. He's punishing the older sibling, the mother. He wants them to know the youngest is dead, that he stole away that bright light, snuffed it out. He might even tell the mother. Maybe that's why Debra Besson came at him like a wildcat." She rubbed at her brows, grimacing.

"That bad?" asked Saunders quietly.

Meredith shrugged the sympathy off and forced herself to drop her hands into her lap. "The men he's killed so far— and there have been two, alcoholic boyfriends, each—he shoots, but not with his usual efficiency, not with his astounding accuracy. He usually needs two shots at the most, but in the Matreaux case, he shot the boyfriend five times, and antemortem, unlike what he did to poor Debra Besson in there. The coroner says the man bled out, that the first gunshots incapacitated him, left him unable to move, to fight. They think the boyfriend surprised the killer, that he wasn't expecting a man to be there."

"You don't?" asked Kevin.

Meredeth shook her head. "This guy is organized, Chief. He's—"

"Call me Kevin."

She nodded to indicate she'd heard him and carried on. "He knows exactly which trailer contains the family he wants. He knows the layout of the trailers, the best way in, where each child sleeps. He knew that man was there before he set foot inside. You can put money on it."

"Then..."

"He didn't want to give him a clean death. The unsub wanted him to suffer."

"But not the other victims?"

"One shot to the left eye, administered while the child is sleeping. Up until last night, he put the mothers down without a struggle, also a single bullet to the left eye."

Saunders nodded and grimaced. "Right." He waved his hand at the Besson trailer. "And Katrin?"

"If the past indicates a pattern, he killed little..." A thunderstorm of sharp, mind-wracking pain rolled through her head as she thought of the boy's room once again. "...little Brad...he killed him first, then went down the hall to the master bedroom. Something woke Debra, and when he went to her bedroom to deal with her, she went after him, fought him. Or at least tried to. That might be what woke Katrin. Whatever the reason, she got up, slipped out her window, and ran like hell. She almost escaped him. That made him angry."

"The postmortem injuries to Ms. Besson?"

Meredeth nodded. "Five more shots"—she tapped her chest five times—"and the number of shots, like stab wounds, indicates the degree of the unsub's anger. The first two, the ones he fired before Katrin made her escape attempt, were almost...utilitarian. Stand her up, stop her, put her down for good. The post-mortem rounds tore through her breasts. This is the first time he's done that."

"Lucky us," said Chief Saunders in a morose tone. "I thought it might be sexual sadism."

"Maybe, but I don't think so."

"Why?" asked Kevin, quirking an eyebrow.

"Well, because I don't think he's motivated by sexual gratification. Deep-seated anger drives our unsub, one that's been a part of his emotional makeup for so long that he might not even recognize it as anger. Our unsub *hates*, Kevin. Most likely he hates his own mother for not protecting them—the unsub and his sibling—from something. Given the injuries he inflicts on the boyfriends..."

"Right. The unsub comes from a broken home where the father-figure is displaced by an abuser."

"Yeah, I think so. I mean, the adult male in his household may not have been a physical abuser, but the fact that abuse took place is almost guaranteed." Meredeth shrugged. "Then again, Berkowitz did his thing because his biological mother and sister rejected him, while his adopted parents loved and cherished him, so the abuse might only have existed in the unsub's mind."

"Then why isn't he off somewhere killing drunk assholes who beat their wife and kids?"

"Because that's just gravy." She waved her hand at the Besson's trailer. "It's like dessert. He'll taste it, enjoy it while it lasts, but it's not what feeds him."

Kevin shook his head. "Then..."

"What our unsub wants, Kevin, is a perfect family. Where nothing changes; where they are happy with each other forever. He wants a return to the kind of happiness he's convinced he felt before the abuse. He kills the baby first, cementing the kid's happiness, not putting him through the terror of the unsub's attack. Then, the mother. If there's a boyfriend, he incapacitates them and leaves them for dead—which they soon are. Last, the older sibling—a metaphor for himself."

"He's punishing himself?"

"Maybe. Maybe he's just teaching his younger self a lesson. The younger self that didn't protect his sibling. Teaching the older sibling that they should've done more to protect the baby." She shrugged, staring at the trailer. "He might even talk to the older child. Then, he sends them on to join the others." She turned to Kevin and looked him in the eye. "You see? He's cementing them in time. He teaches the ones that need a lesson, sure, but then he puts them out of their momentary misery. In his mind, he's collecting this 'perfect little family,' replacing the one he lost. You see?"

Kevin nodded slowly, his bright gaze on her. "I owe you an apology, FBI."

"What for?"

"I don't have anything like the experience you have."

For a moment, Meredeth wobbled on the edge of tears, but she swallowed hard, swallowing the pain, and said, "Be glad, Kevin. Be very glad."

"Hey, I only meant—"

"I know," she said in a voice as unlike her professional FBI profiler voice as day was to night. Her head throbbed, and her vision warbled, blurring Kevin's face, his expression, and a soft groan escaped her.

"Hanable's Valley is small, Meredeth, but our doctor is top-notch. He takes walk-ins."

"Thanks, but—"

"I can have you at his place in about four minutes. Three, if I run the flashers."

"Thanks, Kevin, really. But I'm—"

"I used to be that, too. 'Fine.' Stubborn. Convinced that I couldn't show 'weakness' by asking for help."

Meredeth laughed a single time—maybe more of a grunt. "You sure you're not a profiler?"

"Yeah," he said, with a wry grin. "You don't have to be a profiler when you've walked that same mile yourself."

CHAPTER 3

GOOD OLD GOODE

Buffalo, NY

MEREDETH SAT AT the room's small round table, her dinner arrayed before her. She had little appetite, but she needed the calories, the nourishment. With a sigh, she picked up the remote and found a local station, WUTV, and tuned in to the six o'clock news.

Abner Postwaite gave a stern look at the camera, his steel-blue eyes seeming to skewer any watcher who intended to turn away. "And now, ladies and gentlemen, we turn our attention to the string of murders plaguing Western New York and the Southern Tier. Janet, I understand we have an old friend with us tonight?" He half-turned to skewer his co-host, Janet Murray, with his steely stare.

"That's right, Abner." Janet looked into the camera and flashed her thousand-watt smile, her perfect white teeth framed by her bright red lipstick amidst her perfect, porcelain skin. She flipped her perfectly coifed shoulder-length hair, making it gleam under the studio lights in a fetching way. "Our viewers may remember Jeremy Goode, who was once part of the WUTV team."

"That's right," said Abner. "Jeremy covered the crime beat for us. I enjoyed his reports."

"He is one of the best," said Janet, treating Abner to a slow nod. "And for this evening, ladies and gentlemen, we are lucky enough to have him back. He's outside the FBI field office, here in Buffalo, and he has some information to share with us. Are you there, Jeremy?"

The scene changed from the news studio to an outdoor shot on the corner of Niagara Street and South Elmwood Avenue. A tall, dark-haired man stood beneath the FBI seal hanging from the concrete wall next to a tall bank of black-tinted windows. His dark tan contrasted nicely with the pale concrete. "Good evening, Janet, Abner. And you're correct, Janet. I've discovered that the Department of Justice is taking the State of New York's request for assistance quite seriously."

"Oh?" said Abner. "And what has the DOJ done?"

"I'm glad you asked, Abner, but allow me a small digression to remind our viewers of the current crisis." Without waiting for Abner's reply, Goode plunged ahead. "As many will recall, the terror began a month ago, with the gruesome discovery of the remains of the Maynard family in their trailer located in Franklinville. It wasn't long before the Jones family of Cuba went missing and were subsequently discovered in the family's trailer. A week later, a similar ugly scene was discovered in Limestone with the unfortunate end of the Evreds—also found in their rented mobile home. And just ten days ago, Richburg joined the ranks of small Southern Tier towns mourning the murder of an entire family—this time, the Browns."

"That's a lot of grief spread through the region."

For just a moment, a hot expression of pure contempt flashed across Jeremy Goode's face. "That's right, Abner. It's a horrible progression of mayhem. And it continues to spread, with the newest crime scene in Hanable's Valley, where the Bessons were discovered just yesterday. The New York State Police have been doing their best to assist local agencies, but following the Besson murders, the governor put in a formal request with the director of the FBI himself. It seems the two were college roommates, and—"

"You mentioned they've taken the request seriously?" asked Janet.

"Yes, Janet. I have it on good authority that the somewhat controversial FBI 'superprofiler,' Meredeth Connelly, has recently arrived in Buffalo—and is, in fact, staying in a hotel not four blocks from the corner on which I stand. With her, came her partner, Robert Van Zandt."

"'Superprofiler,' Jeremy?" asked Abner as the view switched back to the studio—just in time to catch Abner's patented forward-lean, quirked-eyebrow, and head-tilt while staring into the camera. After a moment, the scene switched back to Goode.

"That's right, Abner. You may recall the pair recently solved the Sandman case in Daytona Beach, Florida—though that investigation spanned five years—and immediately prior to that, on the Savannah Strangler case in Georgia."

"Oh, my," said Janet.

"Yes," said Goode. "The pair certainly gets around. In any case, the Volusia County Sheriff gave Connelly the 'superprofiler' nickname, claiming her profile was so precise that he believed she must have superpowers. But—"

"Or she could have ESP," said Abner with a chuckle.

"Uh...yes. But Connelly also has her detractors. Many say she works too slowly and doesn't play well with the local departments working the case."

"Sour grapes, I'll warrant," said Abner. "Tell us about the Sandman case."

"Well, as I mentioned, it happened in Volusia County—Daytona Beach—Florida. Warren Montpilar Jefferson murdered eighteen co-eds—mostly during various Spring Breaks—and left them buried in loose, shallow graves on the beach. His spree lasted five years, mainly because he didn't kill on a schedule, and sometimes he went an entire year between murders. He—"

"Pardon the interruption, but he wasn't a spree killer, Jeremy," said Abner. "Spree killers kill—"

"A figure of speech rather than a classification, Abner."

"Oh. Yes."

"As I was saying, Jefferson may have gone on and on, if not for the pair of Connelly and Van Zandt. They'd been on the case in previous years, then returned to Daytona Beach four months ago and worked up a new profile based on the most recent murders. My sources in Florida tell me that the profile almost described what Jefferson would be wearing when he was arrested."

"But that's—"

"Another figure of speech, Abner." Goode almost kept the impatience from his face.

"Right."

"In any case, Connelly led the Volusia County Sheriff's Department to a successful pre-dawn raid of Jefferson's ranch, just twenty-five miles inland, capturing the elusive killer without further violence. Unfortunately, it was just hours too late for his last victim, who was found in a locked freezer located in Jefferson's garage."

"Horrible," said Janet.

"Indeed," added Abner. "And now, we have this powerful team of mind-hunters working for us, for the people of Western New York and the Southern Tier."

"That's right, Abner," said Goode. "It is my opinion that Connelly and Van Zandt have been temporarily shifted to the Buffalo field office and assigned to the .40 Caliber Killer case. I imagine they'll be here until the man is caught."

"Then I hope they aren't here long," said Abner, "though I'm sure they are delightful people."

"I hope so, Abner. I really do. These reports that she's hard to work with..." Goode shrugged. "Well, who among us hasn't rubbed a colleague wrong at one time or another, eh, Abner?" He leaned toward the camera, seeming to almost leer at the screen. "But what concerns me are these allegations that she *slows cases down.* If they are accurate, I'm concerned about the unnecessary loss of life that will ensue."

"Excuse me, Jeremy. Are there public reports of this plodding behavior? And in what way could they be inaccurate?"

"Abner, the issue comes up in the review of several of her cases. As to potential inaccuracy, it's human nature coupled with a misunderstanding of the profiling act. The practice of profiling a criminal requires a lot of data, which can only be acquired in these cases from observing the behaviors of the killers. And that means..."

"Crime scenes," said Janet with a frown that managed to still be pretty. "Murders."

"Exactly, Janet. No one, no matter how skilled at criminal profiling, can join one of these cases and immediately point to the unsub, so there are almost always additional victims. Working up a profile takes time. I imagined this criticism was the typical reaction—she *should have* done more, caught the murderer before he made more kills. I hope I'm right in that."

"Let's pray you are," said Janet.

"Pray all you want, but—and let this serve as a warning to Agent Connelly—*I* will be watching her behavior. I *will* blow the whistle the instant I believe she's strayed from the path that will bring the matter to resolution at the best possible speed."

"One question, Jeremy," said Postwaite.

"Yes, Abner?"

"Could you remind our readers who are not journalists assigned to the crime beat what an unsub is?"

"Of course. It's a law enforcement term coined in the mid-sixties. It means, 'unknown or unidentified subject.'"

"Thank you for the clarification. I know you've covered many criminal cases during your tenure at WUTV," said Abner in a grave voice. "Is it fair to say that as a stringer—that is, since you left us—you've continued in the specialization."

"You are correct on both points, Abner."

The view switched back to the studio and a tight close-up of Abner's smiling face. "Then I can think of no one else I'd rather have on the case. Please keep us informed."

"I will, Abner," said Jeremy from off-screen.

"Our thanks to Jeremy Goode for his invaluable reporting tonight. We'll be back, right after this message from our sponsors."

Meredeth switched the channel to something light—a British baking competition—then looked down at her meal.

She raised an eyebrow at the empty plate, then finished off the carafe of water.

CHAPTER 4

A LITTLE MERCY

An old trailer

WHEN HER FATHER shouted, Little Mercy erupted out of a deep sleep, fear stomping around in her guts wearing steel-toed boots. She sent a panicked gaze fluttering around her small bedroom, checking that she'd lined her toys up on the shelf, that she'd straightened her bedclothes before falling asleep, that her books hadn't fallen over in the night, that she'd tucked her chair into the kneehole of her desk when she'd finished her schoolwork the night before. She had everything in its proper place, but still... There must be something! The thought shouted through her mind, the raucous shriek of a speeding freight train half an hour behind schedule.

Her father's footsteps pounded around in the communal area of the trailer—stomping, grinding footsteps filled with anger, with the promise of a quick slap, a swift boot to the backside. Her gaze darted to the closet, to the relative safety of its dark embrace, but even as her foot twitched off the mattress, she rejected the closet. He would look there, and once she trapped herself inside, there was nowhere to run.

"MERCY!" he yelled, and something crashed in the living room, punctuating his furious shout better than anything else could.

"Garry? Is that you?"

Her mother's tentative voice sounded from the narrow hallway outside her bedroom door, and Mercy bit her lip. *No, Mommy! No!* Mercy thought. She crawled off her bed and took a few unsure steps toward the thin door.

"No, Laura!" Garry snapped in an alcohol-blurred voice. "It's Joe Brendan from the bank. I've just dropped by to yell at your bratty kid."

Outside in the hall, she heard her mother mirror her unsure steps, though her mother walked toward the mounting danger in the living room. "Now, Garry, I think you've—"

"Don't you stick your nose in, Laura! You're always making excuses for the girl, always trying to get between us!"

"No, honey, I'm just—"

"Arguing with me! That's what you're doing!"

"No, Mommy," Mercy whispered. "No, just go back to bed..." But her mother took a few more steps toward the front of the trailer instead. Mercy shook her head violently, but that helped no more than her whispers.

"I'm not! I'm not arguing, Garry!"

"By God, I said you are!" Garry stomped toward them, his thundering steps seeming to shake the entire trailer.

Mercy shook her head, and her mouth formed the word "No!" though no sound issued from her throat. She backed away from the door, backed away from the hall, from the incipient promise of violence in her father's voice.

"Now, just calm down, Garry," said Laura, her voice a tentative tremolo.

Mercy jumped at the sound of the open-handed blow and the sound of her mother crashing against the wall. She turned and ran to her bed, climbed atop it, and wrestled the window open, then turned and stared at her bedroom door, freezing in place to listen.

In the hall, her mother sobbed something she didn't catch, and her father grunted, then shouted, "Then don't make me do it! Every damn time, Laura! Every goddamn time! You don't never learn!"

Her mother blubbered an apology, too late to stop the rolling thunder of her father's drunken wrath, and as another blow rocked her mother into the wall, Mercy turned and slid feet-first into the warm night, hanging for a moment from her windowsill, then dropping to the dirt beneath her window. The lattice that skirted the bottom of the trailer was missing beneath her window—removed to facilitate some project Garry had started, then abandoned half-finished.

The crash of broken glass accompanied her mother's next cry of pain, and Mercy dropped to her knees in the dirt, then scurried into the darkness under the trailer. She crawled deep into the shadows, then turned back toward the entrance and drew her knees up before her, hugging them tight, wanting to squeeze her eyes shut and plug her ears, to deny the sounds of the one-sided ruction coming from the trailer above her—but she didn't dare.

Inside the trailer, blows rained down on her mother, and eventually, her pleading, her cries of pain became first, identical wordless pleas, then faded to nothing more than grunts following each fist, each foot.

Silent, helpless tears rained down Little Mercy's cheeks, and a silent, helpless rage filled her.

Eventually, the sounds from above her stopped—all except for the muted crying of her mother. Mercy snuggled her thumb into her mouth and tried to pretend nothing had happened. Her eyelids grew heavy as the moments drifted past without a renewal of violence, and Little Mercy began to relax.

She'd almost convinced herself she'd escaped her father's anger for the night when the man dropped to his knees outside the open spot in the lattice. He said nothing, just glowered at her, then crawled under the trailer, his narrow-eyed gaze never leaving hers, his snarl feral and terrible.

She scooted away from him, backing farther and farther into the dark shadows, into the feathery spider webs, hands and feet scratching against the cool clay, and he followed her relentlessly. Before she could come up with a way out, a plan to defuse his anger, he reached for her, his hot hand squeezing her ankle, and she screamed.

CHAPTER 5

WAKING UP

Buffalo, New York

MEREDETH AWOKE, A child's cry ringing in her ears. Her room was dark, no light except the feeble glow from the alarm clock on the nightstand. Her head had already started its staccato drumbeat, pounding and pounding. She wondered at the time, but before she could reach for it, her phone shrieked a second time—her special ring tone, the one she used for Bobby's middle of the night calls—and she rolled to her side and scooped it up, swiping away the lock screen and thumbing the accept button. "Connelly," she croaked. "You sound like shit, Mere," said Bobby.

"Yeah, well"—she pulled the phone from her ear and glanced at the time displayed across the top—"it's four in the damn morning, Bobby."

"The .40 Caliber Killer doesn't seem to mind the early hours."

"Another one? So soon?"

"Yes, to both questions, boss. Saddle up. We've got a fresh crime scene."

Meredeth groaned and flung aside the bedclothes. "Close?"

Bobby grunted. "Close to Hanable's Valley. Browncroft, this time."

"Inconvenient. Can't he find a trailer park closer to Buffalo?"

"He does love the Southern Tier. How long do you need?"

Meredeth grimaced at the greasy feel to her face, the roiling in her guts, and the bright, sharp pain behind her eyes. "Twenty minutes. Grab coffee if you're ready sooner."

"Roger that," said Bobby, then hung up.

Swinging her legs off the bed, Meredeth sat up, looking around the dark room, shivering a little in the chilly air. For a moment, a snippet of her nightmare came back to haunt her—trapped in the dark, someone coming after her. She tried not to groan as she switched on the bedside light to banish the gloaming. Her vision blurred, making the room seem like an underwater scene. The inside of her skull itched and itched, a harbinger of migrainous doom. She closed her eyes for a moment, hoping to banish the monster ravaging her skull.

Her dream had fuzzed in her memory, faded to mottled monochrome, though she never remembered much from her nightmares, to be honest. Mostly, she remembered the terror and sadness embedded in the nightmares that came part and parcel with a tough case or an ugly cluster of headaches. *Migraines*, said a soft voice inside her. She couldn't say where the darkness in those dreams came from, beyond the obvious source of her daily professional life. Her childhood had been idyllic—except for the tragic death of her parents in a car accident when she was ten.

She rushed through her morning ablutions, then threw on what she loosely referred to as her uniform—a tailored navy-blue business suit with a white button-down worn open at the collar. She slipped her service weapon into its custom-made holster and slid the whole contraption inside the waistband of her suit pants, making sure the clip caught her belt.

Meredeth glanced at herself in the vanity mirror and smoothed her shoulder-length auburn hair absently. She grimaced at the black bags under her eyes, briefly considering trying to hide the blemishes with a little concealer, but then she shook her head. It was hard enough being a woman in a largely male-dominated organization. The last thing she needed was a bunch of gunk on her face emphasizing her difference from the rest.

She rode the elevator down from her floor and caught Bobby stepping away from the reception desk, a large Styrofoam cup in either hand. She held out a hand and smiled at the night clerk—though that was the last expression she felt like wearing at that moment. "Thank you," she said to the clerk. "I'll be sure to mention your kindness to the management when I check out."

"It was nothing," said the clerk, though he smiled at the praise, nonetheless.

Bobby had the car idling under the portico, with the heat already on, her seat-heater on maximum against the early morning spring chill. She sank into the passenger seat with a groan. "You know, Bobby, you're all right. I don't care what the HRT guys say about you."

He flashed his patented Bobby Van Zandt grin at her and slipped the car into drive. "Not for nothing, Mere, but you look like shit. Headache got you by the tail again?"

"Yeah," she said with a sigh. "This coffee will fix me up, though. You wait and see." She pretended not to see him roll his eyes. She glanced down at her phone, grimacing at the blinding quality of the light the high-resolution screen put out, and frowned at the numbers hovering above her email application. The number never seemed to go away, never seemed to get smaller, only grew and grew and grew. As she looked at it, her phone made the obnoxious noise associated with her anonymous pen pal, then vibrated in her palm.

"I recognize that ringtone. Is it—"

"My secret sicko? Yeah, and it's just what I need this morning."

"Persistent sicko, isn't he?"

"Oh, I forgot to tell you. I got one at the crime scene yesterday. While you and Garson were arranging for the CSI team."

"Yeah? What did it say?"

"Didn't look at it."

"No?"

"No."

Bobby glanced at her for a heartbeat, then snapped his gaze back to the road. "That doesn't sound like you, Mere."

"Tell me about the scene we're headed to." She successfully repressed the sigh of irritation, but somehow, Bobby knew.

"I'm interested, that's all. At one time, we wondered if he was trying to help you out on the active case."

"Yeah, but in Savannah, it seemed more like he was trying to steer my thinking, remember?"

"But—"

"Tell me." She opened the email app, checked to be sure the special rule had fired; the rule that forwarded messages from her cyberstalker to the tech team her boss had assigned to tracking the idiot down. After confirming the messages had been sent along, she deleted the emails and dropped her phone in her lap. "Let's go, Bobby. Tell me about the new scene."

After a short nod, he put the car in gear and got them pointed south. "Park View Estates," he said. "Just a little southwest of Browncroft, but out in the county jurisdiction."

"Still in Cattaraugus County?"

"Yeah. Browncroft is on the eastern edge of the county. Almost due east of Hanable's Valley. We're about an hour away."

"Close to Hanable's Valley, you say?"

Bobby flashed her a one-sided grin. "Oh, Meredeth's got a boyfriend."

"What are you, twelve?"

"That doesn't sound remotely like a denial."

Meredeth rolled her eyes. "Good grief, Van Zandt."

"That also isn't a denial, Mere."

"Okay, then. Wrap your FBI profiler ears around this: I am not interested in Kevin Saunders." She turned in her seat and fixed him with a savage glare, fighting to keep from smiling. "Is that enough of a denial?"

He glanced at her, saw the small smile playing around the corners of her mouth, and grinned. "Your voice says one thing, but your body says another."

"You must be a profiler for the F-B-I." She said the first two initials of their organization in a clipped, staccato tone, but drew out the last one and added a Georgia twang to it. "Turn that razor wit of yours on the .40 Caliber Killer, and we'll be out of here before the week's up." She pinched the bridge of her nose.

"Want some aspirin? For real, I mean?" Bobby asked, his teasing tone gone.

"Nah. Aspirin doesn't help."

"It's worth a—"

"At all." She sighed and then drew in a long, deep breath.

"It's not my place to say this, Mere, but—"

"Then don't."

"—but these headaches of yours are getting worse."

"Think so, profiler? Your experience tell you all that?"

"Yeah, I do. And I think they're more than just minor headaches."

"No shit, Sherlock. I've said they're probably migraines at least forty thousand times."

"More than just migraines, too—at least by the colloquial definition."

"Yeah, well, the common definition is just 'a bad headache.' If people knew what they were really like—migraines—the word would be a lot less common." She turned her face toward the blur of black shapes racing by her window, opening her eyes wide, then closing them, then repeating the process.

"And..."

"Oh, go on," she said softly. "In for a penny and all that."

"And I couldn't help noticing your vision problems."

She snapped her head around and glared at him. "What vision problems?"

Bobby shifted in his seat, switching from the hands-at-nine-and-three position to a more laid-back, wrist-hooked-at-twelve position. "The ones when you can't read, can't see farther than arms-length. Sound familiar?" He looked at her askance, his expression set.

"Yeah, well. Don't worry about it, Bobby." She grimaced and snapped her eyes shut as a pickup truck whistled by in the other lane, its LED lights seeming bright enough to flash-melt steel.

"And the sensitivity to light."

"Yeah, yeah," she muttered. "When we get to the Browncroft, look up migraines on the web. Sensitivity to light goes part and parcel."

"Already did that, Mere," Bobby said softly. "Be honest with me. You have ocular migraines, right?"

"Bobby..." Meredeth started, but then she shook her head.

"It's just us here."

She nodded. "I know, Bobby. Can we just—"

"And I'm on your side."

"Yeah, I know that, too, Bobby. But if an allegation like that were to make it into the earholes of certain people back at Quantico, my time in the field would be over quicker than you can say 'sorry.' Do you know that? They'd want me to teach. To sit on my ass in the office while other people catch the bad guys. I'm not okay with that."

Van Zandt gave her a single nod, staring straight ahead. "But I need to know, Meredeth. I can cover for you, but to do it right, I need to know exactly what I'm covering up."

"I'm not covering anything up."

"No?"

"No. I have no diagnosis—not even for regular migraines."

"Yeah, well, that's because you won't go see someone."

Meredeth shrugged. "Medical records..."

"Right. If you had to, could you shoot at a perp and hit them right now? Could you drive this car?"

"I could drive," she said softly. "It would be difficult, especially with all these damn pickups, but I could do it. And I could hit anything I could see."

He glanced at her, his brows drawn down. "*Anything you could see?* How bad is it, Meredeth?"

"Most of the time, it's fine. And it's only in my left eye. It gets a little blurry, maybe, or I see flashing lights."

"Could you pass an eye exam? You know, when one of these ocular migraines has you in its grip?"

"I don't know, but probably," she said, trying to make it sound like she believed it. "And you don't know that these are ocular—"

"*Probably.*" Bobby nodded once to himself. "How long has this vision nonsense been going on?"

"It's not all that—"

"Mere... How long."

"It gets worse when we're on a case. The higher the stress, the worse it gets."

"How long?"

Meredeth shrugged. "Two years."

"*Two years?* I knew about the headaches, but..." Again, Bobby nodded once to himself. "Anything else I need to know about, Meredeth? Any hallucinations or blindness?"

"No, neither of those"—she dropped her gaze to her lap—"or I'd have said."

"Would you?" Bobby asked.

After that, they rode in silence for a while, Bobby's gaze intent on the dark road, Meredeth's on her hands in her lap. She couldn't blame him for being a little angry with her, but with the stone-age institutional attitude toward women held by the Federal Bureau of Investigation, she had to be better than her colleagues, not just their equal. She needed to be tougher, less emotional, with more hardcore fanaticism to the Bureau policies than even the bluest of blue-flamers. Any weakness on her part erased all her hard work, all her sacrifices, in the eyes of many of her male colleagues. Not Bobby, probably, and maybe not many of the newer agents, but among the senior agents for certain.

She glanced at Van Zandt and found him studiously staring out at the empty road ahead. "Look, Bobby, you're right—we both know that. I should have told you. The only thing I can say in my defense is that you don't understand what it's like for female agents."

He glanced at her and sniffed. "I do understand, Mere, but we're partners, right? Do you think I'd cut you off at the knees?"

"Not on purpose, no." His face hardened, and she held up her hand. "I didn't mean that the way it sounded. All I mean is that I know you've got my back and would never intentionally betray my trust. The problem, Bobby, is that others in the Bureau would have no problem betraying you to get at me."

"They'd have to have something to betray me with, Mere. They'd never hear a word of this from my lips."

Meredeth nodded. "Like I said, Bobby—I know you've got my back. Maybe I'm paranoid." She couldn't say why she felt the need to diminish the truth—she wasn't paranoid, and the constant stream of federal lawsuits for sexual harassment, hostile work environments, and discrimination proved it without a doubt, but the compulsion to smooth things over, not to make waves, was ingrained, as natural as drawing the next breath. "But you know what? Even if you're paranoid, sometimes they're still after you, watching you, waiting for you to slip up a little. All I know is that I might as well roll over and die if they put me on a desk. After all the years of sacrifice, of giving up everything for the Bureau, I don't have anything else. I can't let this get out."

Bobby drove in silence for a few moments, darting penetrating glances at her while her head tried to crack apart from the inside out. Her left eye ached, and nausea stumbled around in her guts like a drunken sailor on leave. "They might not take you off the street."

She shook her head. "No, Bobby, they might not take *you* off the street for a migraine. *Me*, they would. In half a heartbeat. One hundred percent. Me, or any other female agent. They'd stamp our files 'unsuitable for fieldwork,' claiming we were unable to meet the minimum requirements of the job. They'd push us toward early retirement."

Bobby shook his head. "Sometimes I think we work at different agencies."

"We do, Bobby," Meredeth said softly. "We always have. For you, the Bureau is an institution that will reward your hard work, your effort, your dedication."

"It's not that for you?"

"No," she said simply. "For a woman, being a blue-flamer is the minimum requirement. We're not rewarded for that level of dedication. It's expected."

Bobby shrugged. "I don't know what to say."

"There's nothing you can say, Bobby. All you can do is make sure the misogynistic culture left over from the Hoover days dies a cold death. All you can do is promise me you'll be different, that you'll aspire to a higher standard, and that you'll hold your male counterparts to that higher standard."

"Of course," he said. "If it's the way you described, it's abhorrent."

"Did you hear it?"

"Hear what?"

"You said, 'If it's the way you described.' You're already discounting my experiences."

"That's not what I meant. I—"

"I get it, Bobby, but the culture is ingrained from Quantico on up. *If* it's the way I described. *If* I'm not being overly emotional. *If* I'm not blowing a joke out of proportion. *If* I'm not being a good sport." She turned her gaze on his profile. "You see?"

He opened his mouth but closed it without a sound. His expression grew pensive. "I was just trying to remember how many times I've heard a senior male agent make comments like that after a female agent made a complaint." He shook his head.

"Right. The best of you will think the man making that comment is wrong, but you won't say anything. The worst of you will laugh and give him a slap on the back."

Bobby nodded. "I always felt..."

"Right," Meredeth said again. "You always felt those kinds of comments were in poor taste but essentially harmless."

"Well...yeah."

"They're not harmless."

He glanced at her and nodded once. "I'm beginning to see that."

"Enough of the lecture," she said, trying to make her voice bright. "How do I fix this, Bobby? How can I make it up to you?"

He quirked a one-sided grin at her. "Did you hear it, Mere?"

"Hear what?"

"You're apologizing."

"Of course. I should have told you."

"Don't minimize the reasons you didn't. The culture is ingrained in you, too."

Meredeth closed her eyes and pressed them hard with her thumb and fingers. "Yeah. How could it be otherwise?"

Bobby cleared his throat. "As to how you can fix this, Senior Special Blue-Flamer Meredeth Connelly, it's simple. Moving forward, you *will communicate* any special needs you have in full—no matter how or when they develop—to your partner. And for my part, I will keep your confidence and do my best to help you out. Fair enough?"

"Fair enough," Meredeth said. "And thanks."

"Gratitude is not necessary, Mere. We're partners."

"Gratitude is always necessary, Bobby."

"Well, we'll leave it there then. Let's practice. What do you need right this moment?"

"Nothing."

"Come on, Mere. Play nice with the other children." He glanced at her from the corner of his eye. "Anything."

"Anything?"

Bobby nodded.

"Shoot the next guy driving toward us in a pickup with LED headlights."

Bobby chuckled at that. "Want my sunglasses?"

"It's half-past-four in the morning, Van Zandt. The sun ain't even up." Her old accent twanged in the last three words, and she grimaced.

Bobby shrugged the shoulder closest to her. "For the assholes in pickups."

"Nah. Just shoot them." She made a gun from her fingers and thumb, pretending to shoot out the windshield, then to blow away the smoke from her forefinger.

"Okay, if you say so." He hit her with another corner-of-the-eye peek. "But seriously..."

"Right. Tell me about this crime scene. Distract me from my head."

"Here's what the sheriff passed along: The scene is in Park View Estates, a trailer park southwest of—"

"You told me that part. How many?"

"Bodies?"

"No, boxes of breakfast cereal."

"I'll have to get back to you on the cereal. You think the .40 Caliber Killer is a serial cereal killer?"

"Boo."

Bobby pretended to preen. "Everyone's a critic." He sobered and tapped the top of the steering wheel with his thumb. "Okay. Five bodies—two adults, male and female, and three kids, one of whom—"

"Great," said Meredeth in a dark tone. She pinched her nose. "How old?"

"Oh, that's not the worst of it. One of the kids was a sleep-over guest."

"Christ."

"The family name is Eider. The mother was Beth, expired from three bullet wounds. The boyfriend, Randy Martin, put up a fight, and the unsub had to shoot him nine times. The coroner thinks he got up after being shot a few times and re-engaged—"

"Good for you, Randy," she whispered.

"—which really pissed off the unsub. He knee-capped him in both legs, then pumped four rounds into his guts. Hard way to go."

"You're damn right about that. Tell me about the kids." Her head felt swollen to ten times its normal size, and she squeezed her eyes shut.

"Are you sure, Mere? By the look of you—"

"I'm sure. I'd rather know what I'm stepping into."

"Well...okay. The fourteen-year-old daughter was named for her mother—Elizabeth, but she went by Liz. One round in the left eye. Her little brother, Brent, was nine. From the initial forensics, he and his friend must have heard something. Brent's buddy was Mark Roberts, also nine years old. Both boys were out of bed, both shot in the face, but not with the .40 Caliber Killer's usual accuracy."

"The kill order was different?"

"The daughter's bedroom was closest to the living room. Sheriff Jackstral thinks the kids recently switched bedrooms—both rooms were decked out with furniture and things that matched the occupants, but the girl's bedroom was painted sky-blue and has a racetrack mural with the characters from the Cars franchise. Brent's—"

"A girl can't like sky-blue? She can't like Cars?"

"Brent's room was painted pink."

"Oh. Then he made his first mistake."

"Maybe," said Bobby. "Or he doesn't care about birth order. It might be about the proximity to the door."

Meredeth shrugged. She gazed out at Browncroft as they raced through the sleepy little town. "Are we close?"

"Five minutes," said Bobby. He glanced at her. "Time to get your game-face on, Mere."

She nodded once and forced herself to sit up straight, gazing straight out the windshield. "Anything else about the scene? Anything like..."

"Like Mildred Constantine? No. He caught them all inside the trailer and dispatched them with little trouble."

"Except for Randy Martin."

"Right."

"Did Martin do damage to the unsub?"

Bobby shook his head. "I don't know."

"Did he pick the lock again?"

"Seems so."

"I wish these people would buy better locks."

Bobby grunted and flicked on his turn signal. "Park View Estates. Why do all trailer parks have a name like that? Like it's something special?"

Meredeth shrugged. "Even people who live in trailer parks want to feel like they live in a nice place. We can't name them 'Tornado Target Number Twelve,' or 'Cheap Housing Community.'"

"I suppose not."

"And anyway, apartment complexes are no better...names like Marquis Estates."

"Regular neighborhoods either, for that matter," said Bobby. "I grew up in Elk Run."

"You're kidding."

"Nope. Middle-class neighborhood outside Denver. It had streets like Manitoban Way, Rocky Mountain Run, Tule Road, and Roosevelt's Circle." He glanced at her and saw her puzzled look. "Those are all species of elk. Manitoban Elk, Rocky Mountain Elk, et cetera."

"Ah," she said.

"How's the head?" He pulled off NY 242 onto Whig Street.

"It's okay. I'll tell you if it gets any worse."

Bobby gave her a one-shouldered shrug and turned into the trailer park, slowing to idle speed as the car crunched down the loose gravel road. "What's the plan, boss?"

"Same as always. Keep them off me until I'm ready to talk."

"You got it." He pointed to the southeast. "There."

She followed his gaze, setting her facial expression into the stone-faced professional non-expression she adopted at crime scenes. The trailer glowed like a Christmas party was going full-swing, inside and out, with three Cattaraugus County Sheriff's Deputy cruisers and the county coroner's van pulled into the front lawn. Her gaze lingered on the Hanable's Valley cruiser parked on the shoulder across the street.

"Is that—"

"Park behind Hanable's Valley," she said, a small grin on her lips.

Bobby pulled in behind Kevin Saunders's cruiser and switched off the engine. "Strange that—"

"You see him?"

"Chief Sau—"

"No, the Easter Bunny!" Meredeth snapped.

He treated her to a reproachful glance. "He's over there by the coroner's van. With the sheriff. I think—"

Meredeth popped out of the door and strode across the street, head pounding in time with her steps. Her gaze burned on the back of Kevin Saunders's head, and he turned as she stepped from the gravel into the poor excuse for a lawn.

"Agent Connelly, this is—"

"What are you doing here?" Meredeth asked.

Kevin Saunders cocked his head to the side and raised an eyebrow at her.

"This isn't your jurisdiction, is it?"

"No," he said slowly.

"I asked him to come," said the man over-filling a Cattaraugus County Sheriff's Department uniform. He was a giant of a man—at least six foot six inches tall, and close to three hundred and fifty pounds if he weighed an ounce.

"Agent Meredeth Connelly, meet Sheriff John Jackstral," said Kevin with a barely suppressed grin.

"I've known Kevin since he was with the troopers," said Jackstral. "I call on his expertise from time to time."

Meredeth's gaze flicked from Saunders to the huge sheriff, then back. "I see."

Bobby came up beside her and nodded to Kevin.

"And the underwear model is Bobby Van Zandt, also of the special agent persuasion," said Kevin with an answering nod.

"Agent," said Jackstral. "Tell me what you need." His gaze rested on Bobby's face as though Meredeth didn't exist.

Bobby half-turned to face her. "What do you want to do, boss?" he asked.

Jackstral cocked an eyebrow and turned his gaze on her.

"I'd like a few minutes to review the scene. Has the coroner—"

"He's inside," said the sheriff, pointing at the trailer with a thick thumb. "Fair warning: it's pretty gruesome in there."

Meredeth nodded. "Your people inside?"

Never taking his gaze from her face, Sheriff Jackstral narrowed his eyes. "Why?"

"Because I need peace and quiet for this, Sheriff," she said. "I need to form my own first impressions. It helps with the profile if I have a blank slate, so to speak."

With an arched-eyebrow glance at Kevin, Jackstral turned, put both index fingers in his mouth, and whistled. Meredeth winced, pinching her eyes shut, and when she opened them, she found Kevin Saunders's calm gaze resting on her face.

A Cattaraugus County Sheriff's Deputy poked his head out the door, his expression stiff, grim but with all the telltale signs of tight emotional control. "Yeah, Sheriff?"

"You boys come up out of there," said Jackstral. "The FBI is here, and they want it quiet inside while they poke through the underwear drawers."

The deputy's gaze danced over Meredeth and Bobby, then back to the sheriff. "Ten-four." He disappeared inside, then reappeared ninety seconds later. "Doc wants to know if that means him, too."

Jackstral turned back to Meredeth, his slab-face set in hard, grim lines, his eyes hooded. "Well?"

"The doc can stay. It'll only take me a few minutes, then your people can get back—"

"Well, we're all here to accommodate you, Agent Connelly." Jackstral turned his gaze on Saunders and rolled his eyes.

Bobby took half a step forward. "Are there any updates from the information your dispatcher gave me earlier?"

Sheriff Jackstral turned his head slowly to look at Bobby. "Hard to say."

With a wide grin, Bobby went into his "Oh, shucks, ain't I stupid?" routine. Meredeth stepped around the coroner's van and walked toward the trailer. Behind her, the sheriff chuckled at one of Bobby's lines. A solemn line of flinty-faced deputies exited the trailer, passing her without a word as she climbed up onto the stoop, then walked inside.

The smell washed over her as she pulled on a pair of blue nitrile gloves. The odor wasn't as bad as the one at the Hanable's Valley scene as this one was much fresher, but still bad enough. She wished for a little Vicks VapoRub to smear under her nostrils, but she'd left it back in Virginia, and, what with her head pounding all the time, she kept forgetting to drop by a local drug store to pick up another bottle. She glanced at the comfortable-looking living room and the spotless kitchen beyond, then turned down the hall toward the bedrooms.

She stepped inside the first bedroom, noting the blue walls and the Cars mural, then coming to rest on the cheap white headboard with hot pink flourishes at the edges. She drew in a deep breath and dipped her gaze to the teenager's face, freezing her non-expressive expression in place.

Liz Eider lay in the utter stillness of near-instant death, almost as peaceful as if in a deep sleep. Tiny pink-gold hearts adorned her ears. No blemishes marred her skin, no worry-lines, no bruises—nothing to indicate her life had been anything other than as perfect as it could be.

The unsub had shot her at point-blank range. The girl's left eye was gone, gun powder stippling her eyelid instead of mascara and eyeliner, and a bit of gore splattered her orbital socket. She was a pretty girl, or had been anyway, on the cusp of her metamorphosis into a beautiful woman. Meredeth shook her head, unable—or perhaps, unwilling—to imagine why anyone would desire her death, even as painless as hers had been.

Liz had slept—and died—with the bedclothes around her shoulders, her hands folded on her chest. Meredeth's gaze lingered on the gore that had puddled beneath her head, wondering if the unsub had dug the slug out as he had with all his other victims. She moved closer and knelt beside the bed. "I'm so sorry," she whispered. "I'm sorry we didn't get him before he found you." The ache behind her left eye swelled and swelled, a tsunami wave approaching the shore, and her right eye watered a little in sympathy. The nausea she'd suffered on the ride down from Buffalo returned with a vengeance, and she clamped her teeth together, trying to take tiny, shallow sips of the fetid air. She let her eyelids slip shut, focusing on keeping the coffee she'd drank down in her stomach where it belonged. She'd always hated throwing up, ever since she was ten or so.

"Such a shame," said a man behind her.

Meredeth cranked her head around, snapped her eyes open, ground her teeth together against the swell of puke in her guts the sudden movement brought. Red and blue circles danced in her vision, flashing brightly for a heartbeat, then dimming, leaving her with the vague memory of police lights dancing on the ceiling.

The man wore a white bunny-suit with black latex gloves. He had a black rectangular case slung over his shoulder on a strap. He held up his hands. "Sorry. I didn't mean to disturb you. I'm Ted Williams—the coroner."

Meredeth let a breath whistle out between her teeth and gave him a grim nod. "Meredeth Connelly. Nice to meet you, Dr. Williams."

"You're the profiler?"

"Yep." She turned her gaze back on the girl. "And you're right, it's a shame...and worse. You haven't examined her yet?"

"Not beyond an initial check for vitals, no," said Dr. Williams. "I started in the back."

"But she was the first killed?"

"I'm ninety percent sure."

She raised an eyebrow and glanced back at him. "Only ninety percent?"

A wry grin flashed across his face. "I'm only ninety-one percent sure of my name at this time of the morning."

Meredeth surprised herself by grinning. "I see."

"You mind if I... I mean, I can wait if you're not finished with your examination."

Meredeth shook her head and gave Liz Eider a final glance. She stood slowly, and as the dizziness struck, she put her hand on the wall beside the bed to steady herself. She blinked hard a few times, trying to banish the motes of light dancing before her.

"You okay, Agent Connelly?" asked the coroner.

She lifted her other hand and rubbed her eyes. "Sure," she said in a voice that crackled with exhaustion.

"I'm a doctor, you know," Williams said in a soft voice. "Anything you tell me will be kept in the strictest of confidence."

"I'm fine," she said. "A headache. I don't much like waking up at four in the morning."

"Then I'd say you picked the wrong profession." Williams moved into the room and lowered his black case to the carpet.

"Let me get out of your way, Doctor."

"Stick around if you'd like."

Meredeth shook her head and instantly regretted it as the room swam around her. "Thanks, but I like to get my first view of a new scene on my own."

"As you will," said Dr. Williams. He looked at her, his probing gaze assessing. "Are you sure you're okay?"

"Too many scenes like this," Meredeth said.

"That, I understand."

Stepping back into the hall, Meredeth gave him a single, slow nod. "Let's talk afterward. I'd like your initial impressions."

"Sure," said Williams, but his gaze had drifted to the bed, to Liz Eider's corpse.

Meredeth turned and walked down the hall toward the back end of the trailer. She walked past the second bedroom, not feeling up to looking in on the two dead nine-year-old boys—not yet. She glanced in on the gleaming bathroom and frowned. The Eider trailer didn't fit the pattern of the others—no domestic nightmares, no booze or beer bottles littering the place, none of the typical paraphernalia indicating drug use, no decaying furniture. It wasn't the lap of luxury by any means, but it looked cared for, well-maintained. Brow furrowed, she retraced her steps to Liz's bedroom, where she knocked softly on the door frame. "Sorry to disturb you, Dr. Williams…"

The man knelt next to the bed, his hands curled in his lap, just staring at Liz's young face. "My granddaughter is her age," he murmured, then shook himself and looked up at her. "What can I do for you?"

"Were either of the adults drunk?"

Dr. Williams frowned at her. "I see no evidence of that."

"Drugs? Marijuana?"

The coroner shook his head. "No evidence of that, either. I'll run the labs, of course, and I could be wrong, but look around, Agent Connelly—"

"Meredeth, please."

"—these people didn't live that kind of life."

She nodded, her frown deepening. "No, it appears they didn't." For a moment, she heard the cry of a small child from down the hall, and her eyes widened. But Dr. Williams didn't react, except to raise his eyebrows at her. Shaking her head, she turned and strode down the hall and into the master bedroom.

Beth Eider lay crumpled against the wall near the door, blood splatter and powder burns painting the picture of two nearly point-blank gunshots. Meredeth looked at the bed and found blood splatter there—the first of the three shots the unsub had put into Beth. "Almost made it, momma," she whispered. The woman was nude. She had obviously darted from her bed bleeding from the first round and tried to make it to her babies.

Randy Martin lay near Beth—separated by six feet or so, also buck naked—and Meredeth knelt near him, her gaze traversing his body, noting each gunshot wound but also noting the powder stippling, then the skinned knuckles, the soot injected into four of the wounds, indicating close-contact shots. "Good for you, Randy," she murmured. "You got your licks in. You distracted him...almost got Beth past him, too. You died a hero." She looked around the room, looking for blood splatter, trying to figure out where Randy had been when each bullet had pounded into his body.

Her head pounded and pounded and pounded, and Meredeth let her eyes slide closed, shutting out the scene, but not able to banish the scene from her memory. An image formed in her mind's eye—a man and a woman, shouting at each other, both faces contorted with rage, with something akin to hatred, spittle flying—and she shook her head, denying the image.

She forced herself to focus on Randy Martin once more, imagining him leaping from the bed, fists flying, slicing the air, coming at the unsub as naked as a baby, but coming anyway. A challenging thing, to fight naked, but he'd done it without hesitation, and his skinned knuckles proved he'd made contact. *Hopefully, he's got the unsub's DNA on those knuckles,* she thought.

She spun in place, examining the room, and gasped as a man's angry glower blazed at her from the shadowy closet. She rocked back, her hand scrabbling at her holster, her breath ragged in her throat, but by the time she pulled her Glock, the man's face had dissolved into nothing more than shadows. She squeezed her eyes shut and rubbed a shaking hand across her forehead. "This is getting ridiculous," she muttered.

The unsub had put a round in each of Martin's knees—horrible, painful wounds designed to put Randy on the ground and keep him there—clearly after the man had attacked him. Then, the unsub had riddled Randy's torso with wounds, including the four rounds to the belly that he'd delivered at extremely close range—possible contact wounds if she'd read the injected powder right. She shook her head, looking at the state of the man. The damage he'd taken... He'd been lucky that none of the first few rounds had struck close enough to a vital organ to cause systemic collapse.

Not that it mattered in the end.

Like the previous scenes, it didn't appear that the unsub had stolen anything, or even disturbed the neatness of the room—except for the blood splatter and the bodies, of course. With a final glance at the closet, Meredeth rose to her feet and left the bedroom.

As she lingered outside Brent's room, reluctant to go inside, Dr. Williams stuck his head out of Liz's room and beckoned her. "You'll want to see this," he said.

She joined him in the girl's room, where he'd pulled back the top sheet and comforter, exposing the girl's torso. She wore a long T-shirt, but that wasn't what drew Meredeth's attention.

A glossy photograph lay on the girl's chest beneath her folded hands...a photograph of Meredeth standing in the ragged lawn between the Besson trailer and Mildred Constantine's. She was looking intently at the wall of Constantine's trailer, her back rigid, her hands curled into fists.

"Do you recognize that?" asked Williams.

"It's the Hanable's Valley crime scene. Yesterday," she said and frowned. She made a cursory examination of the boys in the room next door—that did nothing but make the jackhammer in her head flog her harder—while Dr. Williams bagged the photo. When she returned to the front bedroom, Williams held the evidence bag out to her, and she took it and walked back through the trailer and out into the crisp early-morning air, carrying the photograph by the corner of its evidence bag. Though she'd told herself not to, and though she knew it was silly, she paused as she crossed the threshold, her gaze darting toward the nearby tree line. The photo was meant as a taunt: "See how close I can get to you if I want to?" but she didn't want it to serve as a distraction, to divert resources from the investigation to some silly protective detail.

She felt Bobby's assessing gaze on her, heard him stop speaking mid-joke, and glanced at him. He stared into the darkness, scanning the same tree line she'd just looked at. Chief Saunders stood beside him, a narrow-eyed gaze resting on Meredeth, while Sheriff Jackstral looked back and forth between them.

She trotted down the steps and approached the three men, watching Bobby as he turned a questioning gaze on her. She held up the evidence bag. "The unsub left us a message."

"A message?" asked Jackstral.

Saunders stared at her, a vertical line etched between his eyebrows, but he didn't waste his breath on questions. Instead, he waited for her to approach, to hold the photo out to Bobby, then leaned in close to look at it. His expression darkened.

"What is it?" asked the sheriff.

"A picture of me at the Hanable's Valley crime scene. I was looking for bullet holes in the neighboring trailer."

Sheriff Jackstral frowned, then belatedly turned his gaze toward the woods. "He could be out there right now?"

"It's possible," said Meredeth.

"Probable, even," said Bobby. "He'd want to see your reaction.

Meredeth pumped her shoulders up and down. "Maybe."

"I'll send my deputies to—"

"He'd see them coming and ghost before your men could get close," said Meredeth, shaking her head.

"But still—"

"No, she's right, John. If you raise the alarm, he'll fade away into the trees. Better if we bring out a canine unit. A tracking dog from the warrants division preferably."

Meredeth nodded. "Good idea. Then we can follow his backtrail, find out how he got there, maybe get a description of him or his vehicle."

"Right," said Kevin, his gaze resting on hers.

"What if he's in one of these trailers?" asked Jackstral.

"So unlikely we might as well discard the idea," said Meredeth. She waved her hand at Beth Eider's trailer. "This is the only trailer that interested him."

"Yeah? Why?" asked the sheriff, his tone edging past irritated and into hostile.

"Because of how this guy works, John," said Kevin. Briefly, he sketched the profile Meredeth had given him the day before, then nodded at her. "Unless any of that has changed in light of the new behaviors?"

"I'm not sure yet," she said with a nod. "It's true that the signature is a little different—he killed the older child first—but that may not represent a true change. It might have been convenience. More worrisome, though, is that this family doesn't match the others. No alcohol, no...squalor."

"And there's the visiting kid," added Bobby. "He'd have known the kid was here. He could have aborted, come back tomorrow."

"But he wanted to deliver his message," said Kevin.

With a massive throb that made Meredeth want to close her eyes and crawl in the nearest bed, red and blue lights began to strobe in the tails of her eyes. "I'd say he did that," she said, "but he also made mistakes. He rushed things, killed the girl, let Randy Martin get close to him, almost let Beth Eider get past him."

"And," said Bobby, "he let us know he was there yesterday. There might be physical evidence in those woods, and with that photo, we can figure out where he stood to take it."

With a half-grin on her face, Meredeth nodded.

"How are you going to do that?" asked Jackstral.

Bobby held out his hand, and Meredeth put the evidence bag in it. He pointed at the Besson trailer, then the Constantine home. "See this, Sheriff? We can use the parallax between the two trailers and things in the far background. Then, at the edge of the woods, we just have to walk back and forth until we find the right angle. After that, it's just a matter of figuring out how close he was."

Jackstral's face clouded. "If you say so."

"It's not as complicated as I made it sound," said Bobby, his inner salesman coming out. "If you want to come with us, I can show you. I'm sure you'll see what I mean immediately."

Jackstral jerked his chin at the Eider trailer. "I'd better stay here. How would it look if I went traipsing off somewhere while the bodies are still inside?"

Meredeth was relieved. There was something about the sheriff that bothered her, though she couldn't say what. She had the impression he disliked her intensely, but that wasn't the reason. Whatever the reason, something about him raised the hair on the back of her neck as if he were a predator and she was nothing but a scared little rabbit.

"Right," said Kevin. "We'll head back to HV, John. Can you call your canine unit? Or would it be better to get BCI involved?"

Jackstral waved a thick slab of a hand. "I'll take care of it."

CHAPTER 6

WHO WATCHES THE WATCHERS?

Hanable's Valley, NY

MEREDETH RELEASED HER seat belt and let it clunk against the door. She looked out at the Besson trailer in the early morning light, finding it different in a nameless—but significant—way. Kevin Saunders parked his cruiser on her side of the car, looked at her askance for a heartbeat and a half, then killed the ignition and got out. He stepped over and opened the door for her, giving her a little grin.

"Thanks," she said and got out, carefully not seeing Bobby's smirk.

"This might sound odd," said Kevin, "but it looks—"

"Different this morning," Meredeth finished for him.

"Well...yeah. I guess so."

"It's the photo," said Bobby as he got out. "Knowing how close he was while we all felt safe and secure. Knowing our impressions of the place yesterday were dead wrong."

"Maybe not dead wrong," said Meredeth.

"Let's see that photo, Bobby," said Kevin. "The quicker we find the spot, the quicker we can start the search." With a shrug, Bobby handed over the clear plastic evidence bag containing the photo. Kevin took it, glanced down at it, and said, "Around back."

Together, the three of them walked around the rear of the trailer and stood halfway between the trailer and the woods bordering the community. Saunders glanced down at the photo, then up at the space between the Besson and Constantine trailers, noting the position of the taped-off rectangle where Katrin Besson's life had drained out into the rich black soil.

"We're too close," said Bobby. "Meredeth would've seen him if he was standing out here in the open."

Without a word, Kevin turned and walked back through the tree line into the woods. He stopped and peered through the foliage, then took a few steps to the left. He repeated the process—making a small move, checking the photo and the view, then doing it all again from a new position—until the photograph and the view matched.

"Not bad," said Bobby, and Kevin shrugged.

They stood in an area of beaten-down underbrush about six feet in diameter, ringed with cottonwood, towering black ash, and sugar maple trees. Looking at the ground, Bobby turned and moved deeper into the woods, looking for a trail. Meredeth and Kevin exchanged a glance, then she stepped closer and looked at the photo. "No question," she said. "This is the right angle. This is where he stood while taking that photo."

"Agreed." Saunders turned in place, his gaze on the ground. "We'll never find footprints in this."

"Maybe Bobby will," said Meredeth. "Should we call for a team of tracking dogs?"

Saunders shook his head. "Not yet." He made another full-circle turn, but this time, his gaze jumped from trunk to trunk of the trees edging the circle of flattened brush. "There." He pointed at a sugar maple with his chin. "See it?"

"The scuffed bark?'"

"Exactly," he said. "You might not know this, being from down south—"

"We do have maple trees down there."

"—but the mark is made by jumping up to catch a low branch, then walking up the trunk. He probably had on hiking boots, given the depth of those scratches." He looked at her sideways. "You don't look so good, Meredeth."

"Aw, you say the sweetest things, Saunders." She closed the distance to the tree and bent at the waist to look at the scuff marks up close.

"Yeah, I didn't mean it like that. I meant that you look like your headache—"

"We all have our crosses to bear." She straightened and glanced at him over her shoulder, a one-sided grin on her face. "But I think you were right about the hiking boots."

"What are you? The strong, stoic type or something?"

"Isn't it obvious?" She sighed and turned to face him. "Look, Kevin, I do appreciate your concern, but there's no help for these headaches, and talking about the situation doesn't help. Instead, it focuses my attention on it; it distracts me from my job."

Kevin gave a little shrug of his shoulders. "Okay, I won't mention it again. But keep my offer in mind. Maybe there's something a doctor can do to help."

She nodded and turned her attention back to the tree. "Will do. Now, get over here and climb the tree."

"Yeah, I know the drill, FBI." Saunders walked over to the sugar maple, then jumped for a low-hanging branch and swung himself up. He peered at the trunk, tilting his head to the left and the right, then shook his head. "Nothing." He turned his head and peered toward the mobile home park. "But there is a great view of the back end of the Besson's trailer."

"He probably spent a good bit of time up there, watching them, learning their routines."

"Yeah." Kevin glanced at the branches above him, craning his neck this way and that. "Ah." He slid closer to the trunk, then stood on the branch, contorting his torso so it fit between two branches above, one hand on the trunk.

"What?" asked Meredeth.

"There's a bit of stripped bark up here."

"Stripped by a person or..."

"The scarring looks fresh like someone sat up here in the past week and used a folding knife to peel the bark."

"The unsub."

Kevin's shoulders hitched. "Maybe. Or maybe Brad Besson."

"Can you take a photo?"

"Yeah." Kevin inched his way closer to the trunk, the bough he stood on bending under his weight.

"Be careful," said Meredeth. "I'm not carrying you out of here, though I promise I will radio for help back at the cars."

Saunders grunted and rolled his eyes. He wrapped his arm around the trunk, digging his phone out of his pocket with the other, his gaze locked on the stripped area. "There's something marked on the wood—a shape or a symbol. Traced or very lightly carved. No, definitely scored into the wood—probably with the same folding knife used to strip the bark. It looks like one of those Celtic tattoos every woman has these days."

"I don't have one."

"Almost every woman."

"Make sure to capture a good image of it."

"Duh, FBI." He leaned toward the tree, then his phone made that artificial shutter sound. He peered at the screen and grimaced, then leaned closer for another take. This time, the LED flash went off like a bolt of lightning.

Meredeth felt woozy for a moment after the flash and dropped her gaze. "Do me a favor and warn me next time you're going to set that off."

79   E.H. VICK

"Sorry," he said, "but I've got it." He slipped the phone into his pocket and climbed to the ground. He stepped to her side, his arm brushing hers, and lifted the phone.

She glanced at him, one eyebrow arched delicately, but his eyes were on the phone's screen. She glanced down at the figure to see a circle intertwined with a Triquetra—a single line that interweaved with itself to form three eye-shaped figures, one pointing up, one down and to the right, and the last down and to the left.

"See? Celtic tattoo, right?"

"Yeah. They have meaning, don't they? Celtic knots?"

"You've got me there, FBI. I'm just a dumb policeman from the sticks."

Meredeth gave him a one-sided smile. "Hardly." She caught the beginnings of a blush before he dropped his gaze, and she smiled. "Email that to me, will you? I can send it on to Quantico, and one of the tattoo and graffiti team geeks will get back to me with its meaning."

The electronic swoosh from his phone sounded, followed by a vibration on her phone. She took her device out and forwarded the image to the Cryptanalysis and Racketeering Records Unit. When she raised her gaze, she caught Saunders looking at her, but he quickly turned his gaze to the woods behind her.

"I wonder what Van Zandt found back in that mess."

"A trail," said Van Zandt, a moment before he stepped into the clearing. "Come on."

"Take a look at this first," said Meredeth, holding out her phone. Bobby frowned down at the Celtic knot for a moment.

"Thinking of getting a tattoo, Meredeth?"

"Right?" Kevin grinned at her in that I-told-you-so way. "I found it up in that tree. Someone sliced away a section of bark and carved this in the tree's flesh." He pointed at the bare spot.

"Hmm," said Bobby. "I found a trail through the woods. I followed it for a bit. It leads to a parking lot over there." He pointed in the opposite direction to the trailer park.

The chief quirked an eyebrow at him. "A trail? A path cut through the brush?"

"No."

"He was Force Recon," said Meredeth. "He means he tracked the unsub."

Kevin narrowed his eyes at Bobby for half a heartbeat, then smiled. "Sempre fi."

Bobby nodded once. "Sempre fi."

"It sounds like the old quarry. Abandoned years ago." Kevin turned and looked into the woods.

"Come on." Bobby turned and slid into the forest as if born to it. He led them through the woods on a circuitous route, then stopped as they approached the tree line on the other side. He lifted his hand and pointed toward a crumbling asphalt parking lot. It was empty.

"The old quarry," said Kevin. He frowned at the broken glass, the trash, and the scorched marks in the macadam. "I suppose high school kids use it to party. Better add this place to the patrol rotation on weekends."

Bobby stepped out of the woods and moved toward a close spot. "I'd bet he parked here."

"More tracks?" asked Kevin. "Didn't know you FORECON boys could track on asphalt."

Bobby shrugged, then grinned at the chief. "It's the closest to where he entered the woods."

Kevin and Meredeth joined him on the macadam, gazing down at the ghosts of white lines defining the spot. "Nothing helpful here," said the chief.

"No," agreed Bobby.

"I don't know," said Meredeth. "You said this place was abandoned years ago."

Kevin nodded.

"Then it tells us one thing: the unsub knows the area pretty well. Wouldn't you need to be a local to know about this spot?"

"Maybe."

"I mean, this place isn't active, and so it probably isn't listed on the web. Am I right?"

Kevin shrugged and pulled out his phone. "Google Maps has everything, Meredeth."

"Yeah, I guess you're right. But that means he looked up the trailer park in Google Maps at the very least, then took a virtual spin around it, looking for an out-of-the-way place to park. Maybe we can get them to share the IP addresses of people who did that."

Bobby grinned. "That sounds like a pipe dream. It's Google, after all."

"Bet you need a subpoena at the very least," said Kevin.

"But the photo, the clearing, all of it... All of this tells us something that can't be argued."

"What's that, Bobby?" asked Meredeth, a lopsided smile decorating her lips.

"The unsub isn't scared of us. Not in the least."

Meredeth pursed her lips and nodded. "True. He's in the vicinity, watching the investigation." She and Bobby exchanged a weighted glance.

"I think you might be in danger, Meredeth," said Kevin.

"Nah," she said, waving it away.

"He took your photograph. Not while Van Zandt and Garson were with you, either." Kevin glanced at Bobby, wearing a solemn expression. "He waited until you were all alone, then he took your picture from thirty yards away. I wasn't here, and I don't know how long you were alone, but—"

"Five minutes max."

"—he could have grabbed you as easily as snapping this photograph."

"No, not as easily. I may be a woman, Kevin, but I'm also an armed FBI agent with years of training and experience. And twenty or twenty-five of those yards separating us were in the clear. I could've easily drawn on him and emptied the magazine into his torso."

"And even if he managed to evade that fire," said Bobby, "Meredeth is a badass. You should've seen her kicking the shit out of the asshole down in Savannah."

"Maybe so," said Kevin with a slow grin. "But *this* asshole waited until you were focused on Constantine's trailer, until your mind was wrapped up in the search for stray rounds. He could've snuck up on you, I bet."

"I'd have heard him come out of the brush—"

"Look, Meredeth, I acknowledge the obvious. Like Bobby said, you are a badass, okay? I'm just saying that an active serial killer has taken a special interest in you."

Bobby nodded. "And he wanted you to know it."

Meredeth bounced her gaze back and forth between the two men, then nodded. "Okay. Message received."

Kevin turned his gaze on Bobby. "How about you?"

"Me? I'm not even in the picture."

Saunders pointed at Meredeth with his chin.

"Oh. Yeah, well, I'm always her Personal Security Detachment. That goes without saying."

For a moment, their laughter rang through the decaying parking lot, and the world didn't seem such a dark place.

"Come on, boys," said Meredeth. "Let's get out of here. We won't catch anything but flies hanging out in this parking lot."

CHAPTER 7

GOODE ON YOU

Buffalo, NY

At the end of another long day of waiting, of trying to piece it all together, of trying to get into the head of the unsub, Meredeth wanted nothing more than bed. But her stomach had given up on grumbling and had turned to jabs of sharp, empty pain, and without feeding the beast, she'd get no rest at all. It was always like that on a case—she had to force herself to eat, then force the food to stay down as the headaches rolled on and on and on. So, she ordered a Filet Mignon with a loaded baked potato and a wedge salad with gorgonzola dressing, then sat in front of the television and tuned in to the same channel again, hoping the evening news would work similar magic as it had the previous night.

The screen faded from the intro graphics on a shot of Abner Postwaite and Janet Murray sitting at the anchor desk, busily shuffling papers everyone knew were blank. Postwaite smiled at the camera and set his stack of paper down, laying his hand atop it. "Good evening, and welcome to tonight's edition of WUTV's Evening News. I'm Abner

Postwaite." He grinned at the camera as if no one watching needed that introduction, yet the smile felt forced.

"And I'm Janet Murray, and this is the Evening News."

Abner turned to look at his partner. "Janet, I understand we have Jeremy Goode back tonight. Two nights in a row. It's almost like old times." His artificial grin faded, growing grave in discrete steps.

"Isn't it, though? However, it isn't pure pleasure to have him back, given the subject matter."

Postwaite's grin crumpled into a frown of distaste—yet one that seemed almost as artificial as the smile. "Yes. It's a horrible business, these murders of entire families. And it's getting worse with the addition of the Eiders from outside Browncroft, New York. Do I have that right, Janet?"

"You do, Abner. The family was discovered early this morning, and Park View Estates has been a beehive of law enforcement activity ever since. Our correspondent, Jeremy Goode, has spent the day in Cattaraugus County, working his sources and gathering the latest intel on the .40 Caliber Killer."

"Let's bring Jeremy on and let him tell us what he's found out. Jeremy?" The view switched from the WUTV news studio to a view behind the Besson trailer.

Meredeth froze, her fork halfway to her mouth. The view was almost a pixel-perfect match of the unsub's little photographic message.

"Good evening, Abner and Janet. This is Jeremy Goode, reporting live from Hanable's Valley in Cattaraugus County."

He waved a hand at the trailer in the background. "This isn't today's crime scene but the penultimate site of terror and mayhem."

"I'm confused," said Abner.

"I'll explain in a moment, but I find that nickname—the .40 Caliber Killer—has become inaccurate. We should be calling him the Dollhouse Killer."

"How so, Jeremy?"

"You see, this unsub—this *killer*—invades the homes of single-parents. In fact, so-called superprofiler Meredeth Connelly identifies the families as 'poor' and 'burdened with two children.' She goes on to say that if an adult male is present, he's always a 'loser or a drunk.'"

"She said *that*?"

"No, she didn't," murmured Meredeth around a mouthful of potato.

Jeremy nodded, staring into the camera lens with an angry gaze. "She says the unsub always kills the baby of the family first and that he 'collects' the family members. She calls him 'interesting.'"

"How macabre!"

Jeremy nodded. "Given that this madman is killing families in order to collect them somehow, it's like he's playing with dolls, playing in his dollhouse."

"Ah, I see," said Abner. "Clever."

"Thank you, Abner."

"And this Agent Connelly thinks the killer should be called the Dollhouse Killer?"

"No, Abner, that's my view. So often, we in the Press, play a part in these kinds of atrocities. We romanticize these serial killers, giving them nicknames that feed their ego, their need for power. The .40 Caliber Killer is one such nickname. It's time we named them for the cowards they are."

"I see."

"And we need to increase our activity on these cases. We need to be proactive—to dig for evidence that is being suppressed by the FBI, and to share it with the public, so they are informed with everything law enforcement knows."

"You idiot," said Meredeth, her fork suspended in midair, forgotten. "Don't do it."

"Getting back to your question, Abner, I *was* in Browncroft most of the morning, watching the fine officers in the Cattaraugus County Sheriff's Department do their work, but I've driven here to Hanable's Valley on the trail of Senior Special Agent Meredeth Connelly and HVPD's very own Chief of Police, Kevin Saunders—both of whom visited the Browncroft scene early this morning. They—"

"Pardon me, Jeremy. Did you say the police chief from Hanable's Valley visited the Browncroft scene?"

"I did indeed, Abner."

The scene switched back to the studio, and a screen-in-screen inset showed a close-up of Goode holding a WUTV microphone. Abner quirked an eyebrow. "Isn't that unusual? For the police chief from a neighboring jurisdiction to visit a crime scene?"

"Yes, Abner, in normal circumstances. My sources say that Sheriff John Jackstral invited Chief Saunders to the scene, given his former position with the New York State Police Bureau of Criminal Investigations."

"Ah!" exclaimed Abner. "I was unaware of the chief's background. Most interesting. Please go on."

"Thank you, Abner. My sources tell me that Chief Saunders arrived before the FBI agents, which makes a bit of sense, given the proximity of Hanable's Valley to Browncroft and the distance from Buffalo." Jeremy disappeared, replaced by a map of the area with Browncroft circled in red, and to the west, Hanable's Valley circled in green. "The agents drove down in the early darkness this morning and caused quite a ruckus within the CCSD when they arrived."

"How so, Jeremy?" asked Janet.

"If you recall last night's report, Janet, you will remember I mentioned the rumors that Agent Connelly doesn't play well with local departments. That was certainly the case this morning, according to my sources, when she came on the scene and immediately ordered everyone out of the trailer, interrupting the Cattaraugus County Sheriff's Department's evidence collection team and booting the county's medical examiner to the curb so she could have the run of the trailer. Rumor has it, she demands exclusive access to every crime scene, claiming a desire to avoid distraction."

"Bullshit," Meredeth whispered, remembering her fork and lowering it to her plate. "Jackstral, you lying bastard!"

"How rude," said Abner.

"Indeed, Abner. Indeed." The map disappeared and Jeremy took its place. "And this morning, her antics caused a delay in finding key evidence—a photograph left by the killer."

"Oh my God!" hissed Meredeth. She took her eyes off the screen for a moment to look for her phone. She speed-dialed Bobby's number, and he picked it up on the first ring. "Turn to channel 31."

"A photo of what, Jeremy?" asked Abner Postwaite on the television.

"Already watching it," said Bobby. "Can you believe this guy?"

"I'll call you back when it's over." Meredeth disconnected the call and dropped her phone onto the table next to her side salad.

"That's where it gets interesting, Abner. The photograph was of Senior Special Agent Meredeth Connelly. And that brings me to my reason for reporting live from Hanable's Valley, and for picking this backdrop. Sources indicate the photo showed Connelly standing alone right over there." Goode pointed at the staked rectangle where poor Katrin Besson met her fate. "Evidently, she ran out of the Besson trailer and came around back here to escape the gruesome scene—only to be confronted with yet another scene." He waved his free hand at the rectangle.

"And this photograph was left by the .40 Caliber Killer?" asked Janet.

"The Dollhouse Killer, but yes, Janet."

"And that means the killer was there *at the same time* as the FBI agents," said Abner. "That he was *watching* them investigate."

"It would seem so, Abner," said Jeremy in a grim tone.

Abner made a show of peering at the monitor set in his desk. "I don't see where the man could have hidden."

The camera followed Jeremy as he walked in a semicircle until the woods appeared at his back. "Again, my sources tell me that the unsub stood—"

"Unsub?" asked Postwaite. "Can you remind our viewers what that term means?"

"It means 'unknown subject,' Abner. It's law enforcement shorthand."

"Of course."

"My sources indicate the unsub stood back in the trees you see behind me. That he observed Agent Connelly, and indeed, took her picture. He then left that photo under the body of one of this morning's victims."

"That's just awful," murmured Janet.

"Oh, I agree. A terrible, terrible thing to do," said Goode. "Sources say that the FBI agents found the exact spot where the unsub observed Connelly from, using advanced photo software only available to the Federal Bureau of Investigation. What's more, they found a Celtic knot carved into a tree." Again, Jeremy disappeared, replaced by an image of the peeled part of the tree trunk. "This Trinity Knot is the Celtic symbol for family."

"Poignant," said Abner, "given the Dollhouse Killer's interest in murdering entire families."

"Indeed, Abner. Meanwhile, it seems strange that the FBI would sanction their agents spending the afternoon in their hotel rooms —which is what Connelly seemed content to do today."

"After the fresh murder this morning?" asked Janet in an incredulous tone.

"Yes, Janet. They returned from the Southern Tier just after midday and entered their hotel."

Meredeth slapped the table. "It was almost four in the afternoon!"

"That can't be good, Jeremy."

"It isn't. If you again recall last night's report, you will remember another criticism leveled at Agent Connelly is her plodding pursuit of the killers in the cases she works. I assumed she would consider *this case* important enough to work it with all possible speed, Abner. It seems I was wrong."

"Agent Connelly is dragging her heels? Is that what you're saying, Jeremy?"

"Absolutely, Abner. Let's take today. After a brief visit to the latest crime scene, Special Agent Connelly spent the rest of the morning hiking in these woods with Chief Saunders."

"Well, that makes sense," said Janet. "Given the photograph."

"I thought so, too, Janet, but a reliable witness says the two—that is, Meredeth Connelly and Kevin Saunders—spent much of the time alone, standing close to one another, smiling... I'm sure you get the picture."

"I'm afraid I might," said Abner. "Your sources say there is a *romantic* relationship between this Connelly and Chief Saunders?"

Jeremy nodded somberly. "And they met just yesterday. At any rate, Connelly spent the morning here in Hanable's Valley, first in the woods, then ensconced in Kevin Saunders's office. And get this, they spent hours trying to track down the IP address of everyone who looked up Hanable's Valley in Google Maps."

"*Dammit!*" hissed Meredeth. Her head felt as though it would explode at any moment.

"Astounding. Even I know that must be thousands of people, given the recent murders there."

"Yes, Abner, and I'm one of them. I hope the officials at the Buffalo field office of the Federal Bureau of Investigation are tuning in tonight. I hope they recognize the need to exchange Connelly for someone suitable to the task. I hope word reaches Washington, and the FBI recalls this troublesome agent, that they take her in hand and send someone more interested in stopping these murders than finding a new boyfriend."

"Your mouth to the Good Lord's ears, Jeremy," said Postwaite with a special wink for the camera.

With numb fingers, Meredeth scrabbled for the remote, groaning as she hit the volume button by mistake. As she picked it up, her vision wavered, then faded toward a deep purple. She mashed the buttons but couldn't get the television turned off before necessity required a lunge toward the bathroom, her stomach betraying her at last.

As she vomited up her dinner, her cell phone rang from the other room, sending a lance of pure pain through her left eye and into her head. Her stomach heaved again, expelling the rest of the food she'd eaten, and stars danced in her eyes. She rocked back, her guts still in full rebellion, her eyes squeezed shut, and reached back to swing the door shut on her ringing phone, on the noxious odor of her dinner, on WUTV, on the world. With that accomplished, she lay on the cold tile floor and shut her eyes.

CHAPTER 8

FINGER PAINTING

In a darkened room

LITTLE MERCY COCKED her head to the side and examined her painting with a critical eye. Her only pot held crimson paint, but that seemed natural and right to her young mind. The white wall was filled with bright red images, stick figures, entire families of them. The scenes depicted various family activities—sitting down to picnic lunch, riding in a car, playing ball at the park, that type of thing—and she judged them good.

Dipping her finger into a puddle of thick, red goop, she picked a blank space on the white wall. It was just big enough to house the trailer she lived in with her mommy and daddy. She sketched the living room and added red furniture. Then she painted herself into the scene, a half-height stick figure with streaks of red for braids. Her stick-figure mother joined her in the living room, a wide red smile on her face. Next, Little Mercy painted another half-height figure, a boy, a tad shorter than her own stick figure.

She frowned at the boy stick figure for a moment, not knowing why, only knowing that the boy felt...wrong...a lie... She shook her head and shrugged. It didn't matter if she added a brother she didn't have. It was just a painting.

She added a bigger male stick figure next to the one representing her mother, but his face came out looking angry, and in a moment of fear, she smeared his features away. Her heart thudded beneath her breastbone, and her stomach hurt a little as she sat back and looked down at her hands in her lap.

Red covered her hands, and worse yet, she had fouled her pretty yellow dress. Tears stung her eyes—she'd never be able to get the paint out. Not even her dry cleaner in Virginia was that good.

She caught movement in the tail of her eye and looked up. The smeared face of her daddy stick figure had grown, gotten bigger until it nearly blotted out the others. As she watched, eyes appeared in the red face, as if someone had wiped away the blood. Then a zigzag-mouth appeared, only to become an angry sneer a moment later.

Little Mercy scooted away from the wall, slapping both hands over her mouth to stifle her involuntary cry, smearing blood-red paint on her cheeks. The stick figure froze for a moment, then turned its head this way and that, as though searching for her, his zigzag frown back in place. Then the zigzag mouth opened into a wide oval, and the figure turned his back on her and stomped back into the painting of the living room.

"No..." Mercy said breathlessly.

The stick figure paused, then half-turned to glare in her direction. After a moment of narrow-eyed rage, he continued on his way. When he re-entered the living room, his mouth flashed open and closed, as though he were yelling at the other two stick figures. The brother figure began to cry red tears, and the mother figure moved to comfort him. This only served to stoke the stick figure father's rage, and he stomped toward the mother figure, his arms waving wildly, lightning bolts of red paint flashing around him.

"No!" screeched Little Mercy. "You leave her alone!"

The father figure stopped and turned a wide-eyed glare in her direction. Again, he performed the pantomime of looking for her, of searching the limits of his vision, then gave up and, with a crafty smile, he reached behind one stick-leg and brought forth a hammer. He showed the hammer to the mother figure, then the boy. Then he half-turned and showed the hammer to Little Mercy.

She sobbed and scooted a little farther away.

The father stick figure nodded his rotund head and turned his attention back to the other two stick figures. The hammer rose and fell, rose and fell, rose and fell, and huge splashes of red paint covered the wall, blotting out the scenes of familial bliss, then dripped down toward the plywood floor, revealing more violence, more hammer blows, more red splashes, in its wake.

Mercy leaped to her feet and shouted, "You leave them alone! Leave them alone, you...you..." Her mouth worked, but no sounds came from her throat.

On the wall, the father stick figure narrowed his eyes, but his grin stretched from one edge of his circular head to the other. When he turned back to the stick figure family, Little Mercy turned away and ran. Behind her, she could feel his silent laughter...and the hammer blows. She tromped toward the door and banged out through it.

Meredeth erupted into the brisk spring morning, squinting her eyes shut against the savage pain that lanced through her left eye.

"We found them out back," a voice said.

"Want me to club him to death with a hammer?" another voice asked—a voice that sounded like Bobby Van Zandt's.

"Too much paperwork," Meredeth said as she descended the steps to the dew-filled grass, grimacing at the mud that covered her bare feet and licked at the hem of her dark-blue suit pants— she'd never be able to get the mud out. Not even her dry cleaner in Virginia was that good.

She sprinted around the short side of the trailer—each footfall driving a spike of pain into her brain—and slid to a stop. One window of the trailer was open, and beneath it, the mud showed signs of a struggle.

"They fell," said the first voice. "Looks like they landed on their hips. Do stick figures have hips?"

"Huh-who...who...who..."

"What are you, an owl?" growled a voice in the trees.

Meredeth's gaze darted from the splattered mud to the trees and then to the open window.

"He got her over there by Ms. Constantine's trailer," said the first voice.

"Damn right I did," growled the voice in the trees.

"Where...where did he hit them?" asked Meredeth.

"In the head, of course," the voice from the trees growled.

"With a...with a...with a hammer?"

"What else?" asked Bobby's voice.

Meredeth lowered her gaze to the mud and nodded. She plodded toward the twin rectangles staked out in the yard of the Constantine trailer—they'd almost made it.

"What do you think you're going to find?" growled that mean voice. "You think you're better than me, Ms. FBI? What do you think you know about me?"

Meredeth turned to survey the trailer behind her. Her gaze flicked from one bloom of bright red to the next, and she frowned. She knew where the hostility came from—after all, she'd seen it at least a thousand times before—and she knew that angry voice would only grow more and more furious, no matter what she said, but she had to try. "Nothing," she said. She raised a limp hand and twirled it in the air next to her head. "It's just these headaches."

A harsh grunt came from the trees, and she snatched a quick glance over her shoulder, then turned to run but froze in place, one bare, blood-covered foot raised mid-step. Across the narrow lawn lay two stick figures, both of their circular heads distended—one lumpy and looking more like an amoeba than a circle, the other a lopsided egg-shape—their faces giant red stains on the grass.

"Mommy!" Little Mercy screamed. She looked around in a frantic fury of frightfulness. She turned toward the trees, barely able to raise her eyes and take in the wooded ken, lip trembling, one hand absently twirling in her auburn locks. "Mommy!" she cried. "Mommy!"

Footsteps pounded around the red-splotched trailer, and she whirled to meet what was coming for her. Bobby Van Zandt charged around the corner holding his pistol ready—of course—concern for her splashed all over his chiseled face, his black aviators winking in the sun, blinding her, the spring sunlight stabbing at her eyes. He slid to a halt at her side.

KA-BLAM! KA-BLAM!

Little Mercy slapped her hands over her ears, pulse thudding away a million miles an hour, almost as frightened by the sound of Bobby discharging his Glock as fast as he could pull the trigger as she was of the stick figure hiding in the trees. Bobby fired eight more shots, then stopped, staring at the trees with a scary intensity.

Finally, he relaxed a little and smiled down at her. "Don't worry, Meredeth. I'm always your Personal Security Detachment. No matter how young you get. That goes without saying."

She beamed up at him, feeling the vague stirring of hope deep within.

But then, the stick figure in the trees roared, an earth-shaking, skull-splitting sound, and Little Mercy screamed along with it. Bobby's attention snapped back to the trees, his Glock 19M snapping back into firing position as if by instinct alone, and he rattled off six more shots in rapid succession. The roar from the trees came again, and Little Mercy backed away five quick steps.

Bobby's feet flew out from under him, though Mercy could see no reason why. He slammed down into the grass, his breath exploding out of him, then his body flattened as if crushed by a massive hammer striking from the sky. The color of his skin faded, and his black aviators became red-smudged lines flattening along his brow.

"Now we'll see!" growled that hateful voice.

Mercy's gaze snapped up from what was happening to Bobby, and she saw him step from the trees, the red stick figure from her painting. He held a hammer resting against his shoulder, and his eyes blazed fire-red. She turned and fled, running as fast as possible through the blood-red grass, but her blood-slicked feet slipped and slid more often than not. She'd run about ten feet when she felt the stick figure looming behind her. She cried out, yelling, "Sorry! Sorry! I'm sorry!" as loud and as fast as she could.

Stick figure hands, fingers shaped more like talons, slipped around her neck from behind, cutting off her cries, cutting off her breath, lifting her from her feet, and holding her kicking, high up in the air.

101   E.H. VICK

Pain lanced through Mercy's head as she tried to pry the claws from her neck, tried to loosen them enough that she could suck in a cool breath of air, tried to wrench them loose.

"Cut that out, Meredeth!" the stick figure shouted, shaking her hard. But she kept right on prying at the fingers, pushing and shoving...

CHAPTER 9

THE TRAIN WRECK

Buffalo, NY

MEREDETH SWATTED AT the hand, clawed at the fingers pressed to her throat, and cried out, coming awake with little transition between dreaming and wakefulness. She snapped her eyes open, catching a blurred image of the man hunched over her. Confusion spun and danced in her mind.

"Dammit, Meredeth! Stop it!" Bobby said.

She turned her wild-eyed gaze on her partner and relaxed, all at once, her chest heaving, her head throbbing, her left eye a miasma of sharp pain and burning fire.

"Just relax and let me take your pulse."

"I'm fine," she grated, her voice sounding like a saw on rusty metal. Even so, she allowed his fingers to find her pulse, breathing deeply, closing her eyes.

"Like hell," said Bobby.

"What are you doing here? Why are you in my room?"

Bobby made a sound of exasperation and, evidently satisfied she would live, removed his fingers. "Gee,

Meredeth, I just thought I'd come and disturb your restful sleep here on the bathroom floor.

She slit her eyes and looked up at him, but his gaze wasn't on hers. Instead, he was frowning at the toilet. He reached across her and flushed it, the sound of it prompting an explosion in the middle of her head, and she groaned.

"Do you even know what time it is? Do you even remember coming in here to puke? How long have you been in here?" His questions came rapid-fire, scarcely a heartbeat between them.

"Is she all right, then?" someone asked.

Meredeth's eyes snapped toward the bathroom door, where the hotel desk clerk and hotel security stood, looking down at her with pity and a little distaste. "Out!" she croaked. "Everyone but Bobby, get out!"

"Come on, Meredeth," said Bobby. "Without them, you'd still be lying here unconscious. It's ten-forty in case you were wondering. It's been over four hours since you called me about the reporter." He glared down at her, his exasperation clear.

"Get them out of here, Bobby, then you can yell at me."

For a moment, his eyes hardened, but then the telltale curl started in the corners of his mouth. He turned to the hotel employees and smiled. "Thanks, folks. I do appreciate you getting me in here, but she seems...well, not dead."

A flicker of a smile flashed across the security officer's face, and he nodded. "Call me if you need me." He tossed a wink at Meredeth before turning to leave.

"Shall I call an ambulance?" asked the front desk clerk.

"Not if you want to live to see the dawn," muttered Meredeth.

"No," said Bobby. "Thank you, but no." He rose smoothly to his feet, flicking his gaze down at Meredeth. "Don't you dare move." Then he turned back to the clerk, put on his best warm smile, and walked her out of the room.

Meredeth blew out her cheeks and slid herself closer to the wall. Her right arm had gone all pins and needles—she must have slept on it—and her head no longer seemed apocalyptic but moving brought dancing motes and bright flashes of blue and red to her vision. She leaned against the wall and took a shaky breath, letting her eyes slide closed for a moment but resisting sleep's call.

"Bad one?" asked Bobby from the door.

"Are they gone?"

"Yeah. I told them it was food poisoning. You've got a free meal on the books."

"Grand," she said but then grinned at him.

"All this..." Bobby spread his hands. "It's because of the news report? That Jerry Goode?"

"Jeremy. Jeremy Goode. The prick." She wiped her lips with her hand, feeling something gummed across them and *not* wanting to know what it was. "And, no, not all because of his stupid report. Most of this is because of the .40 Caliber Killer."

"Don't you mean the Dollhouse Killer?"

"Don't you start, Bobby."

He spread his hands, then dropped them to his sides. "I don't know if I should tell you this, but the report got picked up by the AP. The cable pundits are all calling him the Dollhouse Killer already."

"Oh, great." She pushed herself straighter. "How did he know all that, Bobby?"

"The picture? The moonlit stroll on the beach with Chief Saunders?"

"Yeah."

Bobby shrugged. "You know how it works, Meredeth. You pissed off Jackstral or one of his deputies, and Goode slid them a buck or two." He shrugged again.

"But he put so much out there...the photo, the Celtic symbol, the Google subpoena."

"So maybe it was someone in Hanable's Valley." He half-turned but stared at her from the corner of his eye. "Maybe it was Kevin Saunders."

"You don't believe that, and neither do I."

Bobby loosed yet another shrug on the world. "Let's get you up and out of the bathroom, Meredeth. Maybe get you a fresh, hot meal."

Meredeth's stomach roiled, and she groaned. "Let's not talk about F-O-O-D."

"Want me to find a Doc-In-The-Box?"

"Hell, no."

"But this—"

She turned a hot, withering glare his direction.

He took a deep breath and let it out slowly. "Okay, no Doc-In-The-Box. We can call the field office's on-call physician, and—"

"We've been through that, Bobby," said Meredeth. "Come on, help me up." She held up a hand and beckoned him impatiently. "All I need is sleep. There's no medicine that helps these. Just sleep."

"Right, because you do so well at sleeping during these cases."

"I've got some Benadryl."

He watched her for a moment, his gaze assessing and critical, but then he stepped into the bathroom and pulled her up. "I really think this has gone beyond—"

"I know, Bobby," she said softly. "Let's talk about it tomorrow...or do you want to see me puke?"

He kept his grip on her hand and wrapped his other arm around her to keep her steady. "Fine. But tomorrow—"

"Yeah. Tomorrow, we'll talk. Bed." As they moved toward the bed, Meredeth wrinkled her nose at the smell wafting from the remains of her dinner, and her stomach twitched in feeble protest. "Gross."

"I'll get it," said Bobby, but then he hesitated. "When I... Before, in the bathroom...when I tried to take your pulse..."

"What is it, Bobby?"

"Well...you seemed like you were having a nightmare."

Meredeth sighed and shrugged. "I was."

"Want to tell me about it?"

She gazed up at him. "Not tonight."

Nodding, Bobby guided her to the bed, then turned and packed away her room-service dinner, sliding the tray out into the hall. He found the remote and fished it from under the table, putting it and her phone on the nightstand next to her. "I'm going to ask the clerk to give me the room next door," he said softly.

"Fine, Bobby. Fine." She collapsed on the bed more than sat on it. "But tomorrow. Now, get out of here so I can get out of these stinking clothes and go to bed."

He cocked his head to the side for a moment, but then he nodded and turned toward the door without another word. He closed it behind him with a soft click, and Meredeth breathed a sigh of relief.

She unbuttoned her blouse and slid out of her brassiere, finding her too-big T-shirt and pulling it over her head. She kicked off her trousers, for once not worrying about wrinkles—she was going to dry clean everything before wearing them again. The smell of her own emesis still lingered in her nostrils, and she felt sure the stench had invaded her clothes.

Meredeth pulled back the hotel-fare bedclothes and slipped beneath them with a soft groan. She flicked off the light and curled up on her side, eyes open in the darkness, unfocused. Before they drifted shut, her phone rang, and she picked it up, readying a razor-sharp jab to zing Bobby with, but when she looked at the caller ID, a trace of a smile flickered across her face. She accepted the call and pressed the phone to her ear. "Hello, Kevin," she said.

"Meredeth," Saunders said in an even tone.

"I didn't expect—"

"Hold on a minute. I just got off the phone with Bobby."

"That traitor." Her voice sounded bitter, but even so, there was something soft about it.

"I know you don't want to talk about it. That's fine," said Kevin. "*I'll* do the talking for now. You listen."

She felt the urge to snap at him but merely shrugged instead. "I'm too wiped out to argue."

"Good, because you need to hear what I have to say. Your partner is worried sick about you, Meredeth, and he's too good a man to dangle over the precipice like this."

"I don't—"

"*Listen*, FBI. That's your part in this, remember?"

She grunted but kept her mouth shut.

"You don't think you're dangling him in midair, but you are. You heard him this afternoon. He said he's always your Personal Security Detachment, and we all laughed like it was a joke. It *wasn't*. That man feels responsible. If something were to happen to you on his watch, it would eat at him."

"I never asked him to—"

"Shut up," said Kevin in a gentle voice. "Shut up and listen to me, FBI."

"Okay," she said in a small voice.

"He looks up to you, admires you, even. He cares about you and is frustrated watching you slide over the edge of a cliff with his hand half an inch from yours. You think you're in this alone, that *you're* all alone, and I get that. I've been there. But you aren't alone, Meredeth Connelly. Bobby Van Zandt is always a step behind you, watching your back. And we just met, but..." He sniffed. "Look, you can't keep on like this. You're in no shape to face the .40 Caliber Killer, no shape to hunt him. Bobby told me about your conversation this morning, and I get it. I do. But your career isn't worth an early grave, Meredeth."

"Kevin, I'm not taking myself off this case. I—"

"Forget the case! I'm talking about..." He blew out a sigh. "Listen, FBI, you need to get checked out. You don't want a hospital record getting back to your bosses. Fine. Let me come up. I'll take you in. I'll pull out my badge and act like a police chief. I'll insist they treat you as a Jane Doe."

"They won't do it, Kevin. They need to be paid, and that means insurance, and *that* means a medical record." She closed her eyes, absently rubbing at her temple with her free hand. "I appreciate it, though. I really do."

"Oh, they would do it. You haven't known me that long, but anyone who has could tell you I know how to throw my weight around pretty good."

"No hospital, Kevin," she said gently.

Another sigh gusted over the line. "Okay. No hospital, and Bobby already said no Urgent Care. I'll drop those two ideas, but if I do, you're coming down to the Valley tomorrow. Not only is our doctor top-notch like I told you, but he's also my neighbor and good friend. He'll see you tomorrow at ten. No arguments. I already set it up, seeing as how you're stubborn and all."

She closed her eyes against the prickling there. "Okay," she said softly.

"No, he'll... Wait. What did you say?"

"I said, 'okay,' Kevin. I'll be there at ten."

"Well...good. That's good."

"It's time," she whispered. "I...need to get a handle on this. It's impacting every part of the train wreck I lovingly call my life."

"Is it more than just headaches?" asked Kevin.

Meredeth puffed out her cheeks with a huge sigh. "This doesn't get back to Bobby."

"He's got your back, Meredeth."

"I know that, Kevin, but he doesn't need more to worry about, does he?"

For a moment, Kevin said nothing, and Meredeth imagined his face, a look of pure concern pulling his brows together. "That doesn't sound good."

"It's not that bad, but Bobby would worry about it."

"Tell me."

"Nuh-uh. Not until you agree. Until you give me your word."

Kevin sniffed. "Yeah, okay. I give you my word I won't tell Bobby. It's your funeral, but you really should consider trusting someone."

"I am, Kevin. I'm trusting *you*."

"Okay. What's the big secret."

"This case...the children... Something's woken up in my brain."

"I'm not sure what that means."

"It started at the Besson scene. Something about that little boy's room set it off."

"Set what off?"

"Unwanted thoughts. Flights of imagination, I guess. Dark daydreams. And nightmares."

"You can't do this job without some psychic fallout. I still dream about my first body. Staring. Following me around and staring at me."

"You didn't solve it?"

"No, I did, but I'm still haunted. It was...brutal—a brutal beating. Eightball hemorrhages in both eyes, fluid from the ears."

"Ah."

"But this isn't about me, FBI. Tell me about these flights of fancy."

Meredeth shrugged, knowing he couldn't see it but doing it anyway. "I was in the boy's room, looking at his bed—or rather trying *not* to look at it. Know what I mean?"

"Sure."

"The smells..."

"Yeah, there's nothing like it, the smell of a murder scene."

"Right. Well, something in the odor evoked a... I don't know what to call it. An episode of imagination. Whatever. I was somewhere humid, and the air stank of earth and mold and sweat. Above me, something creaked, but it wasn't a *good* creak—not like a boat moored or a rocking chair or anything. It was like I was in a crawl space, and people were fighting above me."

"Hmm," said Kevin.

"A little later, when the headache really got serious, I saw lights flashing in my eyes. Red and blue lights. With the lights, the scene I told you about came back, and that time I also smelled copper and butcher shop and heat."

"You smelled the heat?"

"Yeah. It's something from back home. A... Well, I don't know if it's actually a smell or... I don't know. I think of it as a smell, so maybe it is."

"Okay."

"Then a door slammed—either in my head or out front where Bobby had taken Garson. It... It scared me, Kevin, and for some reason, I wanted to hide in the closet."

"That's pretty specific for an episode of pure imagination. Are you sure it's not a memory?"

"If it is, it's not a memory of my childhood. I grew up with my grandparents. My...my folks were killed when I was young. Car accident."

"I'm sorry to hear that," said Kevin.

"It was a long time ago," she said with a sigh. "I don't remember them. Not really."

"Was that all of it?"

"Yeah. At the scene. Well...almost all of it. I... You know how Debra Besson fought him? Even shot, she fought him." Her throat grew hot and began to ache. "There's something about that kind of heroism that...I don't know."

"It touches you."

"Well, yeah. I guess that's right," said Meredeth.

"What else?"

"That night, I had a dream. There was a little girl in it—a girl named Mercy. Little Mercy."

"Mercy... Not you?"

Meredeth shook her head. "No. When I was little, my grandmother sometimes called me 'Little Merry,' but never Mercy. Anyway, once I hit adolescence, she stopped calling me Merry in favor of my 'big girl name' except for special occasions. Hell, maybe I made her... And the events in the dream...they never happened to me. It's like one of those dreams where you see something horrible, and then later, your brain puts you in the middle of it."

"What happened in the dream?"

"Mercy gets woken up by her father screaming her name out in the front of the trailer. Her first thought, and this is sad, is to check to make sure she's cleaned up her bedroom, that she'd made her bed look nice before she'd fallen asleep, that nothing had fallen over while she slept, that she'd pushed in the chair of her desk. You know how they do...abused kids trying to eliminate anything that might set off their abuser."

"Yeah. Unfortunately, I do."

"Her dad is still out in the living room, but I can hear him stomping around. She wants to hide in the closet, but she does this little calculation: he'd look in there if he didn't find her in bed, and then she'd be trapped. He screams again, and her mother wakes up. I hear the mother out in the hall, taking wincing, little steps toward the living room. Her mother realizes the dad is drunk and tries to calm him down, but it's no use. It just winds him up tighter."

"Right."

"Mercy knows what's coming. She whispers for her mother to stop, but..."

"It doesn't work."

"No, it doesn't. The mom tells the dad to calm down, and—"

"Big mistake."

"Right. I hear an open-handed slap, and the mom crashes into the wall. The little girl turns and runs to a window...opens it. The dad keeps beating the mom, and the little girl scoots right out the window. There's a piece of missing skirting right under her window—just like at the Besson scene—and she crawls under the trailer. Inside, the beating is in full swing, and glass is getting broken up there. Finally, the dad gets tired of beating on mom and slams out of the trailer. She thinks he's leaving and tries not to make a sound, tries not to let him know where she is, but he knows. He crawls in under the trailer with her...and...and..."

"And he catches her. Catches *you*."

"Right. That's when I woke up." Meredeth's pulse thudded in her temples, and purple sprigs of light danced in her vision. "Weird, huh?"

"I don't know as it is," said Kevin. "This job—*your* job especially—puts us into those moments a lot. We have to empathize with the victims, *and* you have to empathize with the perp—"

"Never," she almost snarled. "I try to imagine how they think. What motivates their behavior. That's all."

"Okay. But you're in the minds of both perp and victim. And these murders, with the children...it's a whole other level of hard."

"You can say that again."

"You said you had another nightmare tonight?"

"Yeah, after I passed out—or whatever that was."

Thirty silent seconds ticked away between them, then Kevin said, "Tell me about the dream. We can come back to the passing out part later."

"Not yet," said Meredeth. "At the Eider scene...when I was first looking at the girl...at *Liz*...I..." She swallowed noisily.

"It's okay, Meredeth," said Kevin. "I've stood in my share of crime scenes, trying not to see—"

"It's not that. Well, I mean, it *is*, but I'm used to that part. I was distracted by these flashes. That I'm *not* used to."

"Like at the Besson trailer."

"Yes, but worse in a way."

"How so?"

"It started with more red and blue lights—giant circles flashing bright, then dimming. That much is like the Besson scene, but this time... This time, as they faded, I saw police lights on the ceiling."

"From the cars out front?"

"I didn't *really* see them on the Eider trailer ceiling. It was one of those memories-that's-not-mine kind of thing."

"Okay," Kevin said, not a single hint of judgment, just simple acceptance. "What else?"

"Dr. Williams wanted to examine the girl—*Liz*—so I offered to go examine the master and give him space. It struck me that the Eider household wasn't quite like the others. Everything was clean...no hint of boozing or drugs. I stepped back into Liz's room to ask him about it and...well, I heard a small child crying out in the hall. Or maybe down in the room with the two dead boys." She shrugged, even though she knew the gesture was worthless over the phone. "But Williams didn't hear it."

"A crime scene like that... Who can blame you for getting the hinkies? It wasn't a pleasant scene."

"No. But..." Again, a worthless shrug. "I *heard* it, Kevin. I didn't imagine it. It wasn't something that sounded like a kid crying." She rolled on her side, squeezing her eyes shut. "I ignored it, played it off, and went back to the master. As I was trying to make sense of the blood splatter, I saw a man and a woman shouting at each other, both so full of hate for the other. They screamed and screamed, but I couldn't hear a single word. Then, right before I left the room, I turned a full circle. You know, checking to see if I overlooked something. I saw... I saw a man in the closet. Or I thought I saw him. He was pissed at me, glaring at me with Hell-bright eyes."

"Tell me about tonight's dream."

Meredeth took a deep breath and recounted the dream, the stick figures coming to life, her switches between Little Mercy and Meredeth, Bobby's death, all of it. When she finished, her breath came hard and fast, the dream still too close for comfort.

"Anything else?"

"Isn't that enough?"

"Stress has—"

"I don't think this is stress, Kevin. I've been stressed before."

"Maybe so, Meredeth, but this case involves children. No one takes that in stride. Some just hide it better than others—and I'm putting you in that category."

"What I mean is that these images...these dreams... They feel more like something coming undone inside my head."

"Well, duh," said Kevin with a chuckle. "How could they not? But you said yourself, they aren't *your* memories."

"Yeah..." Her voice wasn't as firm as she would've liked. "But, Kevin, this stuff...it scares me."

"Of course it does, Meredeth."

"I don't mean I'm spooked or uneasy. How'd you put it? I don't mean I've got a case of the hinkies. I'm *scared*, Kevin." She drew a deep breath and held it for a moment, building her courage, reassuring herself that she could trust Saunders...and that if she was wrong about that, his blabbing could never reach the right ears in Washington. "What if... I mean, what if the stress is getting to be too much? What if I... What if I lose it at a crime scene? Washington would jerk me out of the field so fast there'd be a sonic boom in my wake. I'd never get back out here."

Kevin hesitated, and when he spoke, his voice was gentle. "Would that be such a terrible thing, Meredeth?"

"Of course, it would!"

"I only ask because it seems like the job has started eating you alive. These migraines, all these dreams and visions or whatever they are..."

"Kevin, my job is my life."

"I know, FBI. That's what worries me." He sighed, a staccato rumble across the phone lines. "The last year I spent in BCI, the last year I spent as a New York State Trooper, it was...well, it was pretty bad. I took to drinking to manage the stress. Don't get me wrong, I wasn't an alcoholic or anything like that, but I drank a lot, starting almost the minute I signed out of work until I fell asleep. It...and this is a real 'no shit, Sherlock' moment, so get ready for it. It wasn't healthy. It wasn't conducive to my life, to *anyone's* life. And, of course, the job suffered. You have to ask yourself: is it worth doing the job if you can no longer do it well?"

"I can still do it better than almost anyone," said Meredeth, iron behind the words. "I won't let this stop me."

"But you're not a superhero, FBI. You can't control your body, no matter what you think. That's what these visions are trying to tell you. It's why your migraines are mounting up."

"I'm not taking myself out of the field," Meredeth insisted. "I've given up everything to do this job, Kevin. I chose this life, eyes open, but still...the cost is too high to let it all mean nothing. I'll be fine." Kevin said nothing, and Meredeth allowed a moment of silence to stretch between them, then said, "Anyway, I don't know what I'm getting all oogly-boogly about. This isn't like it's the first time I've worked cases with children. I spent seven years in the Crimes Against Children unit. It's not even the first time I've stood in trailers and looked at murdered kids..." She sucked in a deep breath. *"Oh my God!"* she cried. "How could I have missed it?" Her voice rang with new energy, her migraine forgotten for the moment.

"What? Missed what?"

"Seventeen or eighteen years ago, I worked a string of kidnappings." Her voice shook with strong emotion—excitement and fear. "I... These crimes are like those! *Right here in Western New York!*"

"Kidnappings."

"Yeah, but the unsub *killed the mother and younger child.* Don't you see? *He only took the middle child!*" She gasped. "And they were never found, neither alive nor dead."

"Coincidence, Meredeth. The two sets of cases can't be related. It's been so long—"

"Maybe he was in prison. I've got to search ViCAP. Maybe there were other similar crimes elsewhere. Maybe he was in another state." She sat up too fast, and a wave of bright pain washed through her head. "I've got to dig out my notes—"

"Wait a minute, Meredeth. I'm not saying this might not be a lead, but someone else can do the grunt work. Call it in, request the files, whatever you FBI wunderkind do. But in the meantime, you need rest. You've got to unplug, Meredeth. You keep running yourself ragged like this, you're really going to blow a cog."

She relaxed back against the headboard. "Maybe you're right."

"I mean, we don't *know* the cases are related. There are similarities, that much is undeniable, but the fact that our unsub murders the middle child is enough to distinguish the signatures, right?"

"Well...yeah. But the fundamentals are the same—the mother is punished, the youngest is killed painlessly. And signatures *can* change, especially over two decades."

"Okay, we'll look into it. Hard. I promise. But *tomorrow*, FBI. Am I right in assuming your kidnapping cases are still open?"

"Yeah," said Meredeth with a sigh, her previous energy leaving her like an outgoing tide. "Cold, but open."

"Then it's not like we can just open the file and then go visit the kidnapper from two decades ago. At best, we might stamp closed on those cases when we solve these murders. That's not worth making your migraine worse by staying up all night."

"Yeah, but I need to read over my notes. Get a feel for those kidnapping cases again. Connect with them." The sound of her enervated voice disturbed her. She sounded...*old*.

"What you need to do is rest."

"But—"

"No buts, FBI." His firm voice left little room for argument. "I'll call Bobby when I hang up and have *him* retrieve the case files. We can go over them tomorrow. *After* you see Darren."

"Darren?"

"Yeah. My neighbor. Darren Taber, M.D."

"Ah. Right."

"And don't think you can weasel out of it."

"Wouldn't think of it," she said, a faint smile cracking her lips.

"Are you going to sleep, or do I have to call Bobby to come up there and babysit you?"

Meredeth bit her lip and hesitated, wondering if she had the nerve to say it. "*You* could come up and babysit me."

Kevin said nothing for the space of a long breath, then said, "I'm flattered, Meredeth. And very, very tempted. But I meant it when I said you need to rest."

"Yeah," she said with a sigh. She punched two of the pink Benadryl out of the foil pack and tossed them into her mouth, dry swallowing the pills with a grimace. "Benadryl deployed."

"Good. I'll take a raincheck on that other thing."

CHAPTER 10

THE CALM

Hanable's Valley, NY

MEREDETH DELICATELY SCOOPED the last of her eggs to her mouth and smiled at Kevin, who sat wedged into the vinyl booth beside Bobby. Both men had coffee and toast in front of them, and both watched her eat rather than consume their own breakfasts. Her phone chirped, and she glanced down at it and smiled. "You two better eat up, because when I finish my toast, we're out of here. We've got work to do"—she tapped the screen of her phone—"that's the email from Quantico with the cold kidnapping cases in it." Her voice was bright and filled with laughter, and her smile came easy—she'd awakened after eight solid hours of uninterrupted slumber feeling refreshed, and most importantly, headache-free. It felt like a sunny day after a horrible storm.

Bobby grinned and took a bite of his toast.

Kevin sipped his coffee. "You're still going," he said staring down at the black liquid. He raised his gaze and pinned her with it. "Isn't that right, Bobby?"

Without losing his smile, Bobby nodded. "And if I have to go along and babysit you, who will print out all those old files?"

"But I feel so much better," said Meredeth. Even so, her heart was only half in the argument. Deep down, she knew the respite was just that—a temporary peace. She'd had breaks like this before, and when the migraine returned, it would be a bear.

"I *will* arrest you, FBI," said Kevin. "I'll lock you in my holding cell and get Darren to swing by the station for a house call."

"A cell call, you mean," she said and dimpled. "But don't worry. I'm just giving you a hard time."

Kevin sipped his coffee, watching her over his thick mug's rim. "Meantime, Bobby here can get those case files printed like he said."

Bobby gazed at her a moment, his chiseled face impassive, and his lips parted as though he meant to speak, but in the end, he said nothing, only giving her a grave nod. He reached for the check, but Meredeth beat him to it.

"I'll get it," she said. "After all, it doesn't matter whose per diem we put this on." She grinned, and he rewarded her with one of his trademark smiles in return, then slid his dark aviators on.

"You two have fun," he said, then turned to Kevin. "If she gives you any crap, call me, and I'll come on the run. I'll hold her down if need be." As he said the last, he swiveled his gaze toward her and flicked his dark aviators down so he could glare at her over their frames. "Understood?"

Meredeth held up her hands at shoulder height, palms out in surrender. "Hey, I'm game. I'm game." She watched him turn and saunter out of the diner, check the street, then jog across to the police station.

"You lucked out with him, FBI," said Kevin in a soft voice.

"You think? You don't have to put up with his mother-hen routine."

Kevin wrinkled his brow. "He's only trying—"

She repeated her gesture of surrender. "Kidding, Chief. Geesh." She took the bill up to the old cash register enthroned at the end of the counter and paid it with her FBI-issued credit card. While she did that, Kevin dashed down the last of his coffee, then slid a ten onto the table before getting up and walking to the door.

As they stepped out into the perfect spring morning, Meredeth tilted her head back, enjoying the warmth of the sun on her face—not ducking her head to keep the sun out of her eyes, not even bothering to shield her eyes for the first time in days. "All right, Saunders. Let's get this over with."

He grunted and shook his head a little, then beckoned with his left hand and turned to walk around the block. He stopped in front of an old house that had been painted a soft gray and trimmed in white. That the door had a hand-lettered sign attached to it was the only hint that the house was, in fact, a physician's office. Meredeth frowned at it and cocked her head to the side.

"Yeah, don't sweat the small stuff, FBI. He was a specialist at Mount Sinai in Manhattan but got tired of the city life. Neurosurgeon. He came out here to relax, he says, but he's still top-notch."

"If you say so," said Meredeth, "that's good enough for me."

"*And* he's doing this off the books."

"*And* I appreciate that," she said, smiling.

"I'll wait in the waiting room," said Kevin, reaching for the door.

"Nah. I'm a big girl, Saunders. Head back to your station and do your job. I'll come straight over there after the appointment and fill you in."

He shrugged a little and glanced in the direction of the police station. "You sure? It's no big deal if—"

"I'm sure," she said, giving him a gentle push back in the direction they'd come. "I'll be fine."

He treated her to a narrowed-eyed gaze for a moment. "We're friends, remember? Darren and me. He'll tell me if you ditch and then try to run a line of bull at me."

Meredeth chuckled. "Yes, Dad." That earned her a little grin. She turned away and opened the door, then walked into the little room lined with old chairs, a few end tables, and heaps of old magazines. She pulled the door closed behind her and surveyed the room—there was a doorbell screwed to the doorframe of a closed door opposite the entrance, and she crossed the room and rang it. A buzzer sounded deeper in the office, and after a few minutes, a short, olive-complected man with dark curly hair and round glasses, a la John Lennon, opened the door.

"Agent Connelly?" he asked with a grin.

"The one and only."

"You can come on back," he said as though there was a waiting room full of people behind her. He led her deeper into the old house and into a room that appeared to have once been a small parlor or a dining room. He held out his hand, and his lips twisted in a grin as if he could read her mind. "It's not Mount Sinai," he said, "but it's home." He shrugged, and his grin widened. "For now." The room was perhaps ten feet by ten feet and filled with antique medical cabinets, a single treatment table, and, shoehorned into the back corner, two upholstered chairs. "We can skip the table."

Meredeth walked back to the chairs and sank into the one that put her back to the corner, then smiled at the quirky man as he sat next to her.

"Kev said you're having trouble. Headaches?"

"Migraines," she said with a single nod.

"That word has been colloquialized until it's rather meaningless, so let's start off by dealing with that. To me, a migraine is a vascular headache caused by rapid changes of blood vessels in the head. Generally speaking, they are caused by an abnormal sensitivity of the cranial arteries to certain triggers and subsequent spasms. Not all migraines are severe, and not all headaches are migraines."

"What kind of triggers?"

Taber nodded. "Stress, food, weather, menstruation, menopause." He shrugged. "If you'll pardon the observation, you seem to be in the right employment and age bracket for most of those." He spread his hands.

She grimaced. "Way to make a girl feel old, Doc."

He grinned and shrugged. "You asked. Now, migraines are idiosyncratic, and your symptoms may or may not match those of another patient, but the list is pretty specific in terms of diagnostic criteria."

"I'm pretty sure these are migraines," she said. "I get these flashes of light, pain in or behind my eye and eyebrow, and nothing helps once they get rolling. Well, nothing except going to sleep."

"Are they throbbing headaches?"

"Oh, yes."

"Any nausea? Vomiting?"

Meredeth tilted her head back and forth. "Sometimes. With bad ones."

Taber nodded. "Do they always occur in your eyes? Your brows?"

"Yeah. The headache may start somewhere else, but once it's rolling, it's right here." She gestured toward her left eye.

"Always the left?"

She rolled her eyes up toward the ceiling and squinted. "Seems like it."

"And light? Sound? You haven't mentioned either."

"Does the Pope shit in the woods?"

"I'll take that as a 'yes,'" he said with a sparkle in his eye. "What else? What are you holding back?"

"What makes you think I'm holding something back?"

A sly grin spread across his face like dawn breaking from a dark night. "You don't have to be an FBI profiler to be a student of human behavior."

Meredeth felt an answering grin on her lips. "Yeah, okay. I'm having vision problems."

Taber's grin faded, and his brows knitted. "What do you mean?"

"Well, things go..." She waved a hand next to her head. "Wonky." She shook her head. "I can't describe it."

"Try," he said.

"It's important?"

Taber shrugged. "We're talking about something 'wonky' in the general region of your most important organ."

"My stomach?" He grinned at that, but it wasn't as sunny as his previous smile. "Yeah, okay. It's"—she lifted her hand to the side of her face and waved her fingers— "like there's something there, but there isn't. I can see through it, but it's in the way. It's just there, doing its thing, and whatever I want to focus on is on a layer underneath it. Sort of."

"What's it look like?"

Meredeth shrugged. "Lights? No...sparkles? Flashes? I don't know. It's in the shape of a lopsided C most of the time. The stuff behind it, the stuff I'm trying to see, it goes all blurry. Like I'm looking at it through a cloudy prism or water with crud in it."

"Both eyes?"

She shook her head and tapped her left temple. "Only over here." Her expression darkened. "So far."

Taber nodded at that. "Go on."

"I don't know what else to say."

"Yes, you do."

Meredeth frowned and shook her head. "You'd make a good interrogator, Doc."

Taber said nothing, only looked at her, his intelligent gaze resting on her face.

"Okay." She pumped her shoulders up and down, rapid-fire. "I'm getting these...flashes."

"Flashes?"

"Wrong word in this context. Like a half-remembered dream."

"Hallucinations?" He leaned forward, his focus razor-sharp.

"No. I know they aren't...*real*... They're not some kind of thought or false memory or..." She waved her hands. "They are more like images I've seen in a movie or something. I'm in them, they are from my perspective, but it's nothing I've ever experienced in person. I..." She gave him a tight glance.

"I hear things also. The same kind of thing. A kid crying. An ambulance. A gunshot. Like that."

Taber gave a crisp, curt nod. "I don't think those symptoms are related to the headaches."

"That stuff only just started."

"On this particular case?"

Meredeth nodded, her lips pressed tightly together.

Taber's gaze darted down to take in her lips, then flashed to her eyes, then down to her hands tightly clasped in her lap. "Let's get back to the headaches, but before we do, I want to say that your job isn't an easy one. Dealing with what you have to deal with, *seeing* what you have to see..." He shook his head. "Frankly, I'd be concerned if you tried to tell me none of it bothered you."

She nodded again, once.

"These symptoms—the flashbacks—could be—"

"Whoa, whoa, whoa. I didn't say *flashbacks*, I said *flashes*."

He blinked at her vehemence a moment, then lifted a hand. "Okay. These *flashes* don't seem like harmless..." He shook his head and held his hand out toward her.

"Brain bubbles."

"Brain bubbles?" he asked, laughing.

"You mean that isn't a medical term?" she asked with a grin.

"If it isn't, it should be." He grinned a little but sobered quickly. "I think these 'flashes,' as you call them, are important. I don't think you should discount them, but I can't treat you for them."

Meredeth's shoulders bounced in a shrug. "Then who?"

"I can refer you. A psychologist friend of mine—"

"A head-shrinker?"

He cocked his head at her. "Your background includes a lot of psychology—unless your FBI profile page is a complete fiction."

"That's true, but it's...*functional* psychology. It's not about feelings and—" She drew her head back. "Wait a minute... You checked me out?"

He nodded. "Of course, I did. But this is the important thing here: you could benefit from an impartial listener. Someone who can help you get to the root of the trauma—"

"I said these things aren't related to me. They aren't memories, Dr. Taber, they are...whatever they are."

"There's no shame in talking to someone. I've done it myself." He leaned back and looked her in the eye. "Your symptoms...these flashes. They remind me of symptoms one of my other patients has discussed. He is a vet. Afghanistan, Special Forces."

"PTSD?" she asked with a half-laugh as punctuation. "Doesn't that require some kind of trauma?"

"Meredeth," said Taber in a quiet voice. "You experience trauma every time you visit a crime scene. You have coping mechanisms—you couldn't do your job without them—but everything has its limit."

"I thought a trauma was something..." She shrugged and jerked her chin to the side. "Something like what your patient went through over there."

Taber smiled. "When I was at Mount Sinai, I had a patient who, due to medical complications to other procedures, suffered osteonecrosis in both legs. He—"

"Osteonecrosis?"

"Small parts of his femurs died. The only treatment is a period of complete rest—no weight on the impacted bones for eight weeks or more. This triggered severe muscle spasms in his thighs. He reported that the pain was brutal—the worst thing he's ever experienced, and he's dealt with chronic pain for over a decade. His wife told me he couldn't stop himself from screaming when the spasms set off." He shook his head. "It was enough to give him PTSD symptoms. For years, seeing people in severe pain—even on television—brought him right back to those moments where he couldn't control his screaming." He nodded at her. "You see? Trauma is trauma. The source, the severity, all of that is meaningless. What matters is that your mind, your body, categorizes the experience as trauma."

"But still—"

"Let me tell you the symptoms of PTSD. You don't need to say so, but I want you to think about them and see if you recognize them. Okay?"

Meredeth shrugged.

"Trying to avoid thinking or talking about the traumatic event. Avoiding places, activities, or people that remind you of the event. Negative thoughts—about yourself, the world, others, whatever. A feeling of hopelessness. Memory impairment—including not remembering the traumatic event or important aspects of it. Difficulty maintaining close relationships. Detachment, withdrawal from family or friends. Emotional numbness. Sleep trouble. Chronic hypervigilance or being easily startled. Irritability, anger, aggression. Guilt or shame." He closed his mouth and looked at her, his focus bouncing back and forth between her eyes. "If you recognize yourself in those symptoms, please find someone to help you through it." He leaned closer. "Like I said, there's no shame in it, and there are avenues of treatment that don't involve psychoactive medications."

Meredeth said nothing but nodded.

"Okay, back to the migraines—and that is what I think you are suffering from. Ocular migraines to be more specific. I can help you with some medication, but I'd like you to see a retina specialist."

"Why?"

"There may be something physically wrong with your retina, and that might be impacting or even causing your migraines." He gave her a stern look. "Though, if pressed, I'd say your profession has a serious, if not the biggest, impact on your condition. The stress of it. The trauma of it."

Meredeth nodded. "Okay. Can you..."

"I will speak to a colleague on your behalf. I'll explain your concerns about privacy without explaining why and ask if she will see you off the books. I believe she will."

"That would be awesome."

"Good. Let's talk about the medications—and there will be three to start with. The first—"

"Three?"

Taber nodded. "Migraine treatment takes two forms. One side of it is prophylactic—intended to stop the migraine before it happens—and the other side is for relief in a crisis. For prevention, I'd like to start you on amitriptyline and propranolol. The first is a tricyclic antidepressant, but it is useful in the prevention of migraines because it helps control the serotonin levels in your brain, and serotonin is one of the chemical triggers involved in migraine spasms. The second, the propranolol, is a beta-blocker. It's going to do the heavy lifting. It will help by restricting blood flow in the brain, reducing neurological activity, maintaining serotonin..." He paused, then smiled. "In short, it helps reduce stress."

"Will they impact my job performance? Can I still work?"

"No and yes." He grinned at her. "In that order."

"And the relief side of the coin?"

He nodded. "One over-the-counter medicine— Excedrin—and—"

"Aspirin doesn't work."

Again, he nodded. "Yes, I know. The Excedrin is caffeine and aspirin combined, which helps with the spasms, and is only a helper med. The main treatment is sumatriptan, which will act as a pain reliever."

"I don't know if I want to take pain relievers. I have to maintain my focus, my sharpness."

Dr. Taber smiled and tilted his head a little to the left. "But are you maintaining your sharpness through your headaches? Besides, you won't know how the medication affects you until you try it. Some patients report no cognitive effects at all."

"But it's an opiate, right?"

"No. Sumatriptan is a selective serotonin receptor agonist. Basically, it narrows those blood vessels in your brain, as we've already discussed, but also blocks the release of chemicals and hormones that cause pain, nausea, and your other symptoms. And I have to warn you, it may make your headaches worse or increase the frequency of the migraines, especially if you use it too often."

"Great. Do you have any medicine that doesn't cause migraines?" Meredeth grinned.

Taber smiled a little. "That's the nature of my profession. Believe me, I wish it were different."

"Okay, let's talk about other side effects."

"What you might expect," said the doctor with a shrug. "Drowsiness, dizziness, nausea, flushing, a tingling feeling."

"I can handle those." She barked a harsh chuckle. "I already am."

"What I would like you to try is taking the sumatriptan at the first hint of an oncoming attack. Take it when you experience an aura, or anything else that signals a migraine for you."

"Why? Why not wait until it hurts?"

"Two reasons. First, it takes time to get into your bloodstream and to take effect. Second, the nature of pain and pain relief. If you can take a pain reliever *before* you are in serious pain, it will be easier to control it. Wait until the pain is really kicking, and it becomes harder to wrestle it back into the corner."

Meredeth pursed her lips and looked at the floor. "What I've been doing isn't working, so I guess I'll give all this a shot. What happens if none of it works?"

"There are other avenues we can explore."

With a shrug, Meredeth lifted her gaze and looked the doctor in the eye. "Thanks for seeing me like this. I know it's unusual."

Taber shrugged. "It's no problem. I need to monitor your progress, however. Come by in person when you can. When you can't, call me."

"I can do that. How often."

"Let's get you started on the prevention treatment, then let it run a week. Call me at the end of the first week, and we'll either schedule an in-person visit or another call, depending on how well you do." He got to his feet and extended his hand.

Rising, Meredeth took his hand and gave it a firm shake. "Thanks again," she said. "I do appreciate the extra...efforts."

Taber nodded and held out his arm, motioning her to precede him back to the front of the office.

As she stepped out into the morning sunshine, her phone danced in her pocket and played the obnoxious Rick Astley song she'd let Bobby talk her into assigning to her secret admirer's emails. With half a snarl, she cleared the notification, then did away with the special notification. She no longer wanted to know when the stalker dropped her a line. *Let the techs read them*, she thought. *I need some peace for a while.*

CHAPTER 11

BAD NEWS

Hanable's Valley, NY

BOBBY DROPPED THE three case file binders on the conference room table and sat with a grunt. He'd spent the last hour and a half printing and copying them and looked a little worse for wear. "I'm wasted on office work," he said with a grin. "My true value is standing by, looking svelte and dangerous, while someone else does the office work."

Saunders hooked one of the binders with his index finger and pulled it to him. He flipped open the cover, staring down at the case file's contents. "Too ugly to work in public," added Kevin without looking up.

"Oh, ho," said Meredeth in a sing-song voice, smiling wide. She opened her own binder and read the first few lines of the summary page. "This case..." She shook her head. "This case really bothered me at the time. It's weird I didn't think of it sooner."

"Yeah," said Bobby, his own gaze glued to the page. "I mean, it took you like *five whole days* to remember a case from what? Twenty years ago?"

"There about," she said. "Still."

"Meredeth Connelly, not perfect after all," said Bobby but grinned and winked at her to take any sting out of it.

"Says here these kidnappings ranged all over the Southern Tier," said Kevin. "All from trailer parks."

"All from single-parent homes—mothers and kids, exclusively," said Meredeth with a nod. "At least two kids."

"And he took only one of the kids?" asked Bobby. "Always killed everyone else?"

Meredeth shook her head. "No, he only killed the mothers if they woke up and caused a stink." She frowned, then cocked her head to the side. "No, I take that back. He killed every mother that woke up. The rest slept through the crimes."

"But he always took the oldest child, killing the other children?" asked Bobby.

Meredeth nodded. "Sounds familiar, doesn't it?"

"Says here the unsub used a .22 caliber." Kevin thumped the binder with his thumb. "Not a .40."

"Were .40 caliber pistols even a thing way back then?" asked Bobby.

"'*Way back then*,'" Meredeth said and grinned at Kevin, hooking her thumb at her partner. "Can you believe it?"

"Kids these days," said Kevin with an answering grin.

"And to answer your question, my svelte young'un: yes, .40 caliber rounds came out in early 1990. The Bureau didn't adopt the caliber until 1997, though."

Bobby shrugged and went back to reading. "Then they were available?"

"Yeah," said Kevin, looking up. "But they were expensive back then, and .22s have always been available on the cheap, and the ammo is even cheaper. And it says here that the FBI ballistics lab thought he used a homemade silencer."

Meredeth nodded. "They suspected the unsub made one out of a lawnmower muffler and a passel of steel wool, and the forensics team made something similar for around thirty bucks. It wasn't perfect, and it didn't perform one hundred percent of the time, but..." She shrugged.

"Good enough for nineteen kidnappings and twenty-nine corpses."

"Right," said Meredeth with a grimace. "But it would never work with a bigger caliber."

"Why stop at nineteen?" asked Bobby. "Were you close? Did you scare him off?"

Meredeth's frown deepened, and she shook her head. "No, we were never close. He just...stopped."

"It does happen," said Kevin. "Look at BTK."

Shrugging, Meredeth said, "It doesn't happen all that often. Rader was unusual in that."

"Just that?" Bobby asked with a quirked eyebrow and half-smile.

"And he wasn't exactly inactive. He was still stalking, still hunting... His family life got in the way of carrying out his 'projects.' He was a power-control serial killer. He got more out of the process than the act."

"Still," said Kevin.

"And he returned to killing," said Meredeth. "Until it got him apprehended and put away." She looked down at the case file. "This guy just stopped taking kids."

"Maybe he started killing them," said Bobby. "Maybe in another place, another state."

Meredeth shook her head. "We checked ViCAP, Bobby. The .40 Caliber Killer is new—or at least this signature is."

"I don't know," said Kevin, thumping the case file again. "This case seems like a pretty good match."

"Let's compare," said Meredeth with a nod. "Let's not go with 'seems like.' Let's make sure."

"Right," said Kevin. "We've got the exclusivity of the scenes—all trailer parks, all Southern Tier."

"And the single-parent homes," said Bobby.

"No fathers," added Meredeth.

"Multiple children." Kevin looked up at Meredeth. "Any sense of who he killed and who he took?"

"Always in reverse age order. He killed the youngest, took the oldest."

"That's a match, then."

Meredeth shook her head. "You're forgetting the Eiders. He killed the youngest last."

"Right, but they'd just switched rooms."

Bobby arched an eyebrow. "And there was an able-bodied man in the home."

"Maybe he rushed this one." Kevin sighed and shook his head.

"Maybe," said Meredeth, slowly, "but my gut says otherwise."

"Okay, so scratch the 'match' comment, but there's something here. He killed all the younger kids, and he killed them *first*. Let's call it a high-probability similarity."

"Right," said Bobby with laughter in his voice. "He used a gun—a silenced pistol—just like our current unsub."

Meredeth nodded. "Yes, but both the gun and the silencer have been upgraded."

Bobby shrugged his shoulders. "Maybe he's got more money now."

"What else?" asked Kevin.

"He left no evidence at the crime scenes," said Bobby.

"But there were witness reports about various older cars, and we found multiple burned-out cars of matching vintage."

"We don't have anything like that with this present case."

"And then there's the photograph and the symbol he left for us to find. I take it you never found anything like that twenty years ago."

Meredeth nodded. "That's right. The kidnapping unsub didn't do anything like that. Observing from a hidden spot, I mean. No photos, no marks, and no messages, either."

"That you know of," said Bobby, and Meredeth nodded again.

"You said the odds of him being from Hanable's Valley were so low we should treat them as zero."

"Yes," she said. "And I still think that's true."

Kevin cocked his head. "Despite the parking lot? I thought you—"

"I said I think he's from the area, from the Southern Tier. We've established that he doesn't have to be a Hanable's Valley resident to know about the abandoned lot."

"What other areas can we exclude? The towns from the old cases?"

"Hold up. We don't *know* the two are connected. But even if we did, crimes separated by two decades..." She shook her head. "I'm not sure how comfortable I'd be drawing conclusions based on that. But we can feed them into a geospatial hunting modeler."

"You mean we feed in all the locations of the present crimes to narrow down where the unsub might live?" asked Kevin. "Geographic profiling?"

"That's an idea," said Meredeth with a wink at Bobby. "We could do the same for the kidnappings and see if the data sets overlap."

"Worth a try," said Kevin with a shrug. "Let's see what we can rule out."

"Exactly," said Meredeth. "That's all the hunting modeler does—help us prioritize our information. These kidnapping cases might have no impact—they might be nothing more than irrelevant distractions—they might do nothing but reinforce the modeling from the present crimes, or they might help us narrow the window of locations with a high probability. Bobby can get the data for this current series into the program later." She pursed her lips, frowned, and looked up at the ceiling. "The more I think about them, the more I question spending time on these old cases, though."

"Why?"

"The murders during the kidnappings seemed more like crimes of convenience. He killed, yes, but not to serve some internal need. He killed the mothers that woke up; those that might have seen him, interfered. The others he let sleep on blissfully."

"But," said Kevin, holding up an index finger, "he *always* killed the youngest. Couldn't that be his motivation? His signature?"

"Could be," admitted Meredeth. "But the kidnapping bothers me. If he took the older sibling to punish, as we surmise is the point of killing the current older siblings last, why didn't we ever find them?"

"Maybe he took them out of state?" asked Kevin.

"Or buried them deep," added Bobby.

"Or he kept them alive...sold them or something."

"Either way, I'll put them in as separate series for now. We can eyeball them for overlap at the very least."

Kevin made a face. "What I don't understand is: why wait until everyone was home? These are single mothers here. They work. The kids are likely to be latch-key kids—home half the day all alone. Why not grab them when the mother's out?"

"Daylight," said Meredeth with a shrug. "Too many potential witnesses."

"But also, many plausible covers for being around," said Kevin. "Dress up like a utilities guy. Or even drive a white panel van and wear tradesman clothing."

Meredeth shrugged. "Deviant behavior doesn't always make sense."

Kevin chuckled. "That's it? That's all you've got, FBI? Some 'superprofiler.'"

Meredeth shrugged again. "Sometimes the truth is harder to swallow than a convenient fiction. Besides, I don't need to understand the why. I only need to understand the behaviors, and what personality traits are most likely to lead to them."

"But you've got to—" Kevin closed his mouth as his part-time assistant knocked and stuck her head inside.

"Sorry," he said, "I've got a call for Agent Connelly."

"If it's Jeremy Goode, you can give him the standard 'no comment' line we—"

"It's the managing editor of the New York Times."

The two FBI agents and the chief of police exchanged raised-eyebrow glances, then Kevin pointed at the fancy speakerphone in the center of the table. "Put it right there," said Kevin. When the phone rang, he thumped the connect button with his thumb. "This is Chief Saunders of the Hanable's Valley Police—"

"We need Special Agent Connelly," said a gruff voice in Manhattan.

"I'm here," said Meredeth.

"Agent Connelly, this is a courtesy call. My name is Edwin Watts, and I'm the managing editor for the Times. We, that is the New York Times Editorial Board, received a letter with the morning's post. A letter from someone claiming to be the .40 Caliber Killer."

"I see," said Meredeth. "In general, such letters should be sent to the Federal Bureau of Investigation analysis laboratories in Quantico, Virginia, but I'm glad you called as I'd like a copy faxed to me here in Hanable's Valley." She quirked an eyebrow at Kevin.

"Right," he said. "716-555-1212. That's our fax number. Or you can email—"

"As I said, this is a courtesy call. I'm happy to forward the letter to Virginia, but we're running it in a special edition this afternoon."

"You can't do that," said Bobby.

Meredeth raised her hand to stop him. "Mr. Watts, it is Bureau policy to request a hold on publication until we've had a chance to examine the letter. To analyze it for every possible lead. There's no way we can do that in such short time. Workflows being what they are, and the caseload—"

"I understand, Agent Connelly, but once you read it, you'll understand why I'm choosing to disregard the preferences of the FBI and run the drivel this afternoon."

"Mr. Watts, I must not have made it clear how important your cooperation is—"

"I'm faxing you a copy now. Read the letter, read the *threats*, then sing to me about cooperation and—"

"At least, let us review the letter. Perhaps we can suggest edits that will serve both our needs."

"He speaks to that, in his threats. No, we're running it as written."

"We can provide physical security for you," said Bobby.

Watts scoffed. "No, you can't."

"The FBI most certainly can—"

"I'm sure the US Attorney for the Southern District will have no problem getting a court order to stop publication." Meredeth grimaced down at the phone as though trying to force her will through the phone lines.

"We both know that isn't true, Agent. Not in the current political climate. Besides, press time is in less than an hour." The line went dead as Kevin's assistant strode into the room with copies of the fax for each of them.

Meredeth put the printout on top of the binder in front of her, and as she turned her eyes down to read it, she grimaced at a spike of pain drilling through her left eyebrow. She scanned the letter quickly. "Christ," she muttered and swept up her phone. "I've got to call New York," she said without looking at either of the men. "Bobby, call Quantico and let them know what's happening. We might need the big guns on this."

"Right, boss," he said and picked up his own phone and left the room.

Kevin sat, as still as a statue, and stared down at his copy of the letter, his expression growing ever darker the more he read.

CHAPTER 12

EDITS

Letters to the Editor

New York Times

TO THE EDITOR:

Re: The Dollhouse Killer Strikes Again (front page, May 11, Morning Edition)

First, let me begin by saying this "NICKNAME" you've picked up is atrocious. You'd think with an UNKNOWN PERSON (or persons) running around killing folk that you might be a little more circumspect. Alas, this is the world we find ourselves in, though, isn't it? People screaming at their neighbors because they don't agree with one of the so-called parties of our so-called democracy, families coming to blows over which old man is less of a terror when seated in the White House (and here's a clue: they all suck), and literally thousands of equally INANE "reasons."

But enough soapboxing, let's get on with it.

I am the one you are maligning with your nicknames. I am the one FREEING families from the depravities forced upon them by a SICK SOCIETY. I'm sure MEREDETH CONNELLY of the FBI would call me "the UNSUB" and say I'm freeing no one, only murdering them to fulfill some PERVERTED need or another. Let me assure you: nothing could be further from the TRUTH. But more of that later.

I'm happy Agent Connelly has found a friend in the form of KEVIN SAUNDERS, once of Canandaigua and the New York State Police Bureau of Criminal Investigations, but lately chief of Hanable's Valley Police Department in the Southern Tier. This will, no doubt, give her poor slave, ROBERT VAN ZANDT, a bit of a break. I'm sure he needs the rest. I'll not mention anyone else by name—no one else working the case has EARNED my attention. (Do BETTER, idiots.)

I'm unsure if you will take this seriously. After all, I may be a PRANKSTER or other SICK SLOB who wants to take the credit for another's work. I assure you: I am not. To prove this, I will tell you something the AUTHORITIES have kept SECRET: in Hanable's Valley, events necessitated I free [name redacted] from her mortal coil at some distance. I left her where she fell—OUTSIDE. It was not a problem, I'm an excellent shot, and I hit those whom I aim at. I'm sure SPECIAL AGENT CONNELLY can confirm this fact for you and thus establish my bona fides.

Now, to the point. I'm not finished with my work. Not even CLOSE to finished. This is the BEGINNING of my practice, not the end. I will make my nocturnal visits again, and again (and yet again). It is my calling to FREE those living in the gutters, but not by anything they've done themselves. Rather, by means of DIRTBAGS and DRUNKS who leave them saddled with debt and without SKILLS or other MEANS to pay the bills. Life for these families is a DRUDGERY. A bullet from my .40 caliber pistol frees them from that (yet another way to establish my TRUE IDENTITY—a shell casing, if required.)

I'll say this to SPECIAL AGENT CONNELLY: you'd better hurry up, dear. You don't want more bodies on your already fracturing mind. I've KNOWN you for a long time, Meredeth, and you KNOW me, my dear, and not just because of all those EMAILS, either. WAKE UP, girlfriend.

To the publisher of the Times: print this in its entirety, EXACTLY as I've written it, TODAY, or I just might break my preference and hit an upscale neighborhood. Like the one YOU LIVE IN. In fact, for my upscale premier, I might VISIT YOUR HOUSEHOLD or that of your SON who lives at [address redacted]. Don't test me.

To the rest of you drones, I say this: watch for a new work of art from me soon.

Hope that you don't end up as the center piece of my showing.

Yours in DEATH,
ANKOU

(You may call me this without fear of repercussion)

CHAPTER 13

THE STORM

Hanable's Valley, NY

MEREDETH SNARLED AND snapped the special afternoon edition of the Times closed, then folded it in half, and then in half again. Her pulse pounded in her neck, and the pain behind her brows roared, growling and snapping its teeth. She could feel every beat of her heart in her left eye, every erg of anger in the throb of her temples, every ounce of frustration like an icepick driven through her skull. "Dammit!" she rasped. "They ran *all* of it. The US Attorney thought he—"

"All of it except Katrin's name and the address," mused Kevin, "bad grammar and all."

"You don't think he's your secret admirer, do you?" asked Bobby in grave voice.

"Secret admirer?" asked Kevin.

"Yeah," she said and slumped into her chair. "I've had a creep emailing me since... Well, for a long time. Critiquing my work."

Kevin grunted, then turned back to his own copy. "That seems to fit this guy's state of mind. What's with the capitalization?"

With a sigh, she jabbed her thumbnail into the soft tissue above her left eye and grimaced. "Exaggerated self-importance... A belief he is superior to everyone else, and the desire to be recognized as such. Arrogance. Conceit. Pretention."

"Narcissist?" asked Bobby.

Meredeth nodded. "We know he's not a sadistic lust killer, that he's of the assassin archetype. Add to that this admission that he's doing these families—and by extension, society—a favor by committing these crimes. And the letter indicates a powerful thrill-seeking compulsion. He needs to show everyone how much better he is than we are...than the 'drones' are."

"All those fit with the organized crime scenes, the mission-oriented nature of the crimes."

"Yes," Meredeth said, resting her head in her hands and covering her eyes.

"Headache back?" asked Kevin, a symphony of concern in his voice.

"Good Christ, yes," she croaked.

"Give me the scripts Darren wrote you. I'll go get them filled."

"You can't get—"

"The pharmacist lives on the block behind Darren and me. I *can* get those filled, and at wholesale, so shut up, FBI, and hand them over."

"Why is it you only call me 'FBI' when you want to bully me."

"Bully you?" Kevin rolled his eyes. "You've got a gift for expressing gratitude, don't you?"

Meredeth's only reply was a groan as she pressed a hand against her brows and shielded her eyes.

"Do I have to say it twice?"

Meredeth fished in her purse and handed over the written scripts the doctor had given her. "Get me the sumatriptan first. And a big bottle of Excedrin. The other stuff can wait."

"I'll fill them all," said Kevin, "but I'll come back as soon as the sumatriptan is ready. Meantime, Bobby will get the files ready for our review. In the other room." Kevin stepped to the light switch and flicked the overheads off. "You, *FBI*, are to chill out. Tell me if you don't think you can handle that, and I'll lock you in my holding cell."

"I can't just—"

"I *will* put you in a cell, FBI." When he next spoke, his voice softened a touch. "Stop being stupid, Meredeth."

Meredeth flashed a weak grin at him. "You're getting to like this ordering me around stuff."

Kevin glanced at Bobby. "Conference room." Bobby nodded, then exited Kevin's office. He turned his gaze back on Meredeth. "Stay here, Meredeth. Let Bobby handle it until the meds kick in." He pointed at the large, overstuffed couch against one wall. "That's so comfortable that I sometimes want to sleep here, even when nothing is going on. Use it."

Meredeth nodded and smiled, then grimaced and gritted her teeth as the blooms and explosions of light hit her and nausea rolled in like a storm surge. Kevin stepped closer and rested his hand on her shoulder. She squeezed her eyes shut against the deluge of flashing colors and blinding flares, but as usual, it didn't really help, and she opened them again.

"Come on, FBI," said Kevin, but this time, he said the initials in a kind, comforting tone. He slid his hand down her upper arm and cupped it under her elbow. To Meredeth, it felt almost like a caress. He applied gentle pressure to her elbow until she stood, then guided her to the sofa. She sank into its pampering embrace. "Now, shoes off, feet up, lay back, and close those eyes."

Meredith flashed another weak grin at him and did as he bid her.

"Good," he said. "I'll be back as soon as I have the meds." She didn't open her eyes as he slipped out the door and closed it with a soft click. She sighed and let a little groan escape her. The vise closed tighter around her temples, and the icepick in her head drilled deeper. She massaged her forehead with thumb and fingers and fought the weakness in her belly, the hot swirl of nausea. The soft hum of the air handler began to grate on her auditory nerve, and the incessant chatter of a functioning police station seemed to get louder and louder the more she tried to relax. The couch was as good as Kevin had promised, though, and she forced herself to relax into its embrace.

She lay there, trying not to hear the cheerful banter from beyond the door, trying not to notice the rattle-click of the air handler, trying not to *think*. For a woman like Meredeth, for any person with a mind as powerful as hers, stilling it was a tall order. The best she could do was stop herself from following every thought that entered her conscious mind. She drew a cool breath deep into her lungs, focusing on the physical act, feeling each muscle contract and relax, feeling the swell of her rib cage, her diaphragm displacing into her belly.

The din from the outer office died down as a telephone rang, then the murmur of the dispatcher's voice followed as he fielded the call. It wasn't unpleasant, and Meredeth let the low susurration carry her deeper into a state of relaxation. She began a relaxation technique she'd learned from an interview with Chuck Norris, of all people. She tensed the muscles that controlled her toes and relaxed them, then tensed the muscles of her foot and ankle and relaxed them. She carried on that way, moving slowly from her feet toward her head.

She'd gotten to her thighs when she heard the little girl crying. Her eyes snapped open, though she knew she was alone. The sobs swelled to a wail, and in the distance, Meredeth heard the answering wail of an ambulance coming code three. Meredeth sat up, swinging her feet to the floor and finding her shoes on autopilot, but as soon as her heel settled on the insole, the wailing—both from the little girl and then from the ambulance—stopped dead. *Are you going to tell me that wasn't a flashback?* said a cold voice within. She sneered at the thought, not deigning to answer such a stupid question.

She relaxed back into the couch, though she didn't lie down. She released her pent-up breath, closing her eyes and looking for that sense of serenity she'd lost when the little girl cried, but then an image flooded her mind: a woman standing with her back to Meredeth, her shoulders shaking and shivering in her grief. Meredeth reached for her, and as she rested her hand on the woman's shoulder, the woman turned, blood dripping from a ragged cut under her eye.

Meredeth gasped and opened her eyes. "Oh, this is getting ridiculous," she murmured, but in truth, it had gone far past that. *I've got to get a handle on this...get to the bottom of these...images. I need to figure out why they are plaguing me.* She pinched the bridge of her nose. *It's got to be the migraines. Right?* But she sighed and shook her head. *Darren said the migraines and the images weren't likely related.*

Outside, she heard a man's voice swell with anger. "I don't care *what she's doing.* I want to talk to Agent Connelly."

"What now?" Meredeth muttered.

"There's no need to yell, sir," said the dispatcher. "Agent Connelly doesn't work here."

"No? Oh, I must've confused this little shack in this little Podunk town with the FBI Plaza in Buffalo! *I'm so sorry!*"

"There's no need to get nasty, sir."

"Paul? This guy giving you trouble?"

"Oh, here it comes," said the angry man. "Deputy Fife, is it?"

"No, sir. My name is Officer Garson. I can't have you harassing our dispatcher. He's a sworn officer, the same as the rest of us, and you'd do well to show him some respect."

"Then run along and get Connelly!"

"I'm afraid I'm going to have to ask you to stop yelling."

Goode. Meredeth's face distended in a sneer for a heartbeat, then she sighed and pushed herself up, glancing back with longing at the heavenly couch. She walked to the door, hesitating a moment with her hand resting on the knob as the room swam in a lazy circle around her. She took a deep breath, then opened the door and stepped through, recognizing the reporter instantly from the news reports. "I'm not doing interviews, Mr. Goode...not with you, not with anyone," she said in a flat voice.

Behind Goode, a man swung a camera up to his shoulder and flicked on the light attached to it. "Rolling, Jer," he said.

Meredeth shook her head and turned back toward Kevin's office.

"Agent Connelly, what's so interesting in Chief Saunders's office? I noticed your partner is in the other room. Would you care to comment?"

Knowing better, but not able to summon the energy or the patience to care, she turned back to the reporter. "Is that the best you've got, Mr. Goode? Some middle school attempt at slut-shaming?"

Goode's cheeks flushed, and he lifted his tablet, open to the New York Times. "Would you care to comment on the Dollhouse Killer's letter?"

"Why bother? Why not just make up my reply as you have made up the 'facts'"—she hooked her fingers in air quotes—"in your other pieces?"

"I assure you, Connelly, nothing I've ever reported has been anything but the truth."

A hard grin twisted her features. "You and I must have a different definition of that word. Your latest report wasn't even *accurate*, let alone the truth."

He bristled, face flushed, and hid it by shoving his tablet into his pack. "Well, Special Agent Connelly, this is your chance to set it all to rights. What, *exactly*, did I get wrong?" He raised his gaze to meet hers, and his eyes boiled with raw fury despite his controlled tone.

In her mind's eye, Meredeth saw another glare of rage from a man with a dark face due to the suffusion of blood to his skin—and a dark beard. The vision...the memory—or whatever it was—expanded, and in it, she turned and ran from the kitchen of an old trailer and didn't stop running until she was deep in the woods festooned with "Halloween leaves." She heard the door slam far behind her, then a woman's shout of pain and fear and frowned.

"Did I hit a nerve? Was it the length of time you and Chief Saunders have been shacked up? Or maybe the amount of time you've spent in his office rather than out on the streets?" He paused for just enough time for her to open her mouth to reply, then pushed on. "If you're not comfortable with those questions, perhaps you can answer this: is what the Dollhouse Killer said about the Besson girl true? Did he, in fact, shoot her outside and leave her there for the birds to eat?"

Meredeth lifted a hand to rub her left temple. "Mr. Goode..." She sighed and shook her head, the dull throb of anger adding itself to the pounding rhythm of her migraine. "If you weren't such an asshole, *Jeremy*, I might have consented to an interview. Tell me, does this nastiness work out for you? Do people respond to this idiocy? Or do they simply recognize it as the utter lack of intelligence of the duplicitous moron spewing the nonsense?"

Goode sneered at her, his back to the camera, but when he spoke, his voice had the characteristics of emotional turmoil. "Agent Connelly, I don't know what I've done—"

"Shut your mouth. Let me repeat my earlier statement for you. I'll go *really slow* so you can understand. I'm...not...doing...interviews...with...anyone...least...of...all ...a...*fucking pathetic asshole*...like...you. Get it, Goode?"

She snapped her gaze on the cameraman. "Did you get all that? Maybe you can replay it for him if the sentence was too complex for his fifth-grade level of comprehension." Returning her gaze to Goode, she noted the half-smile on his face and grimaced as she recognized she'd just made a huge mistake. "Now, both of you get out of here. These people have real police work to do, and frankly, dealing with scum like you is beneath them." In the corner of her eye, she saw Richie Garson grin, then glance at someone outside her field of view and lose the grin.

His grin widening, Goode nodded. "Oh, I think we've got enough. Thanks for your cooperation, Agent Connelly." He glanced at the cameraman. "Wrap it, Greg. We'll do the transitions out front."

A gunshot sounded, followed almost immediately by a second, and she flinched, then her hand twitched toward her sidearm. No one else reacted.

Across the room, Goode frowned and narrowed his eyes at her, noting her shoulders jerk, her aborted grab at her pistol. "What, you're going to shoot me?"

Shoulders slumped, Meredeth felt a pit yawning in her belly and blinked her eyes against the flashing lights and blooms of color. Nausea sloshed up her throat, and she clamped her jaw against it. A child cried—wailed, really—sounding several rooms away, and an ambulance matched the wailing.

"Mr. Goode, my partner's unwell," said Bobby, earnestness burning in his voice. "That's why she was in

Kevin's office. The chief isn't even here. If you could see your way to—"

"Forget it, Van Zandt," said Goode.

"If you'd allow me to explain—"

With a grin at Meredeth, the reporter said, "Oh, I think Agent Connelly has explained in full. And on camera."

Ragged panting came from Kevin's office—a room she *knew* was empty. It was the kind of hard breathing that beating someone half to death engendered. Despite her knowledge that no one could be in there, Meredeth couldn't resist the urge to glance through the door over her shoulder. As she returned her gaze to the outer room, Bobby was staring at her, a wrinkle of concern spearing the skin between his brows. She shook her head a little, and he turned back to Goode.

"Listen, maybe I can do an interview. We could discuss the case, and I could answer your questions. Within certain parameters, of course." Bobby advanced into the room, one hand out in a placating gesture. "Surely your viewers would rather learn *why* the unsub is—"

"Nah," said Goode. "I think we've got what we came for. See you in the funny papers." He shot one more malicious glance at Meredeth, then turned and made a throat-slitting gesture at the camera.

The red light on the camera winked out, and the man slid it from his shoulder, a sardonic grin on his face. "Masterfully done, Jer," he said. "If only everyone were so easy."

Goode treated the room to one last condescending smile and followed his cameraman outside.

Bobby turned toward her, a frown decorating his face. "Meredeth..."

"I know!" she snapped. "I know, Bobby. I just kicked the dog." A low susurration tickled her eardrums, a murmur of dark consonant dissonance, nonsense syllables of a pleading variety, but unintelligible as if the speaker's mouth was full of viscous fluid—blood, maybe. She turned her gaze toward the hallway leading to the front parking lot, sure the sounds came from that direction, but it was empty.

"On camera, Meredeth."

Meredeth blew her bangs with an exasperated breath. "I know," she said in a calmer voice. She closed her eyes for a moment, wanting nothing more than to go back in time and change things—even if only for five minutes. "I'm..." She sighed and shook her head, turning and going back into Kevin's office. She closed the door and leaned against it, loosing another sigh. "I know," she whispered.

CHAPTER 14

GOODE NEWS

Hanable's Valley, NY

KEVIN GRUNTED AND walked over to the television in the corner of his office. Behind him, Bobby spread out the Chinese take-out containers, opening their tops and burying plastic spoons in their contents. Meredeth sat on the couch, lost in a morose study of the pill bottles in her hands. "God hates a coward," she muttered, getting up and crossing over to the table to grab a bottle of water. She squinted down at the medications, then held them out to Bobby with a sigh.

"Which one?" Bobby asked.

"Sumo-something," she said, peeling the plastic off the Excedrin bottle and popping its top.

"*Suma*," said Bobby, tapping one of the bottles. "Sumatriptan." He looked at Saunders. "Highlighters?"

"Sure," said Kevin, pointing at the desk.

Bobby rummaged in the top drawer a moment. "Yellow is for pain, blue and green are these other two."

"Fine." She opened the bottle he'd marked with a yellow slash, fished out one of the pink triangular pills, and tossed it into her mouth along with the Excedrin, washing both down in a single gulp of the bottled water. She grimaced and sank into one of the chairs, resting her head in her hands.

Saunders bent down, squinting at the front of the television to find the on button, then pressed it. "Let's see what the jerk has to say."

"Let's not and say the whole thing never happened."

"Come on, FBI," said Kevin in a light, teasing tone. "With that personality of yours, this can't be the first time your mouth has run off without you."

Meredeth sucked her teeth. "I'll have you know my personality sparkles like those dumb vampires that are all the rave right now."

Bobby humphed. "Sparkling vampires are so 2005."

"Yeah, well, so am I," grumbled Meredeth.

"Nah, you're at least 2008," said Kevin. "Either of you see the remote?" Bobby pointed at Kevin's desk, where the corner of the remote peeked out from under a mountain of loose papers. "Ah! Right where it should be," said the chief, reaching for the remote and unmuting the television.

"...which the Times ran in a special afternoon edition," said Jeremy Goode. The scene on the screen showed Goode standing across the street from the building they sat in, his back to the front doors.

"Why would they do that?" wondered Abner Postwaite.

"That's answered in the last few paragraphs of the letter," said Goode. He nodded into the camera. "But suffice it to say, the Dollhouse Killer didn't leave them a whole lot of scheduling room."

Abner grunted. "I've read it, as has Janet, but some of our viewers may not have seen it. Can you summarize the letter, Jeremy?"

"But, of course," said Goode. "He begins with a comment about the nickname I dubbed him with—the Dollhouse Killer—which he apparently finds offensive. Included in the comment is a not-so-subtle veiled threat aimed at the media in general, and I suppose, at myself."

"A threat, Jeremy?" asked Janet, and the producer cut to her in time to see the bored expression on her face before her perfect news-anchor mask slid back into place.

"Yes, Janet. He said something along the lines of: 'You'd think people would be more careful what they call the serial killer playing in their backyard. He then comments on the failure of society at large to be open-minded and polite, then segues into a condemnation of American politicians, the president—well, *all* presidents, past and present—and our democratic system."

"I particularly enjoyed that part," said Abner. "Audacious."

"Uh...yeah," said Goode. "But he got all that out of his system in a single paragraph and then moved on to crow about how his perverse, barbaric crimes are a *service* to the community at large. Get this: he claims he is setting those poor people free."

"Setting them free?" asked Janet.

"Yes."

"Free from what?"

"In the Dollhouse Killer's own—"

"Pardon me, Jeremy," said Abner. "Are you sure you want to go on using that nickname? After the threat?"

A lopsided grin broke across Goode's face. "I never back down, Abner. You know that better than most."

"He's a stupid, stupid man," said Kevin around a mouthful of General Tso's Chicken.

"Yeah," said Meredeth.

"A 'duplicitous moron,' I believe is the right description," Bobby said without a hint of a smile.

Meredeth grimaced.

"That works for me," said Kevin, "though I'd have said 'lying prick' and been done with it."

The show switched to a view of the WUTV's studio, and Abner's face crumpled by anxiety. "Er, well... Yes. But in this case, when the person making the threats is a serial—"

"He's a bully and nothing more. And if I may take a moment to address the Dollhouse Killer directly, I'd like him to know that I do not scare easily. In fact, threats of this kind only fuel my initiative, my drive to find the truth."

"Jeremy, I really think—"

"It's okay, Janet," said Goode. "Like all bullies, the unsub will back down as soon as someone stands up to him." The view cut back to the studio, this time catching a moue of concern distorting Janet's pretty features, but she said nothing more, and the broadcast transitioned back to Jeremy. "At any rate, the letter goes on to mention Special Agent Connelly, Special Agent Van Zandt, and Chief Kevin Saunders of the Hanable's Valley Police Department in a positive light. He lumps everyone else working on the investigation into a category of never-do-wells and collectively insults their intelligence, exhorting them to, and I'm quoting here, 'do better, idiots.'"

"How rude," said Abner.

"To confirm his identity, the Dollhouse Killer mentions that one of the Bessons tried to escape him, requiring him to shoot her from a distance. He left her where she fell—evidently outside. Though the Times redacted her name, I've discovered the victim was Katrin Besson—Debra Besson's fourteen-year-old daughter."

"That asshole!" Meredeth snapped. "She was *fourteen*."

"I believe the term is 'fucking pathetic asshole,'" said Bobby, again solemn faced.

"That's enough," she said in an exhausted voice. "I already said I know I made a mistake, Bobby."

Bobby looked down at his food and shook his head a little.

"The Dollhouse Killer then went on to say he's not even close to finished in the taking of innocent lives. He exhorts

Agent Connelly to both 'hurry up' and 'wake up.' It's interesting to note that—"

"What do you suppose he meant by that?" asked Abner.

"I think his meaning is both clear and obvious, Abner."

"Yes...well."

"As I was saying, it is interesting to note that the Dollhouse Killer claims to have known Special Agent Meredeth Connelly for a long time, and worse yet, that she knows the killer personally."

"Do you believe that claim?" asked Janet.

"He used such terms of endearment as 'my dear' and 'girlfriend,' and those terms are generally used between close acquaintances at the very least."

"I agree," said Abner.

"He then goes on to threaten the lives of the New York Times editorial staff to ensure they printed the letter exactly as he'd written it. He closes by promising more 'work' soon."

"Horrible," said Abner.

"Agreed," said Janet.

"Were you able to reach Special Agent Connelly or any of the other officials in charge of the investigation, Jeremy?"

Goode covered what at first appeared as a predatory grin with a grimace. "Indeed I did, Abner, and I must say I'm very concerned by Agent Connelly's mental state and declining behavior."

"Declining behavior?"

"Yes, Janet. I found Agent Connelly working—or perhaps just socializing—at the Hanable's Valley Police Department, which is behind me, earlier this afternoon. I asked her for an interview, and... Well, let's roll the footage and let our viewers judge her actions for themselves."

The view switched to the interior of the police station, a close-up of the HVPD's dispatcher. From off-camera and in a pleasant, professional voice that he hadn't used at all earlier that afternoon, Goode said, "Hello, I'm hoping you can help me. I'd like to ask Special Agent Connelly a few questions about the Dollhouse Killer's letter to the editor. Does she have a moment?"

"There's no need to get nasty, sir. Agent Connelly doesn't work here." said the dispatcher.

The footage cut to a close-up view of Goode wearing a perplexed grin. "I'm sorry. I must have misspoken without realizing. I had no intention of being 'nasty.'" The background was too dark to make out—but it was clearly not shot within the police station. Anyone familiar with the station might see that, but no one else would likely catch it.

"Huh. What was it? Lying prick?" asked Bobby.

"That's it," said Kevin with a grim frown.

"My name is Officer Garson. I can't have you harassing our dispatcher." Garson's voice came from out of the scene, and Goode turned his head to the left."

"Harassing? I was apologizing. Look," said Goode, holding up both hands in supplication. "We've gotten off on the wrong foot. I'm really just trying to—"

From off-camera, Meredeth said, "I'm not doing interviews, Mr. Goode...not with anyone." Her voice was flat, though it contained an undertone that sounded a trifle hostile.

"Would you care to comment on the Dollhouse Killer's letter? He claims to know you."

The camera zoomed in on Meredeth, showing her dark grimace. "Is that the best you've got, Mr. Goode? Some middle school attempt at slut-shaming?"

"I assure you, Agent Connelly, nothing of the kind has ever been my intention. I simply—"

"Why not just make up my reply as you have made up the 'facts'"—she hooked her fingers in air quotes—"in your other pieces?" Her voice and her expression showed what seemed like unwarranted fury and hostility given the editing, the re-cuts of Goode's part.

"I've never reported a single thing that has been anything but the truth—in this story or any other."

A hard grin twisted Meredeth's features. "You and I must have a different definition of that word. Your latest report wasn't even *accurate*, let alone the truth."

The camera switched to a tight close-up of Goode. "I'd love for you to correct anything I've gotten wrong. Our viewers would appreciate it."

"Mr. Goode, my partner's unwell," said Bobby, earnestness burning in his voice, and the scene cut to show him standing outside the conference room in the HVPD station. "We could discuss the case, and I could answer your questions."

From off-camera, Meredeth said, "Do people actually respond to this idiocy? Or do they simply recognize it as the utter lack of intelligence of the duplicitous moron spewing the nonsense?"

"Uh, that would be welcome, Agent Van Zandt," said Jeremy as the view flashed back to his face, his gaze cutting to the side as if switching his view from Connelly to Van Zandt, then cut away an instant later to show Meredeth's narrow-eyed, furious expression.

"If you weren't such an *BEEP*, *Jeremy*, I might have consented to an interview," she said.

The view switched to Jeremy's confused expression. "Agent Connelly, I don't know what I've done to offend you. Whatever it is, I apologize."

"If nothing else," said Kevin, "he's a decent actor."

Bobby scoffed.

On the screen, the view switched back to Meredeth as she lifted a hand to rub her left temple. "Mr. Goode... Shut your mouth. Let me repeat my earlier statement for you. I'll go *really slow* so you can understand. I'm...not...doing...interviews...with...anyone...least...of...all ...a...*BEEP pathetic BEEP*...like...you. Get it, Goode?" She snapped her gaze directly into the camera. "Did you get all that? Maybe you can replay it for him if the sentence was too complex for his fifth-grade level of comprehension."

"I...uh...I'm sorry to have wasted your valuable time, Agent Connelly," said Goode as the scene transitioned back to his face, his expression one of sadness and hurt feelings. "Before I go, could you please confirm the information the Dollhouse Killer mentioned in his letter? About shooting a Besson victim outside the home? Did he leave her where she fell as if murdering her wasn't enough?"

Meredeth flinched, a wild look in her eye, and her hand twitched toward her sidearm. A moment later, she turned and glanced over her shoulder into the shadowy office of the chief behind her. Then her shoulders slumped, and a sick pallor fell over her face.

From off-screen, Bobby repeated, "Mr. Goode, my partner's unwell—"

"Shut your mouth," said Meredeth, her expression crumpling in one of fury and distaste.

The cuts were very good—even Meredeth almost didn't notice.

"Well..." said Abner Postwaite. "That's very..."

"Disturbing," finished Janet. "It seems there is a certain amount of friction between Connelly and Van Zandt?"

"You could say that, Janet," said Goode. "There was more, but we cut it out, as Agent Connelly is obviously under tremendous pressure and unwell—as her partner mentioned." He gave a small shrug. "And her language became unsuitable for the air."

"Foul language from an agent of the Federal Bureau of Investigation is unacceptable," said Abner. "I've a mind to place a call to Washington."

"Let's not be too hasty, Abner," said Goode. "Take the level of stress she must be under into account. Make allowances."

"That's very big of you, Jeremy."

"And compassionate," said Janet.

Again, Goode issued a small shrug. "I can't imagine how hard her job is. I'll continue to monitor the situation. If her behavior becomes any more erratic, we may have to take such drastic measures."

"I find it concerning that she remains in Hanable's Valley," said Abner. "It isn't even the most recent crime."

"No, it isn't," said Goode.

"Is it personal, then? The reason she's spending so much time down there? Is this budding relationship between Chief Saunders and her the reason Hanable's Valley is getting special treatment?"

Bobby cleared his throat, and Meredeth sighed.

"I wasn't aware we were getting special treatment. Or that we were in a relationship, FBI. You could tell a guy."

"Shut it, Saunders."

"I don't know the answer to that, Abner," said Goode with a shrug. "But it is another reason for concern. And there are more..."

"Go on, Jason. Don't be shy," said Abner as the camera switched to him and his wide grin, his bright white teeth gleaming in the studio lights.

"It's Jeremy, Abner," said Goode in a curiously flat voice.

"I beg your pardon, Jeremy. A slip of the tongue."

"It's no problem. But with respect to the causes of concern with Agent Connelly's behavior...well, you know I don't like to cast dispersions without all the facts."

"Of course."

"After her...*breakdown* this afternoon, I did some background on Agent Connelly. Well, I should say I did *additional* background."

"You dug into those previous cases. The reasons for ruffled feathers and whatnot."

"That's right, Abner."

"Go on, then. Our viewers know you are a man of integrity."

With a single nod, Goode stared into the camera. "I previously reported that there was some feeling Agent Connelly had dragged her feet on the Sandman case."

"The fanatic in Savannah, Georgia," said Abner with a knowing grin.

"No, that was the Savannah Strangler, Abner," said Janet. "The Sandman slayings occurred in Daytona Beach, Florida."

"Oh, yes," said Abner.

"Yes, in Daytona Beach," said Goode with a nod. "I placed a few calls to individuals in the position to know and asked them about Connelly's work habits. It seems this penchant for hanging out in her hotel room instead of tracking down the vicious thugs plaguing the areas she was sent to help isn't new behavior."

"No!" said Abner.

"Unfortunately, yes. It seems that while in Daytona"—and here Goode looked down at a notepad—"Connelly spent an average of sixteen hours out of every twenty-four holed up inside her room."

"Six hours working the case! That's—"

"*Eight* hours, Abner," said Goode, "which is a typical workday for many of our viewers."

"But our viewers are not in the business of tracking down dangerous psychopaths stalking our streets."

"*Exactly*, Abner. What's more, there is evidence of the same kind of favoritism shown for the Sheriff of Volusia County as she is showing Chief Saunders. *And* there were rumors of an inappropriate relationship in that case, too."

"You mean she had sexual relations with officials in other cases, too?"

"Well, that is the rumor, Abner—"

"Bullshit!" snapped Meredeth.

"—but I don't really care who Meredeth Connelly is sleeping with. No, what's more important is that in several of the cases I looked at, she could have stopped the serial killer much earlier than she did."

"Surely not, Jeremy!"

"It's true, Abner. Take, for instance, the Sandman case in Daytona. The killer—"

"Warren Montpilar Jefferson," said Abner.

"That's right," said Goode, his bonhomie expression slipping a little. "The *killer* in that case interjected himself into the investigation, as serial killers often do. Jefferson claimed to be a witness to the abduction of his second-to-last victim. Connelly interviewed the guy." Goode turned a scornful glare at the camera. "And for all her vaunted 'superprofiler' status, she didn't identify him, though she did discount his witness statement in its entirety. Tell me, Abner, Janet, with the level of detail her profile contained in that case, how could she not see that Jefferson was who she was looking for? Was she blinded by her...*relationship*...with the Volusia County Sheriff? Was she having a *bad day*? Or was it something else? Some *mind-altering substance*, for instance? Some other *distraction*?"

The scene switched back to the studio, showing both Abner and Janet shaking their heads a little. "I don't know, Jeremy, but none of those...*reasons*...sound acceptable in a case where lives are at stake."

"Indeed," said Goode from off-camera.

"Have you been able to contact Connelly for comment?" asked Janet. "Or anyone with the Federal—"

"You saw how she reacted to a polite request for an interview at the top of my report, Janet." Again, the scene switched back to Jeremy Goode, standing across the street from the Hanable's Valley Police Department. "And there are other cases Connelly let drag on, costing lives and millions of dollars in local law enforcement expenses. Take, for instance, the Red River Killer. In that case, Connelly revised her profile *three times*. And on the TexMex slayings in West Texas, Connelly had the gall to *leave town* for several weeks, no doubt delaying the conclusion of the investigation."

"Shocking, Jeremy," said Abner.

"Yes, it is. It is shocking that the Bureau would allow such behavior to happen *once*, let alone *again and again*. One wonders what kind of oversight the Behavioral Analysis Unit has—that Connelly has—that she can do these things, *again and again,* without consequence."

"Jeremy, I know you cautioned against it, but I'm leaning more and more toward making that call to Washington."

"Well..." Goode plastered a regretful expression on his face. "...I guess...if you think it's best..."

"Yes," said Abner. "I believe I do. I would think so even if we were not under constant threat by this Doll—this *Ankou*. But given the current situation of our viewing community, I feel even stronger about it. We simply cannot allow the Federal Government to—"

"It's all bullshit," said Meredeth in a flat, dead voice.

"*Of course* it is," said Kevin. "Can't expect much else from this character assassination team."

"I don't know..." murmured Bobby. When both Meredeth and Kevin turned incredulous looks on him, he shook his head and said, "I didn't mean that how it sounded. I mean, I did, but I wasn't referring to the content of Goode's nonsense."

Goode and Postwaite rattled on, a constant dribble of drivel underneath the conversation around the table. "Ugh," Meredeth said. "Can you turn him down? He hurts my head."

"I can do you one better." Kevin flicked off the tube and then took another helping of General Tso's. "What did you mean, then, Bobby?"

"Goode..." Bobby waved a hand at the television. "These attacks are so mercenary, so...Machiavellian."

"The Dark Triad," said Meredeth. "You don't think—"

"I don't know what I think," said Bobby, "but—"

"Wait a second. Wait a second," said Kevin. "I get Machiavellianism, at least in the general sense. I think. But Dark Triad?"

Bobby glanced at Meredeth.

"Go ahead."

"Okay," said Bobby. "The Dark Triad is the relationship between three personality traits: narcissism, Machiavellianism, and psychopathy."

"There are several theories explaining serial murder," said Meredeth, "and they all rely on the characteristics associated with the Dark Triad."

"Like?"

"Like a lack of empathy. Impulsive behavior. Manipulation," said Bobby.

"Selfishness and an absence of morality, as well," said Meredeth. "Remember earlier? When I described the unsub in terms of a pragmatic mission-orientated killer?"

Kevin nodded.

"Maybe I was wrong," she said with a shrug. "He might be a power/control-oriented killer. He's exercising the ultimate control over the whole family."

"Okay, but I don't see how that ties in with this Dark Triad thing."

"Narcissistic, Machiavellian, and psychopathic personality types show a high degree of overlap. All three fit into an interpersonal style that can be described as callous and manipulative."

Meredeth nodded. "They show no empathy toward anyone. In fact, they hardly see anyone else as a real person, rather a tool to be used and discarded."

"A killer motivated by power and control tends to rely on manipulation to feed his darker urges and shows zero empathy for anyone else. They may rape to exercise control and degrade their victims, even though sexual gratification isn't the point at all. They may play games with their victim's families—"

"Phone calls. Letters."

Bobby nodded. "Messages that the missing loved one is fine, and that the unsub will let them go in time—"

"Especially if the family does something for him."

Bobby nodded.

"But his letter..." Kevin looked at Meredeth. "You said he fit into that mission-oriented category."

Meredeth nodded. "And the letter still points in that direction."

"As does Goode's behavior," added Bobby. "Which was my point. Goode expresses a Machiavellian personality. He's exploitative, manipulative, amoral, and selfish."

"*And* he's grandiose and prideful."

Bobby nodded.

"In other words," said Kevin in a musing voice, "he's a suspect."

Bobby made a gun from his finger and thumb and shot Kevin with it. "Bullseye, Chief."

CHAPTER 15

THE LONG ROAD HOME

Western NY

KEVIN SMILED AND waved as Bobby reversed them out of the parking lot. For half a heartbeat, he glanced across the street to where Goode had given his report, and his face hardened. Even though the sidewalk was empty, he glared at the spot for a moment, his jaw working as though he chewed on something disgusting. After a moment, and with an obvious effort, he forced a smile and turned back to wave at them again.

"Good grief," muttered Bobby. "Sometimes that man gives me the creeps."

"What? He's the friendly type, Bobby. That's all."

Bobby narrowed his eyes but put on one of his patented "aw-shucks" grins and lifted a hand to wave back. "Yeah? You didn't find that a little strange? The glaring at an empty piece of sidewalk?" He backed into the street and turned the car away, driving northwest on 353.

"No, not really. He's put out with Goode. It's his reputation being smeared alongside mine."

"I don't know, Mere. My hairs are standing up." He lifted his hand to gesture at the back of his head. "Something feels...off."

"Paranoia is an unrelenting mistress."

Bobby barked a harsh laugh. "True, but one of us needs to take a hard look at this whole thing. One of us who isn't wearing rose-colored glasses."

Meredeth snapped her head around to look at him, brows bunched, that telltale line popping up between them. "What do you mean by that?"

Bobby didn't look at her, pretending to check his mirrors instead, and then he lifted a shoulder in a half-hearted shrug. "What was it Goode said about Jefferson? Oh, right. 'He interjected himself into the investigation.' And you like him, Meredeth. Any fool can see that."

"Bobby, that's..." Meredeth turned and glanced back over her shoulder, squinting into the dark. Saunders still stood there, watching their taillights grow ever smaller. "That's crazy," she finished, but her voice sounded much less sure than before. "And yes, I like him, but that's the extent of it."

"Is it?" Bobby repeated.

"Yeah. I can like him and still be objective."

"Then I'm just being paranoid." Bobby kept his gaze on the road ahead of them but drummed the steering wheel with his thumb.

"Yes. Kevin was *already* a part of the investigation. Bodies dropped in his town, Bobby. I'd hardly call that interjecting himself—"

"And the Eider case?"

"You heard the sheriff as well as I did, Bobby. Jackstral *asked* Kevin to come to that scene."

"Sure," said Bobby easily. "But he would, wouldn't he? Once Kevin was already involved?"

Meredeth frowned and glared down the length of the hood. "You're jumping at shadows, Marine. Seeing connections that—"

"Maybe so," said Bobby, "but didn't you teach me to leave no stone unturned, no possibility unexplored?"

"Yes, but there *are* limits."

He shot a quick, bright-eyed glance at her. "Are there?"

"Bobby, he's a *cop*. He's been a cop for a long time."

"And cops can't break? Can't give in to their evil sides?"

"'Evil sides?' Come on, Bobby. That's a stretch. Don't you think he worked major crimes with the NYSP? Don't you think he's seen all of this before?"

"Well, what would you call it then?"

Meredeth lay her head back against the headrest and pushed her thumbs in her eye sockets, pressing upward.

"Bad?"

Meredeth scoffed. "After that hatchet job? What do you think?" She sounded surly, put-upon, half-angry, though she hadn't intended it to be so. "I feel like someone's using a spoon to scoop my eyes right out of my head...or that someone *should* use a spoon to do so. I can't decide which is more accurate."

"I'm sorry," said Bobby. "Let's table this—"

"No, it's not your fault, Bobby." She dropped her hands to her lap and glanced at him sidelong. "But Kevin? No, I don't think so."

Bobby gave another of his peculiar one-shouldered shrugs. "Think about it. The leaks. The evidence he just happened to find up in that tree. The information Goode seems to have access to. The photo that no one saw until after he was on-scene—"

"Woah. Wait a minute, skippy!" she snapped in a voice that twanged like she'd never left the South. "I don't even know if Kevin *went inside* the Eider place. Do you? *I* was inside when the photo turned up, and let me tell you, that girl's body wasn't disturbed. No one had been at her. No one—"

"Except the unsub. *He'd* been at her."

Meredeth heaved a sigh and pressed her eyebrows with the heels of both hands—*hard.* "Look, Bobby, the unsub's activities aren't part of this. We *know* what the unsub did. What I'm saying is that no one messed with her *after* the unsub. She—"

"But you can't know that, Meredeth. You can't—"

"Don't tell me what I can't know, Bobby. I've been doing this—"

"—possibly see whether someone pulled the covers back and—"

"—twenty-three *goddamn* years. When I say I know something you can—"

"—then fixed everything back to how he found them. And anyway, the *unsub* could have done it. I'm just saying that..."

"—bet that I do."

As their raised voices gave way to the tired thump of the frost heaves drifting by under the car's radials, mutual grins slowly blossomed on their faces as the ridiculousness of their argument dawned on them. "Twenty-three *goddamn* years, eh?" said Bobby with a grin.

"Yeah, and tonight, I feel every single one of them." She lifted her hands back to her brow. "Listen, Bobby, you know what to do with these suspicions. You don't need my permission. You don't need my *buy-in*. Which you definitely don't have, if my position isn't clear." She dropped her hands to her lap. "Kevin isn't the unsub—I feel that in my bones—but if the suspicion is there, work it out. Find out for sure. For yourself."

Bobby flicked both shoulders up and down, rapid-fire. "Yeah. I know, Meredeth. I just wanted your take on him."

The frost heaves did all the talking for the next several miles, then Meredeth said, "Now, Goode... I'm on board with Goode. There's something wrong with that little prick. Machiavellian? No doubt. Twisted, amoral? Again, absolutely. The unsub?" She scrunched her lips into a moue.

"That's up to us to prove, so let's get into it. Let's do what Goode spent the last few days doing to us. By end-of-business tomorrow, I want to know everything there is to know about Jeremy Goode."

Bobby grinned like a shark looking at a fat bluefin. "I can do that, boss."

"I know you can, Bobby."

"But, boss?"

"Yeah?" She glanced over at him, watching the dash lights dance in his eyes.

"Don't call me 'skippy.'"

She chuckled. "Yeah, I don't know where that came from." Her smile faded as she turned to look out the windshield. "What do you think about the kidnapping cases? Related or not?"

Bobby shook his head and see-sawed his free hand in the air. "I could go either way. But I don't think it matters much. You didn't have much on your kidnapper, judging by the case files."

Meredeth frowned and gave a single shake of her head. "No, nothing concrete, and he quit before the profile could pay off. He was as much of a mystery at the time as this unsub. But the old profile I developed on the kidnapper might inform our current profile."

"Would it, though? What would it add? What would it change?"

With a one-sided shrug, Meredeth said, "If—and it's a big if—we can tie the cases together, we'd have a better idea of his age, for one thing. He'd be older than we currently believe. Closer to my age than yours. And his motivations... What would the current series of murders tell us about the old kidnappings and murders? And vice versa? Assuming it's the same unsub?"

"Closer to *Kevin's* age, you mean."

She groaned. "Let's not start down that path again."

Bobby pursed his lips. "What kept the kidnapping unsub from offending for the past twenty years?"

"Prison, maybe, as we've already said."

"Or he moved away."

"That, too."

"Or he's like Rader, and his job fed his demons."

"Rader continued to hunt; he just couldn't act on his plans. And his job gave him a feeling of power and control. Word has it he was a real son-of-a-bitch as a compliance officer."

Bobby grunted. "Yeah."

"Let's look at it backward. What does this present series of offenses tell us about the old cases?"

"The trailer thing is high on his list of motivations."

Meredeth nodded. "And the single mother. With the exception of the last case, the dirtbag boyfriends, too. All the pain he rained down on them, the suffering he dished out."

"Anything like that in the kidnappings?"

"Nothing," she said, shaking her head. "Like I told Kevin, the murder of the adults seemed to be a matter of convenience. If he didn't need to kill the mothers, he didn't. And unless my memory has skipped tracks, there were no boyfriends around at the time of the kidnappings."

"But he did kill the youngest child."

"Like the present series, yes. Possibly to protect them from the pain of what he was going to do with the older sib."

"What if it didn't have anything to do with protecting them?"

Meredeth glanced at him askance, her head inclined away. "That's a big part of the profile. The protection."

"I know. What if it's wrong?"

"Then... But if he doesn't care about protecting the younger kids, why kill them first?"

"Younger kids make more noise. My sister's kids are always screaming, even when they're asleep, it seems like."

"Maybe," she said, tugging at her lip. "Another matter of convenience?"

"Let's say all he really cares about is that older child. Say he wants time with them. Time to...I don't know, talk to them without being interrupted."

"The present unsub shoots them in the eye, too, if he can. At least, he did at the Eider's."

"Was the letter for real, then?" asked Bobby. "Does he really think he's freeing them from drudgery? Maybe that's why he says you know one another."

Meredeth scoffed. "I doubt it. He might tell himself he's freeing them, but he's a serial killer, and at the end of the day, he doesn't really care about anyone outside his own skin."

"Did the unsub care in the kidnapping case? Or did he just want to get his freak on with a young teenager?"

"That's the question, isn't it? We can only guess with no bodies."

"But we know the current guy isn't a hedonistic killer. He's a mission-oriented killer."

"Maybe." Meredeth waved her hand in the air in a vague circle. "All that stuff's on the internet now. What if he's trying to throw us off?"

"It's one thing if he's saying one thing and doing another, but there's no sexual sadism in the current series."

"And we can only assume it in the previous series. No evidence of it, only missing bodies that we must surmise he raped." She shook her head. "No, we deal in evidence. In behaviors we *see*, not behaviors we *assume*."

"Yeah," said Bobby with a sigh. "Then what did he do with them?"

"Well, that's the question, isn't it?"

"What if the Eider killings are the anomaly? What if he shot them *all* as a matter of convenience?"

Meredeth's eyebrows knitted, and she winced as the pain behind them increased at the movement. "A scene where he could leave the photo?"

"That's what I'm thinking."

"But why take the risk? Why kill at all? Why not just mail the damn thing to the Times with his silly letter?"

Bobby could only shake his head. "Maybe he wanted us to *know* it was him. That he—a prolific serial criminal—was that close to us. If he just sent in a photo, it could be anyone. Goode, even, looking to influence the news instead of reporting it."

Meredeth shrugged. "The letter could still be that. Goode already seems to know everything that happens in this case as soon as we do."

"Your kidnapper sent no letters, left no photos, no marks on trees."

"No, he didn't. No communication with law enforcement at all. He did his thing, we did ours."

"Confident? Or the reverse?"

"I really don't think he even cared we were hunting him. Either he was so confident he never thought we could catch him or..." She frowned.

"Or he knew what was happening on the law enforcement side. Was Saunders in BCI back then? Was he with NYSP?"

"I don't know," she said with a long sigh. "You're not going to let that go, are you?"

"I don't want to assume he's in the clear."

"Right," she murmured, sticking her thumbnails into the soft flesh between her eyelids and her brows. "Then do me a favor. Let it rest until you have something more than a suspicious mind."

"Meds didn't work?"

"Oh, they worked," she said. "Just not very well. Taber said it wouldn't work as well if I didn't take it before the pain hit. If only I'd known that letter was coming."

"And Goode," Bobby said with a grim smile. "But the prescription says you could take a second one if the first didn't provide enough relief after two hours."

"Yeah. The more you take them, the higher the chance it will start causing more migraines—at least according to what my new friend, Dr. Taber, told me...and Google backs him up, so he must know something after all." With a sardonic grin, she dropped her hands to her lap. "No, it's helping. I'll be all right." Her tone left whether she was trying to convince him or herself ambiguous.

Bobby sighed.

"Help me keep my mind off it. What other light do the current crimes shine on the kidnappings?"

"Now, the mothers always get it. Then, only those that woke up."

"Yeah."

"So, in the last twenty years, their importance in his motivations has increased."

"Or his anger toward his own mother has ratcheted up. Maybe his need to punish them has started eating away at him."

"I don't know," said Bobby. "He could knee-cap them and leave them to bleed out, too. Maybe he really does want to 'end their suffering.'"

"What about the letter? If it is the same unsub, how would his mission of 'freeing' these families translate to the kidnappings?"

Bobby glanced at her. "He 'freed' all the young kids?"

"What about your theory that they were convenience murders?" Her voice snapped a little, raw tension edging her tone. "Maybe the kidnappings were to 'free' the older child, and everyone else was collateral damage."

He shrugged. "If I knew the answers, boss, we'd be on our way to pick this guy up."

"I know," she said softly. "If we believe the letter, then he might be in the system. As a foster kid, or at least someone the Office of Children and Family Services took an interest in."

"Abused? By his mother's boyfriend? And where? Here in New York?"

"Or neglected to the point that the state had to intervene." They rode on to the sound of the car's ever-present war with the frost heaves for a few minutes. "What was it Goode said the symbol meant?" Meredeth asked. "Father?"

"Family," said Bobby with a frown. "I'd forgotten. That tends to support the claims in the letters, right? Freeing families?"

"Then why break up families in the earlier series? Why kill one child, abduct another, and leave the mother alone?"

One of Bobby's shoulders bounced. "Maybe that was her punishment. One child dead and gone, the other just gone, never knowing if the child was still alive or not."

"Pretty horrible."

"Yeah," said Bobby. "Free the youngest, punish the rest?"

"And now he's done punishing them? He's moved on to freeing the whole kit and caboodle?"

"Could be."

"Yeah, it could," said Meredeth. "It very well could be."

"Does that tell us anything if it's true?"

Meredeth let a breath gust from her. "It tells us we don't know enough about this unsub. It tells us we have tons of work to do before we get close to this guy."

"Unless he screws up."

"Right," said Meredeth. "But we both know that means more bodies."

"Yeah," Bobby agreed sourly.

CHAPTER 16

FREE FOR THE TAKING

In a darkened room

LITTLE MERCY SNAPPED awake as the flooring in the hall creaked, her heart thundering, the blood vessels in her neck throbbing, her head aching. A scream scratched her throat, her head still muddled with sleep and dreams. She didn't know if a nightmare had roused her, or if some telltale sound before the creaking floorboard had nudged her toward consciousness.

"The creak doesn't mean anything," she whispered, but at such a low volume, it was almost inaudible—even to herself. She'd just turned ten and was too old to be scared by dreams and darkness. "It's an old trailer. Or it might be Kenny getting up to pee. Or cryin' out for Daddy." She frowned in the darkness. Who is Kenny? she wondered.

After a few moments of half-drowsing, half-muzzy-headed illogical thinking, she shifted the bedclothes off her thin body and shivered at the early morning chill. It wasn't cold outside—not up-north cold, as her mother said—but in the low forties, which was cold for their neck of the woods. Her father insisted they keep the heat turned low, that "nighttime was sleep time," and the covers would keep them warm.

Mercy put her feet down on the thin, threadbare carpet, not worried about stepping on a toy or a book as she'd put all of that away before bed—another thing that her father insisted on. She stood stock-still, listening to the old trailer breathe in the night, imagining her father's stealthy footsteps out in the hall, creeping back toward the room he shared with her mother. And if Kenny (whoever he was) had cried out, that would make a lot of sense.

Moving with the slow care of a young child aiming for stealth, Mercy tip-toed to her door and pressed her ear against it. She listened hard, but if she had heard stealthy footfalls rather than imagining them, they didn't sound again. Softly, and with exaggerated care, she grasped her doorknob and twisted it, gasping silently and freezing in place at the loud click that sounded when the door's mechanism came unclasped.

After a moment, she opened the door a skosh—just enough that she could press her eye into the inch-wide crack between the door and its frame and peek into the gloaming that swathed the hall. Kenny's bedroom was toward the front of the trailer, and she could just make out its dark maw. That was unusual, as her father also insisted on closed doors after bedtime, but Kenny did get up from time to time to go to the bathroom, and sometimes, he left his door open so he could sprint back, fleeing from the terrors in the dark.

All her thoughts about Kenny getting up to pee took their inevitable course, and she eased her door open. After a quick glance toward the living room to see if her daddy was up and drunk, she darted down the hall to the restroom, leaving her door ajar. The entire trailer had the feel of the library at school—an artificial reverence and soft silence. Mercy found it unnerving—as though she'd awakened in an empty trailer rather than one populated by her family. She finished her business, washed her hands, and opened the door to the hall, enduring a sudden shiver of undefined fear.

When she stepped lightly into the hall, she glanced at the closed door of her parents' bedroom, then at Kenny's open door, frowning and shaking her head. *Where is he? If his door is open, it means he isn't in there... Would he dare sneak into the kitchen for a midnight feast?* She hitched her shoulders in a silent shrug. If Kenny wanted to earn their father's wrath, so be it, but she wasn't going to join him—no matter how good a bowl of Golden Grahams sounded.

As she passed his room, she peeked into the darkness, wondering if he lay in there in silence, watching the hall, waiting for her mother's light step. If he was in there, he made no sound as she passed, and she shared a silent sigh and a little grin with the gloom. She reached her own bedroom, turned the knob, and pushed the door open.

That's when it dawned on her.

She had left her door open. She froze, squinting into the stygian gloom. Maybe Kenny had an accident, she thought. He's almost eight, but everyone can have an accident. *She didn't allow herself to think about the fact that since her father had gotten more and more violent, Kenny's bladder control had regressed.* "Kenny," she hissed, "if you wet your bed and are lying in mine with your gross PJs on, I'ma kill you dead." *She took a step into her room and squinted at her bed—which was empty.*

She froze for the second time, running her memory back like a VCR tape, back to when she'd awakened with a kernel of fear in her belly—well, more like a whole cornfield than a single kernel. Did I close the door? *She couldn't remember one way or another. She peered into the corners of her tiny room, but nothing seemed off-kilter—the room was too small to hide much, in any case. Her shoulders bounced in that fast shrug all little kids seemed to know by instinct and grinned at her own silliness. She turned and pushed the door mostly shut—leaving a gap of a few inches so she could watch for Kenny's return and warn him to clean up after himself in the kitchen. Nothing made the mad dash to make the school bus worse than having to watch Kenny get his butt beat. She shivered, looking forward to snuggling down under the blanket, to pulling the covers up over her head until she was toasty warm. She turned toward her little bed with a little smile and took a single little step.*

That was when the thick-fingered hand clamped down on her shoulder with painful force, and its partner snaked around the side of her head and slipped over her mouth, pinching her lips against her teeth, tweaking her nose.

"Now, little princess, you just shush," whispered the man in a gruff, graveside voice. "I'm not a-goin' to hurt you...unless you make me do it. Understand?" They stood frozen a moment, and then the hand on her shoulder grew tighter. "Nod that pretty little head if you understand that disobedience equals pain."

Little Mercy squeezed her eyes shut, praying she'd strayed back into dreamland without realizing it, feeling the need to pee as though she hadn't just gone and knowing she was awake.

"You nod now, girl," the man rasped, his breath in her ear making her want to shudder.

She nodded, though. Lord, yes.

"Good. Now, a few more rules to get us both through this unhurt. You listenin'?"

Again, Little Mercy nodded.

"Good, because I ain't a-goin' to tell you twice. That one there is rule one: you do what I tell you, when I tell you. And I do mean right now, girl. That includes answering my questions, should I feel the need to ask one. Break rule number one and you'll pay the butcher's bill in pain. Do you understand rule one?"

She wanted to shake her head defiantly, to bite his stupid hand, to stomp his foot, to thrash the way kids did in shows and get away and run and hide...or to have the courage to ignore him. But she'd believed him about the butcher's bill—whatever that was—and the price of disobedience, so instead of doing any of that, she nodded.

"Good girl. Rule number two is even simpler: you don't talk. In fact, you don't make no sounds 'tall. Not now, not ever. Unless, o'course, I ask you a question. Rule number three: you don't whine 'n cry, scream 'n stomp, or any other thing bratty little kids do. Rule number four: you eat what I give you, no questions, no smack-talk, no complainin'. Rule number five: if'n anyone finds you out, I'll kill 'em. Kill 'em dead, as you just threatened to do to your brother. That goes for tonight or any time, years in the future or tomorrow. If I have to kill someone cause o' you, I'll smear their blood all over your face so's you remember the lesson. You understand me, girl?"

Every one of the things he said, all his rules, came in a dead voice that lacked warmth or emotion or anything she'd learned to expect from a person. She sniffled, and a tear raced from the tail of her eye, slid down her cheek, and came to rest against his sausage-sized finger.

"Good," he hissed in her ear. "You might just live to the weekend. Now then, when we leave this little room of yours, you do nothing, girl, but what I say. Do that, and I might leave this trailer with your brother and mommy and daddy still drawing air into they's lungs. You want them to live? Your family?"

She nodded, more tears joining the first.

"Now, I need one hand free, so I'll keep my left on your shoulder, right where 'tis. If I squeeze, it means stop, and stop right now. And you recall them rules. Understand?" His huge hand left her mouth, but the one on her shoulder remained. He turned her back toward her bedroom door and applied just enough pressure to set her moving toward it. He reached around her to twist the knob, then pulled the door open in utter silence, and as he did, Mercy smelled hay and dirt and animals. He marshaled her out into the hall and turned her toward her parents' bedroom. When they reached its door, he turned her to face the wall, and the hand on her shoulder disappeared. He leaned down, putting his lips so close to her ear that his lips tickled her a little. She could smell the soap he'd bathed in—something with the smell of lilacs or something like it.

"Don't move, girl. Disobey me and your brother's dead. Don't make a peep, or he dies. Don't do nothin' but stand there, mind. Stand there and wait on me to come back." He quit whispering, but she could still feel him looming over her, hovering, waiting, watching her, ready to stop any foolishness she got up to. "Good," he whispered. "You done good."

Her mother's door clicked as it did when the knob turned, but the sound was a little one, almost indistinguishable from utter silence. She risked a glance over her shoulder. The man was huge, a veritable giant, filling the doorframe like an ogre or a troll, but he moved like a ghost—silent, smooth, purposeful. She kept watching, tracking his darker shape as it floated through the shadowy room.

"Wuh—" started her mother, but she never finished and never would. Instead, there was a pffft sound and bright flash that left her blind for a heartbeat. Another pffft followed the first, and another flash lit the room for half a second.

It was long enough, though, to see the blood on her mother's pillow, her mother's gaping mouth, the hole where her eye used to be.

As her vision returned, the big man turned back toward her, his shadowed eyes glinting. "Good!" He walked toward her slowly—the way her mommy had taught her to walk by dogs she didn't know—but without stealth, without his previous gliding silence. He stopped next to her and said, "Rule number two." Without warning, he flicked on the overhead light, and pale yellow washed the room.

Little Mercy tore her gaze from his face—his face, his face! a tiny voice in the back of her head screamed. She looked at her mother's flaccid body, one arm flung off the edge of the bed, the other still buried under the threadbare blanket, and her gaze lingered on the gore-splattered hole where her denim-colored eye used to be. She stared at her mother's chest, hoping, but knowing it was still and would remain so.

Her gaze zipped to her daddy's side of the bed, expecting something similar—an eyeless corpse, bloodstained, limp, dead—but the bed was empty. She frowned, her brows bunching in the face her mother had always teased her about, saying, "Your face is going to freeze like that, Little Mercy, and then how you going to land yourself a fine husband?" With the faint beat of hope in her heart, she shifted her gaze back to her mother's side of the bed, but she lay as she had—dead and gone.

When her gaze traveled back to the big man, she gasped— she couldn't help it. The big man was gone, and her father stood in his place, a smoking pistol held down by his side, his furious face burning in the darkness. He glared at her. "Rule two, you little brat," he said and grabbed her by the wrist, squeezing and squeezing, grinding her little bones together with savage fury.

Little Mercy bit back the cry that threatened to escape and swallowed her pain—all except the silent tears that spilled down her cheeks. She glanced toward the hall, sudden cold terror gripping her heart.

"Don't you worry, Little Mercy, I killed that little brat first. I don't want kids his age. Too much goddamn hassle."

A sudden flood of fury flashed through her—insane, horrible, mind-crushing rage—and she jerked her wrist out of her father's malignant grasp, turned, and sprinted for Kenny's room, hearing her daddy's pounding footsteps right behind her. She slid to a stop in Kenny's dark doorway, reached inside for the light switch, but hesitated, her molten-steel anger gone cold in an instant, brutal terror taking its place.

Her daddy came to a stop behind her, and she cringed, though he didn't touch her. "Go on," he said in an iron voice that brooked no disobedience.

209   E.H. VICK

Mercy shook her head.

"Rule one. Go on," he insisted.

Hating him, her wrath impotent and useless, she glared up at him and shook her head, risking his anger, risking pain to show her defiance, her disrespect, but before she could finish the movement, one of his lightning-quick hands darted up and left fire in its wake. Her head snapped around, but unlike what usually happened when he hit her, his expression stayed flat, emotionless.

"Rule one," he said.

With his handprint burning across the entire side of her face, a sob lurking in the back of her throat, Mercy turned back and flicked the switch. Light spilled from Kenny's decrepit and scarred Teletubbies lamp—years out of date, years past what her brother wanted in his room, but the only one he would ever have—its yellow warmth replaced by stark, cold white light. Kenny's smooth, waxen face lay frozen and still, like her mother's. Also like her, Kenny had a cavernous black hole in the space his left eye had once occupied.

Her daddy's hand fell on her shoulder, and she winced. "Don't worry, I ain't gonna hurt you. I said so, didn't I?" He gave her shoulder a gentle squeeze. "Take a good look. Drink it in, the perfection of death, his slow regard of silent things, his respect and reverence for our moment together." He breathed heavily for a moment as if he'd sprinted a mile rather than said a few sentences, then her daddy went on, "Drink it in. Memorize the beauty of it. It's something to aspire to, don't you think, Little Merry?"

She furrowed her brows and gazed up into his face, but her father only smiled, his green eyes dancing.

"Your old name—Mercy—doesn't matter anymore, Merry. I've set you free from this imperfect family, this imperfect existence."

Mercy fought the urge to lift a hand to her eye, to check for the jelly-slick spatter of her eye's fluids on her cheeks, the bloody hole where the orb should be.

Seeming to know her thoughts, her father smiled. "No, not like that. I sacrificed all of us. For you, Merry. For you. Hell, you ain't even my blood, girl, and look at what I done for you." He beamed down at her for a few moments, then grasped her shoulder and pulled her into the hall, allowing her one last look over her shoulder, one last look at Kenny's slowly cooling corpse. "You're free of him, Merry. Free of your worthless mother. Free, too, of me, in a minute or two."

He marshaled her back into her bedroom and told her to fill a black garbage bag with the things she wanted to take, telling her she could never come back. Brows furrowed, Mercy took her teddy, her globe with the light inside, her Soda Pop book with the funny goat on the front, three pencils and a rubber gum eraser, a pair of socks, a pair of underwear, and her dinosaur nightlight. When she looked up at him and nodded, her daddy looked heroic in his uniform, his sheriff's deputy badge glowing softly in the moonlight. He'd gained weight while she packed, and his thick, heavy hand patted her tenderly on the head as he'd never done before. Then it shifted to her shoulder, and he marshaled her out of the trailer and out into the night's embrace, shoeless, coatless, and shivering.

He pointed at the ugly old four-door parked under the great big live oak. As skeevy and broken-down as the car seemed to her, it roared to life as soon as her father touched the key. He looked at her in the rearview mirror, his steel-gray eyes flat, emotionless, dead. "You lie down, girl, so no one sees you. I already killed twice for you tonight." Though a bolt of bright pain raced through her at his words, she did as he bid her.

After a short, twisting ride, the hum of the tires on macadam became the crunch of tires on gravel, and the car slowed, then stopped. The front door creaked open, then slammed shut, and she heard footsteps crunching the gravel.

"Come on, girl!"

Mercy bolted up, staring out the front window at the tall, dark-haired man in a cop's uniform walking toward an old Bronco parked ahead of them. The clothes hung from him as though they were for a much fatter man, but the slacks were far too short, and the shirt sleeves seemed intent on cutting into his armpits. Without turning back, the man lifted a too-tan hand and beckoned her, then turned and unlocked the tailgate of the Bronco.

Mercy got out and walked toward him as slow as winter frost. He stood, back to her, and waited, allowing her to set the pace, to take her own sweet time. When she stepped up *beside him, she saw the box in the back of the Ford—the box with its open drawer, a drawer large enough to hold a ten-year-old girl, and ice filled her guts.*

"Get in," said the man in a familiar voice.

She turned her head with tendon-creaking slowness, not wanting to see, not wanting to know, but unable to do more than slow her head's movement. When their eyes met, Jeremy Goode grinned down at her with a mouth full of wolf fangs, and she stumbled back, her bare feet stuttering in the cold, sharp gravel. She whirled around to run, but his tan hand slapped down on her shoulder and paralyzed her.

"Rule one," said Goode, and Mercy screamed.

CHAPTER 17
DAWN'S DECEPTION
Buffalo, NY

GROANING, MEREDETH SHIVERED at the
memory of the dream and rolled to her side, swiping at her
wet cheeks, her migraine growling and clawing at the back
of her left eye. The dream-image of her mother's face
flashed in her inner eye—her dead face...her face with a
hole where *her* left eye should have been—and Meredeth
groaned a second time in as many seconds. "No, no, no," she
murmured. "Just a dream. She died in a car wreck. Grandma
said so."

She flipped to her other side, trying to sink back into
unconsciousness, into a dreamless void where she didn't
have to think, to remember, to *hurt*. Cold golden light
danced on the outside of her eyelids, and she cracked open
her right eye. She'd forgotten to close the black-out curtain
before she fell asleep, and the only thing between her face
and the sun was the worthless sheer curtain. She grunted
and tried again to sleep, but she couldn't. She couldn't
ignore the gold dancing on her eyelids, couldn't ignore the

pain in her chest and throat and head, and couldn't ignore the memory of Kenny.

Because she remembered him now. Kenny.

Her brother, Kenny.

Did he die in the accident, too? Why would Grandma keep that from me? She sat up, her brain awhirl with thoughts, with suppositions, with the desire for fast answers. She grabbed her watch and glanced at it. It was only a little after six, and her grandmother would still be asleep, but she glanced at her cell phone, the temptation burning in her mind anyway. "It's too early," she chided herself. "She's *old*, Meredeth. She needs what sleep she can get." She grimaced, but it slowly became a smile. "And why are you talking to yourself? *Out loud?*"

She got up and filled the tiny coffee maker, glancing back at her phone every twelve and a half seconds, trying to ignore its siren call. "No," she told herself. "Don't call and wake her up."

Jamming her thumb against her upper eyelid, Meredeth stepped into the bathroom and took care of the need that her dream-self hadn't been able to banish. When she emerged, the coffee maker was burbling along happily, but there wasn't enough for a mug yet. She stood in front of it, arms akimbo, and stared down at the beat-up little machine.

She glanced at her phone, then shook her head and looked away. A heartbeat later, she looked back and sighed, then walked over and swept it up off the nightstand. She lay it on the little countertop that held the coffee maker, then slid it over next to the black machine. She frowned at the coffee machine, then the phone's time display, then the coffee maker. She picked up the cell and checked her email. Curiously, the "secret admirer" who'd been sending her emails for almost a year seemed to have stopped since the Times had run the Ankou letter. She glanced at the time again, studiously ignoring the phone icon on her home screen.

"It's too early," she said, then barked a laugh. "Stop talking to yourself, chick."

She glanced at the television, but the last thing she wanted was a repeat dose of Jeremy Goode's unique style of journalism and was sure the talking heads in the cable news industry had already picked his story up. Allegations of sexual misconduct, incompetence, and the apparent breakdown of an elite FBI agent on camera? There was nothing else going on that was half as juicy.

"She's probably awake. You know she said she can't stay asleep these days." She shook her head. "Stop it. Stop talking to yourself, you crazy old dink." With each word, with each syllable, her head throbbed as if to underscore what she was saying.

She turned and scanned the room, looking for what she'd done with the bag of prescription meds. She wanted to take a sumatriptan and an Excedrin with her coffee. She crossed to the little dinette table and reached for her purse, then froze, staring down at the traitorous cell phone still in her hand. "Uh-uh," she said. She lay the phone down and dug through her handbag until she first heard the rattle of the pill bottles, then felt the cool plastic beneath her fingertips.

Meredeth pulled her menagerie of meds out of her purse and stood staring down at the four bottles and their highlighter slashes to mark their contents. The whole business of the sumatriptan causing the migraines to get worse if she took too many of them bothered her—*a lot*—and she couldn't decide what to do about it. She set them on the table and fished out a propranolol and an amitriptyline, washing them down with the dregs of the water glass she'd set on the nightstand before going to sleep.

Behind her, the coffee pot gurgled and hissed, and as she turned to look at it, a bolt of misery lanced through her skull, seeming to originate in her left eyebrow and diving deep toward the core of her brain. "Good morning to you, too, you bastard," she muttered. She turned and took an Excedrin and a sumatriptan from the bottles, then stood looking at them in her palm. She lifted her hand toward her mouth, then lowered it again, then repeated the song and dance two additional times. "This is stupid." She tossed the pills into her mouth and swallowed them. "Now, do your job and make this thing go back to sleep." She barked another uncomfortable laugh. "And you're still talking to yourself, silly woman."

Shaking her head, she turned to stare at the coffee machine—as if that would make it brew any faster—but her phone kept calling her name. She scooped the cell phone up off the table and looked down at the screen, thumbed the contacts icon, scrolled down to the entry for Dawn Connelly, and stared at the picture of her grandmother—a silver-haired woman approaching eighty. *Why didn't you tell me I have a brother?* Her lip curled in a half-smile. *Heh, at least I didn't ask that out loud.* Her thumb hovered over Dawn's picture, descended toward the screen, then hesitated another beat. "Oh, for Chrissake," she murmured and slapped the pad of her thumb on the picture, then lifted the phone to her ear. Dawn picked it up in the middle of the second ring—a sure sign the woman was awake.

"Meredeth? What's wrong?"

"What? Oh, nothing." She frowned, shaking her head. "Well, maybe something. Maybe a lot."

"I'm lost, dear." Dawn Connelly's voice was like crushed velvet, warm and soft.

"The headache is back. I—"

"Oh, no! I know you are worried about the FBI, dear, but you need to see a doctor."

"I have, Grandma. Yesterday. It's official: I have migraines. But he gave me some medicine, and we'll see how it goes."

"That's good. I'm pleased you finally listened to reason."

Meredeth rolled her eyes. "That's not why I called, though."

"No?"

"No."

Seconds ticked by silently while Dawn waited for her to go on. Finally, the old woman said, "Well? Why did you call at the ass-crack of dawn?"

"This case is..." She turned to stare through the sheers at the budding day. "It's hard, Grandma. There are kids involved."

"Oh, that's terrible. It's so hard to see children hurt." She cleared her throat. "Killed. But you know I understand—maybe not the extent of what you see every day, but the horror of it."

Dawn had been a social worker for thirty-seven years, and she'd seen horrors, but there was nothing Meredeth could imagine that would match a little boy with a gaping gunshot wound where his eye once was. "Yeah. This one is particularly bad. I'm not going to put the image in your head, but...it's...gruesome."

Another few seconds of silence ticked by. "Have you seen the news?" Dawn asked in a tentative tone.

Meredeth grimaced. "Jeremy Goode. Yes, we've seen it."

"He seems to dislike you."

"Don't worry about him, Grandma. We've got it under control."

"Oh. Okay."

"These crime scenes...triggered something, Grandma."

"Triggered?"

"Yeah. Flashes of imagery. Sounds."

"Was this after you started the new medications? Because side-effects can—"

"No. It was before."

"Want to tell me about them?"

"No. I mean, not right now. I have a question I need to ask you."

"Okay."

Meredeth couldn't be certain, but she thought she heard a touch of defensiveness in that word. "I've also had nightmares. Oh, I know they're to be expected, a case like this, but they are particularly vivid."

"None of those sentences were questions, Meredeth."

"I know. The dreams were about a mother, a little girl, and...and a man hurting them—"

"That's understandable. From what I understand of your case—"

"Grandma, this is hard for me. Let me finish."

"Go on, then."

"The dreams have also had a boy in them. He's younger than the girl in my dream—a girl called Little Mercy. Isn't that weird? I mean, you used to call me Little Merry, but—"

"Meredeth, I'm not feeling well. I need to go." The warmth in Dawn's voice had departed, leaving the old woman with a dry croak.

"Wait, Grandma. I need to ask you about—"

221   E.H. VICK

"I need my rest!" Dawn snapped.

"—the boy. His name is Kenny—"

"Didn't you hear me? I'm feeling *unwell*, Meredeth. I need to hang up and go lie down. Why must you harass me when I'm ill?"

Meredeth closed her mouth, brows furrowed though the motion *hurt*, and frowned. Years of law enforcement experience had allowed her to develop a pretty accurate instinct about deception and evasiveness, and her grandmother was ringing every alarm bell she had. "Grandma, I don't understand. What happened to Kenny? Why did you allow me to forget him completely?" Dawn said nothing, but Meredeth could hear her ragged breaths. "Was he in the car? Did he die with—"

"Meredeth Brigitte Connelly! Why are you *pestering* me? I've told you I'm feeling unwell!" Dawn's voice blasted across the phone, driving needles of ice into Meredeth's brain.

"If you could just—"

"*Goddamn it, Meredeth!*" Dawn shouted, then she sobbed, and the call went dead.

Meredeth's frown deepened as she pulled the phone from her ear and stared down at the screen. She lifted her thumb from the edge and moved it toward the redial icon, hesitated, and then shrugged and tapped the button. The phone rang four times, then went to voice mail. With a heavy breath, she hung up and redialed, but the third call went straight to voicemail.

The coffee machine gurgled a final time, then beeped, and Meredeth stared at it for a few moments, then sighed and made herself a cup, stealing secret glances at her phone all the while.

CHAPTER 18
CENSURE
Buffalo, NY

MEREDETH HAD FINISHED her breakfast and was toweling her hair dry when her cell phone rang. She grabbed it, hoping it was her grandmother, then frowned down at the caller ID, which read simply: Jim.

James McCutchins had been her boss in the Behavioral Analysis Unit for the past five years. A dyed in the wool blue-flamer, he was ten years younger than she was, but she didn't care about that—she wanted nothing to do with managerial positions. She wanted to be in the field, not trapped in some admin office at Quantico.

She swiped accept and lifted the phone to her ear. "Hey, Jim. What's the word?"

"Not good, Meredeth."

She frowned a little, looking at herself in the mirror. "Oh yeah?"

"I'm not sure if you've seen it, but—"

"Oh, God."

"—that local reporter up there...what's his name...Goode?"

"Jeremy Goode."

"Right. He's made enough of a stink that last night's report has made it to all of the cable news channels."

"I figured as much. It's a great bit of theater."

Jim said nothing for a moment, and Meredeth imagined him sitting at his desk, staring down at his blotter, maybe twiddling one of the number two pencils he liked so much. "I've been on the phone all morning. The avalanche started before I even made it to the office."

"Grant—"

"Grant called, that much is true, but he was the third call of the morning. It went like this: A.D. Brenton called me at 7:05 while I was brushing my teeth. Then, after he hung up, Mike Wilcox from the Office of Professional Responsibility took over the yelling as I poured my morning joe, and while Wilcox chewed my ass, Brenton called Grant. Then, after OPR was done curdling the cream in my cup, Grant put in his obligatory call as I got into the car."

"Jim, that report—"

"Doesn't matter, Meredeth. The reports *never* matter. What matters is the national attention. The cable outlets are having a field day. They've 'fricasseed the Bureau in front of one hundred and fifty million viewers' as A.D. Brenton put it. You've really stepped in it. I've seen the footage of you yelling at Goode at least twenty times, and you can be sure Brenton has seen it twice that many."

"It didn't happen the way Goode made it look. He shot all his questions *after* the incident. At the time, he was more abusive than I was, and I wasn't his only target. He—"

"Brenton said, and I quote, 'Connelly has given the whole Bureau a black eye. Cursing! Name-calling! One hundred and fifty million viewers watched her little temper tantrum! The pundits will fricassee her and us!'"

Meredeth grimaced, walked over to the edge of the bed, and sat down. "I lost my temper—that much is true—but he was yelling at the HVPD staff. Threatening them and yelling, demanding an interview with me. I—"

"'If you weren't such an *BEEP*, Jeremy, I might have consented to an interview,'" he said, quoting her. "I can only imagine what you called him."

Meredeth sighed. "Out of context."

"'Shut your mouth. Let me repeat my earlier statement for you. I'll go really slow so you can understand. I'm...not...doing...interviews...with...anyone...least...of...all ...a...*BEEP pathetic BEEP*...like...you. Get it, Goode?'"

"That's—"

"You said that, right?"

"I lost my temper, as I said. I had a headache. This case—"

"Lost your temper? A headache?" Jim exploded, his breath in his phone's microphone sounding like an artillery barrage. "You said it on *camera*, Connelly! On *video*!"

She closed her eyes against the flashing red and blue lights, denying them. "I did. But if you'll let me explain—"

"Meredeth, there's nothing you can say that will explain it. You know better. Brenton asked me at least thirty times: 'Doesn't she know better? An agent with her experience?' I told him you did, but this footage... Can it be you don't know better?" His voice rasped with fury.

"I *do* know better, Jim. You know I do. But there were extenuating circumstances."

"No, Meredeth. No circumstances. No explanations. It's gone beyond that. Maybe if it had stayed local, I could have fended the vultures off, but..."

Fear trickled through her, a cold arctic wind bleeding under the door in her belly. "Suspended?" she asked in a weak voice.

Jim paused, then sighed. "No. Not suspended. The AD pushed for it, but Grant pointed out that you're in the middle of a case—a case with a growing audience."

"Then?"

When he spoke, Jim's voice was business-like, matter-of-fact. "Letter of censure."

"*What?*" Meredeth asked.

"You heard me. It's the least you should have expected."

Meredeth shook her head. "Jim, that's unfair. I've seen—"

"*On camera*, Connelly."

She snapped her mouth shut, the click of her teeth audible over the phone.

"It's only a letter of censure. Be glad it's not a suspension. Or worse."

"Where's the investigation? Where's the adjudication committee?"

"Meredeth, don't be—"

"I'll appeal it."

"That's your right, of course," he said in a cold voice, "but I wouldn't recommend it."

"Well, why not? This isn't fair. No one's even asked me what happened. Have they at least asked Bobby?"

"Core values, Connelly. Personal integrity, accountability, leadership." He cleared his throat. "And it's only a letter. No financial hit, no suspension, no reassignment."

"Those things fade over time, Jim. A letter of censure is always there."

He sighed. "That's true, but do they really matter? This week? Sure. You won't get any promotions in the immediate future. Two years from now? No one will even remember why you were censured."

She said nothing, not trusting herself to speak.

"Listen, Meredeth. You're not getting promoted, anyway. You've gone as high as you can go and stay in the field. We both know that's your goal, so let's not make this into something more than it is."

"But it's *not fair*, Jim! That story was cut apart and edited to make it seem like I lashed out without provocation. He tried to make me look crazy—emotional, over-wrought. He *retaped* his whole role in the matter! Ask Bobby!"

"You're not hearing me, Connelly. You're getting the rip. It's already decided. The investigation, the adjudication, those things are never more than window-dressing. Appeal it if you like, but Brenton wants this, and he'll be watching you."

"Yeah," she said with a bitter sigh.

"And the appeals never win. You know that."

"Right," she said in a voice as cold as his.

Jim hesitated a moment, then she heard him get up and close his office door. "And listen, Meredeth... No one's saying you shouldn't have barbequed the guy. Well, maybe Brenton's saying that, but he's got a rod so far up his ass you can see it glint when he yawns. Mormon Mafia...anti-profanity, you know the drill." His tone had warmed, become more friendly.

"Yeah."

"Anyway, as I said, the letter's really the best deal for you. No unpaid suspension. No demotion. It's just a letter in your file."

"Yeah," she repeated in the same arctic tone.,

"And in the meantime, you stay right where you are—in the field, doing what you love. Away from the office politics. Away from asshats like Brenton. That's what you want, right?"

A sigh escaped her. "Yeah," she said softly.

"The way to handle this is to go snatch the .40 Caliber Killer off the street. Do it in record time, with as much public attention as you can get, and all will be forgiven. Not even Brenton will look at you cross-eyed."

"I'd do that regardless. That crap Goode spewed about being slow on the draw is nothing more than—"

"I know," said Jim softly. "You need a thicker skin, Meredeth. Guys like that thrive on pulling your strings. Making you dance to *their* tune and in *their* time."

"I know, Jim. It just chaps my ass."

McCutchins sniffed. "Why did Van Zandt keep repeating you are unwell? What's going on?"

"Nothing," she said. "The headache. And he only said it once. Goode took it out of context and spliced it in multiple times."

He said nothing for the time it took Meredeth to draw and exhale five breaths. "Is there something you need to communicate to me?"

"No, nothing," said Meredeth, her heartbeat accelerating like she was sprinting uphill.

"Are you sure?"

"Yes."

"You can tell me, you know. If there's something going on. Medically, I mean."

"Really, Jim, there's nothing."

"And if I ask Bobby? Will he say the same thing?"

She thought about their conversation in the car and decided to trust Bobby's word. After all, there was nothing she could do, one way or the other. "Yes. Of course. I was taking a rest in the chief's dark office, trying to get rid of a headache from a lack of sleep. It was a bit of downtime, so Bobby said I should grab the quiet time while I could."

"Where was the chief?"

"Off doing chief-stuff."

Jim sniffed again, and Meredeth felt a moment's fear. He'd spent years in the field, too, and he had the same instincts about deception that she did. But then he said, "Okay. Just keep in mind that you can bring things to me if you need to."

"Right. I know that, Jim."

"And if I can give you one last piece of advice, just take the censure and move on. No appeal, no stink in the press, and for God's sake, please no lawsuit about sexual discrimination. The rip's because you got caught on camera with your backside showing. It's got nothing to do with anything else."

"Right. Thanks, Jim," she said, thinking anything but that, but wanting the call to end so she could call Bobby and warn him that Jim might call. They said their goodbyes, and for her part, Meredeth tried to make hers sound upbeat, positive. Truth to tell, she felt anything but that. She felt resentful, abused, hung out to dry. It was bad enough, doing the job she did—out in the field, little in the way of support, the pressure of all the active serial killer cases in the country bearing down on the back of her neck—but getting a rip for Goode's hatchet job was like the rotted cherry atop a second helping of shit.

She settled on texting Bobby in case Jim had hung up with her and then speed-dialed her partner. Van Zandt's reply came instantly: "No problem. I'm on the phone with Saunders now—I'll pass it on to him. You had an exhaustion headache, and I told you to take it easy for an hour." She nodded at the phone, then typed, "You're a superstar, Van Zandt, but if you ever tell anyone I said so, there's gonna be trouble." He replied with one of those laughing emoticons that were all the rage.

Meredeth lay her phone on the bed next to her and collapsed backward, loosening her muscles all at once, and flopping down like a fish on the shore. She felt like screaming, felt like crying, felt like breaking something...like Jeremy Goode's stupid teeth.

Despite the morning's stress, her head felt marginally better after taking the sumatriptan and Excedrin combination, and she counted that as a good thing. Even so, her mood was foul and growing worse by the second. The idea that Brenton would push for a reprimand without knowing the facts, without knowing *her*, made her angrier and angrier with each passing moment. She had the feeling that Jim and Grant hadn't fought very hard to keep her out of trouble, that they hadn't been willing to risk the office politics that would have come from putting up a real fight, and that seethed and sizzled in her mind, inflaming her, filling her with bile. No one had her back—well, with the exception of Bobby and Kevin.

She thought about the way her grandmother had reacted to her questions—more fuel for the fire—and she narrowed her eyes. *What are you hiding, Granny? What's got you running for cover? The fact that I remembered Kenny, or something else?*

When her phone jangled, she had no idea how long she'd lain there stewing, thinking up one plan after another to ruin Jeremy Goode, to trap him, to make him act like an ass on national television, to expose his true colors, but in the end, she had discarded them all as petty or juvenile. She wasn't as oblivious of the FBI's core values as Assistant Director Benton seemed to think.

She accepted the call without looking at the phone, then pressed it to her ear. "Connelly," she said.

"I'd say good morning, FBI, but I don't want to get my ass kicked."

"You're smarter than you look, Chief."

"Ouch," he said with a chuckle.

"Bobby told you, eh?"

"He did. I'm sorry."

"Bullshit politics. What are you gonna do?"

"It still sucks, Meredeth. A stern talking to? Sure, you deserve that for ignoring the camera guy, but a letter in your file? Nah."

"Thanks," she said listlessly.

"Want me to drive down to D.C. and kick some major ass?"

"I'd probably get arrested with my luck," she said. "Inciting a riot or something."

"Nah. They'd never catch me, so there would be no tie back to you."

"Come on, Saunders. It's the Federal Bureau of Investigation, the *premiere* law enforcement agency in the entire world."

"I don't know, FBI. I can be pretty cat-like when I want to."

"Cat-like? You mean you pee in a box of sand?"

"Well, that too, but I meant agile. Light on my feet."

"Ah." Silence stretched between them, but it was a companionable silence. She felt comfortable with Kevin. There was never any pressure, never any undercurrent that she wasn't good enough. "Maybe I really should retire back to home."

"Hell, FBI, you retire, and I'll hire you. Chief of Detectives. How's that sound?"

"You don't have any detectives, Saunders."

"Well, you'd be the first, therefore the chief by default."

"Or I could run for sheriff."

He chuckled warmly. "Not overly impressed with Jackstral, are you?"

"That's one way of saying it. Another way would be: I think he's an asshole."

"He is," said Kevin with another chuckle, "but he's not so bad once you get to hate him. And only a little bit bent, to boot."

"Yeah." She tugged her bottom lip with her free hand, trying to decide if she wanted to ask Kevin for more help. "Listen, can you do me a favor? I need a name run, and it's personal, not work."

"Old boyfriend, heh? Maybe I'll look him up and then give him a call. Scare him off."

"Brother. I think."

Kevin sobered. "I thought you were an only child. Don't know why."

"That's what I thought, too—at least until this morning. I had another dream, and in this one, that boy was back, but I knew his name—Kenny."

"Kenny Connelly? N-E-L-L-Y, right? I'll punch him in right here from home."

"Yeah, Connelly, same as me."

"Give me half a second." She heard him clatter away at his keyboard. "You know, I still don't know what state you're from."

"Georgia."

"Really 'Down South,' heh?"

"That's right. Little town between Hotlanta and Savannah."

"Named?"

"Belle's Crossing."

"Well, that's a name and a half, FBI. Searching." He clattered away some more. "Nothing here."

"No death certificate? Would have been thirty-five years ago."

"Nothing from Oglethorpe County at all for Kenny Connelly."

"Hmm. How about Laura and Garry Connelly? My mother and father. Same time frame."

He typed their names in. "No, nothing."

"That's not possible," she muttered.

"Maybe the courthouse had a fire and lost all the records before they got them digitized."

"No, no courthouse fires."

"Look up Dawn Connelly."

He typed for a minute, then said, "Yeah, she's here. A social worker for the county. Married to Ca-jed-el? K-J-E-T-L?"

Meredeth chuckled. "It's Scandinavian. It sounds like 'cheddar,' but with an 'il' sound on the end instead of the 'ar.' 'Chedil.'"

"Wow, his parents hated him."

"And you don't even know what it means."

"Yeah? Tell me."

"It means, 'bowl for sacrificial blood,' and also, 'helmet.'"

"Oh, that's just awesome. 'Hello, little bowl for sacrificial blood. How are you today?'"

She grinned despite everything else. "My grandfather, and he was as sweet as spun sugar."

"Gone now, I take it?"

"Yeah, fifteen years. Heart attack."

"I'm sorry for dredging that up."

"It was a long time ago. So...Granny is there, and Gramps, but no Mom and Dad, and no Kenny?"

"That's about the size of it. Are you sure you have the names right?"

Meredeth shrugged. "It's what Granny always told me—except for Kenny. She's never mentioned him." She related the story of the early morning phone call.

"In light of these names sounding fictitious, that's pretty strange, FBI."

"Yeah," she said pensively. "I got the feeling she was being evasive and outright dishonest. You know the feeling."

"When you've got a skell in the box and he's dancing as fast as his tongue can wag?"

"That's it."

"Well...maybe she's trying to protect you."

"From what?"

"She's your grandmother, FBI. From *everything*."

"I guess so, but in this case, protecting me seems to be hurting me."

"Yeah, well, you've never raised a child. Sometimes you have to pick the lesser of two hurts."

"Have you? Raised a child, I mean?"

"Three of them. Jennifer's done with her undergrad and is off in Rochester studying to be a doctor. Kevin Junior is at Vanderbilt studying history—because that will land him a great job." He scoffed and laughed at the same time.

"And?"

"And what?"

"You said you've raised three of them, but that's only two."

"Yeah. Sensitive subject. Vanessa passed away."

"I'm sorry, Kevin."

"You didn't know. How could you? She was..." He cleared his throat. "She went out with the local rebel—this was when we lived in Canandaigua. He was a piece of work, but there was nothing I could say that helped her see that. In fact, everything I said just made her hold on tighter to his stupid studded leather jacket. I was a cop. Worse, I was her father. What did I know?" He took a deep breath. "He got her into drugs. First, just pot. No big deal. And drinking—though she was only sixteen. He was a year older. Things...progressed. She never made it to her high school graduation. Overdose."

"That's horrible, Kevin."

"Yeah, it is. At least the bastard died at the same time so I didn't have to go to jail for murdering his skank ass." He drew in a deep breath. "I think they got a hot packet of dope and it killed them both. I should have busted them up. Busted them both, sent them to jail for six months or so on a pot beef, but I couldn't bring myself to do that. I failed her, Meredeth, because I couldn't pick the lesser of the two hurts."

"Is that why... No, that's not my business."

"What do you want to know? I don't mind."

"Is that why you're single?"

"That and the job. The drinking I told you about. Nance couldn't handle how I went off the rails. She also couldn't forgive me for letting Vanessa die. It wasn't rational, and she said as much, but she couldn't stop thinking that way, couldn't forgive me."

"Oh. I'm sorry."

"It was years ago."

"Still."

"Well, I appreciate the sentiment. What about you, FBI? Ever married?"

"Only to the damn job."

"I hear you. Sometimes, I think it would have been better for everyone if I'd gone that route."

"Don't say that, Kevin."

He cleared his throat again. "Anyway, what do we do about tracking down your brother? Have anything more than the name?"

"My folks passed away on March 13, 1986. It was a big crash. Maybe it made the papers."

"Checking." His keyboard clicked and clacked as he typed in the search query. "Hmm, this is strange, FBI."

"Find it?"

"No. No mention of it in any paper in Oglethorpe County. No police bulletin about the accident, either."

Meredeth shrugged and frowned. "Maybe I have the date wrong, but it was definitely in March."

"Let me remove the date from the search string." There was a short pause. "Still nothing."

"That's weird."

"Let me try something."

"Go for it."

After a moment, Kevin grunted and said, "Oh boy."

"Did you find it?"

"No. There's nothing on your folks in the papers, but I found something that mentioned your grandmother. March 15, 1986. The Ides of March."

Meredeth waited a moment, but he didn't go on. "Well? Are you going to read it to me?"

"Maybe you should let it lie, FBI."

"Yeah, that's not going to happen. Especially now."

"This is from the Lexington Examiner."

"That's the county seat."

"Okay. It says here that Dawn Connelly responded to the scene of a violent crime, that she was the social worker looking after a pair of kids in Rockford."

"She did have kids all over the county. But I'm from Belle's Crossing. I told you that."

"I know you did, Meredeth. This case was probably some other kids she was looking after, but it says she took a ten-year-old girl into her own home on an emergency foster basis. She was interviewed for the story. Dawn said: 'The child was traumatized by the violent and deplorable events that occurred in the family mobile home.' It says another child was admitted to the local hospital for observation. He was in rough shape due to neglect."

"I don't remember any foster kids. Maybe it was before the accident."

"Maybe. Yeah, you're probably right."

The way he said it drew a harsh line between Meredeth's brows. "Now, don't you start."

"I'm just saying. You don't remember any of this, so it probably happened like you said."

"But you don't believe it, Kevin. That much's plain by the sound of your voice."

"Well, I'm a jaded old cop. I don't believe much of what I hear these days."

Meredeth sat for a moment, furiously dredging her memory for the events mentioned in the paper but drawing a blank.

"What was the girl's name?"

"Her name was withheld from publication."

"What about the parents? What happened?"

"All this rag says is that domestic violence rendered the trailer unsuitable for the children. Sounds like cop-talk to me. How about you?"

"Right. Sounds like a serious beating."

"Or something worse." Kevin sucked his teeth. "Maybe we are looking at this from the wrong direction."

"Meaning?"

"Your grandmother adopted you, right? Legally, I mean."

"Yes. I remember it. DFCS had to come in and do a home evaluation, even though they were my grandparents, and even though Granny worked for the department. Then there was a hearing. It was my first time in a courtroom."

"Then there will be an adoption petition and ruling."

"Yeah, I suppose."

"You could get your records. Hell, we might be able to do it right now. Let me look around the web."

"Why would I..."

"It might let you find your original identification documents. I'm not sure, FBI. I'm not the one from Georgia." His fingers rattled more keys. "Ah," he said. "There's this website: the Georgia Adoption Reunion Registry. It's a non-profit the state contracted to help with adoption searches. It says here you can find your birth parents—"

"They're dead, Kevin."

"—or siblings. Ah. It will still require a petition for your records to be opened, but you have to contact these people first—evidently, it's required by Georgia law. You can't get your original birth certificate any other way."

"Something to consider," Meredeth said. "But I know my parents' names. I know Kenny's name."

"Do you?" he asked quietly.

"Yes. My grandmother told me their names. Garry and Laura, and I remembered Kenny's name on my own."

"I've got another idea..." He typed for a moment, then said, "Right. I just searched the Georgia state records site for Garry Connelly. There are no vital records for anyone in that name, that spelling. And no marriage records for Garry and Laura. No birth records for Meredeth Connelly or Kenny Connelly. You made it sound like Dawn is your paternal grandmother. Is that right?"

"Yes," whispered Meredeth. A growing feeling of unease had invaded her thoughts—a sense of foreboding and dread, as though something inside her knew where this line of thinking would lead and didn't want her walking that path. "At least, that's what she's always told me."

"Then Garry should have records. Hold on." More keys clacked in the background. "No records that Dawn Connelly ever gave birth. Kjetl, either."

"She always said Daddy was an only child, that she had a difficult delivery and couldn't have any other children."

"Something's off here, FBI. You see that, right?"

"I do," she said in a weak voice. "Dawn's been lying to me my whole life. Who is she to me? If she had no children, she's not my grandmother."

"I've got the 911 call record for a domestic in Rockford on March 15th on my screen, Meredeth. Do you want to hear the details?"

"Do I?"

"It was an ugly scene."

"Tell me. I deal with ugly every day. And it probably has nothing to do with me."

Kevin hesitated, then took a deep breath and started reading.

CHAPTER 19

THE 911 CALL

Rockford, GA

"Oglethorpe County 911. What's your emergency?"

"Hey, something's goin' on next door. Something bad from all that hollering."

"Why do you say that, sir?"

"Well, that Reynolds man... He just ain't right when it comes to his missus. I've called y'all before on him."

"Are you at 19 Loblolly Pine Road in Rockford?"

"Yeah, that's me. Laurel Oaks Mobile Home Park."

"And what is Mr. Reynolds's address?"

"20 Loblolly Pine."

"Okay. What's going on tonight?"

"Lots of hollering, like I said. Some loud noises, stuff being smashed up. Like that. Then that little girl of his came haulin' out of that trailer like her ass was on fire. She didn't even stop to close the door. She can't be more than ten or eleven."

"You saw this?"

"Yeah, I saw it. I was standing at the winder on account of the hollering."

"Was it the girl yelling?"

"Naw. Ain't you listening? I say it was on account of that Reynolds man who lives over there. They been up in there for a year or two. Nothin' but trouble. Screaming and crying, banging, the works, and at all hours. The man drinks. I seen him driving up, weavin' around like a fool, then go a-stumblin' up them steps an' inta that nasty old trailer. Rental, you know."

"And you saw Mr. Reynolds tonight?"

"I ain't *seen* him. I *heard* him. Hollering. You sure you're listening to me?"

"What's the girl's name?"

"The little'un who done ran off?"

"Yes."

"I don't rightly know. Something with an M, I think. Mary. Margie. Like that."

"So Mary or Margie Reynolds?"

"I ain't sure about her last name. I don't think that no-good is her blood kin." The man gasped. "Oh-Lordy-me! Did you hear that?"

"No, sir. What happened?"

"That there was a gunshot, ma'am. You need to get them Johnny Laws on out here. I'm going over."

"Sir, please don't do that. Especially if you just heard gunshots."

"Don't you worry none. I got me a shotgun, and I know how to be sneaky. I learned how over to Nam."

"Still. I need you to stay inside your home and let the police handle it."

"Ma'am, I ain't know you, so I can't judge, but it ain't Christian leaving that man to hurt that woman and them babies. No, I'm a-going over and putting a stop to it."

"Sir, please stay on the line."

Silence.

"Sir?"

Dial tone.

"10-3, 10-3, 10-3. Any car in the vicinity of Rockford, respond to a 10-16 reported in the Laurel Oaks Mobile Home Park located at 20 Loblolly Pine Road. Caller reports shots fired and has left his residence armed with a shotgun. Caller reports a young girl fled the trailer. Respond 10-18 10-40."

"10-4, Dispatch. Show car oscar-two-one responding."

"10-4, oscar twenty-one."

CHAPTER 20

INTERLUDE

Buffalo NY

Meredeth's breath came fast and hot. Something about hearing Kevin read the call bothered her on a level so deep she couldn't identify it. None of it was even vaguely familiar, but at the same time, it felt...*immediate*.

"You okay, FBI?"

"I..." Grimacing at the southern twang in her voice, she took a deep breath and forced herself to calm down. "Yes, I'm fine. I don't know why that made me... I don't remember anything like any of that."

"What about the address? The name of the trailer park?"

"Nothing."

"Look, maybe we should drop this."

"I understand if you want to, Kevin. Really, I do, but I can't drop it. Maybe I could have if we hadn't dug into it this far, if we hadn't learned Dawn's been lying to me my whole life. But now, I have to know all of it."

"Well...I've got the police report from oscar twenty-one."

"Let's hear it."

"Why don't you come down to the Valley? We can read it together."

"I'm fine, Kevin. Read it."

CHAPTER 21

OSCAR TWENTY-ONE

Rockford, GA

POLICE REPORT OGLETHORPE County Sheriff's Department

Case Number: OT912357X
Date: 15 March 1986
Reporting Officer: Corporal Junior Markin, Oscar 21

Incident:
Domestic violence resulting in death, suicide by firearm.

Event Details:
Responded to 20 Loblolly Pine Road, Rockford, GA at 22:28, this date. Complainant reported hearing a lot of yelling, then seeing a young girl run off into the woods, then hearing gunshots. I discovered a white male, approx. 35 years of age, crouched in the shadows near the front stoop of the trailer. He identified himself as Boudreaux Walker, the complainant. He reported no further gunshots, no

yelling since his call to 911. I directed Mr. Walker to return to his home. He refused, stating I needed backup if "all hell breaks loose." I commanded Mr. Walker to stay outside, and he agreed to follow my commands.

Approached the trailer's door, took cover, and knocked. An adult male inside the trailer called out, commanding me to "get the [expletive deleted] off" his porch. At that time, I heard the working of a rifle bolt and drew my weapon. I identified myself as an Oglethorpe County Sheriff's Deputy on a welfare check. Subject repeated his demand that I leave and could be heard overturning furniture. I stated I had to speak to his wife, or I couldn't leave. Subject laughed and said, "Go to hell, cop. You'll have to, 'cause that's where she is."

I requested back up via my portable radio at that time and descended from the stoop to take cover behind a tree in the yard. I covered the trailer's only door, and Mr. Walker assisted me, armed as he was with a Remington 12 ga. pump. The door was thrown open, but the trailer's interior was pitch-black, and I couldn't see a thing. I repeated my identification and directed the subject to come out of there with his hands up. He laughed, and a single gunshot sounded, followed by a clatter and a thump.

When oscar seventeen arrived, Deputy Rogers and myself approached the trailer again, and this time, the adult male made no comment. We made entry with weapons drawn and ready, but it was too late. Subject (later identified as Garry Reynolds, white male, approx. age twenty-five to thirty) lay on the living room floor, a single self-inflicted gunshot wound to the head noted. A deer rifle lay by his side. Examination of the rifle showed it to have been fired.

Upon further investigation, Deputy Rogers and I found the remains of Laura Reynolds, approx. age twenty-two to twenty-five in the kitchen. She'd been shot twice—once in the chest (center of mass, approx. area of the heart), once in the face (left eye). A young boy (later identified as Kenny Reynolds) was found lying next to her, a bullet wound to the chest. Deputy Rogers requested expedited emergency services while I rendered what aid I could.

Before the ambulance arrived, Mr. Walker called for me from out front. Deputy Rogers took over first aid, and I went outside, taking the deer rifle to secure it in my trunk. I found a young girl (age ten), who identified herself as Mercy Reynolds of 20 Loblolly Pine Rd., standing with Walker. She identified the boy inside as Kenny Reynolds, her brother (age seven). The girl was plainly in a state of extreme psychological shock. She stated she had "run to the woods and hid from him" and that her daddy (Garry Reynolds) had "a problem with whisky and getting mad for no reason."

Scene secured for GBI investigators, homicide division. Dispatch notified the children's DFCS caseworker, Dawn Connelly, of the crime and called her to the scene to take possession of Mercy and transport her to appropriate care and accommodations. Kenny was transported to Saint

Luke's Medical Center via Lifeflight. The bodies of Garry and Laura Reynolds were released to the Oglethorpe County Medical Examiner's Office. I released the scene at 01:37, 16 March 1986 to GBI investigator Marty Riggs and returned to the station to write this report prior to going off duty.

CHAPTER 22

DAWN BREAKING

Buffalo, NY

HOT TEARS SLID down Meredeth's cheeks as Kevin fell silent. She had no memory of any of that, but her dream from the night before with her father, dressed as a sheriff's deputy, taking her to her room and allowing her to pack a bag, flashed through her mind like a video on fast forward. "My dream... Do you think last night's dream was a... And Mercy?" Her voice shook, and deep in her guts, something quaked and rumbled, a volcano of emesis looking for a way to the surface.

When he spoke, Kevin's voice was soft, kind. "A lot of similarities to what no doubt happened to Mercy Reynolds. It would take a firm belief in the world's biggest coincidence to overlook that you dreamed your name was Little Mercy, dreamed you had a brother named Kenny, dreamed a man who turned into your father murdered your mother and brother. I don't think I can stretch my suspension of disbelief far enough to accept that. Can you?"

Despite being on a phone call, Meredeth could only shake her head, lips quivering, eyes shining with tears.

"You okay over there, FBI?"

Swallowing hard, forcing the bile, the hurt, the shock down deep, burying it with puke churning in her guts, Meredeth dashed the tears from her cheeks, knowing it wouldn't matter, knowing fresh tears would track back down her cheeks in half a heartbeat, but doing it anyway. She squeezed her lips into a thin white line and swallowed hard, blinking as though dust had gotten in her eyes. "Yes," she quavered. "I'm..." She had to bite her lip then, to keep the words from degenerating into sobs.

"It's okay, Meredeth," Kevin said, empathy singing a slow dirge in his voice. "You survived. Whatever happened, you survived."

"Why don't I remember it?" she sobbed. "Why didn't I remember Kenny? Why did Gran—*Dawn*—try to turn me into someone else?"

"I can't answer that, except to say that maybe it was the only way she could see to help you."

"*Help me?*" Meredeth exploded, and a tidal wave of pain shot from the top of her head down into her neck. "She *lied* to me, Saunders, for my *whole life*! She stole my identity away, stole my brother! How in the hell can you say she helped me?"

"Go easy, Meredeth," Kevin said quietly. "I didn't say she helped you, just that she *thought* she was—and I'm only guessing. I've never met the woman. I know nothing about her, but I have to believe she had your best interests at heart."

Meredeth scoffed, then laughed sourly as the pain retreated from a ripping burn to a dull ache.

"It's clear she loves you, FBI. From the sound of it, she was nothing more to you than a social worker, yet she took you in. Raised you. Clothed, fed, housed you. *Welcomed* you. Made you part of her family. I bet she paid for your education, too. Did she make mistakes? Yeah, and big ones it seems. But I believe she made them from a place of love, not maliciousness."

"I should call her. Call her until she answers, then demand the truth." Where a few moments before Meredeth's voice quavered with heartbreak, it now quivered with pent-up fury. Where hot tears of pain had fallen, cold tears of rage wet her cheeks.

"Go easy," said Kevin. "Confront her, find out the truth, by all means, Meredeth, but *go easy*. Remember this is the woman who served in place of your mother for four-fifths of your life."

Meredeth squeezed her eyes shut, trying to press her emotions into a deep, dark cave within her. Her time in the FBI, all the years full of horrible crime scenes, of kidnappings, of child murders, of serial killers and serial rapists, had given her firm control of her emotions, an ability to store them up for when she was alone, never showing the pain, the horror, the heartbreak—keeping that frozen, professional mask in place. But this...this pain, this anger, the betrayal, the *grief*...it was all too much to contain, too much to repress and deal with in private, and the sobs broke free, the tears escaped the dams, and she cried like a little girl, falling to her side, curling into the fetal position, the phone still pressed to her ear.

Kevin let her cry. He made the right sounds, the comforting croons, the soft-spoken words, and she knew he cared for her—he showed more care than that of an acquaintance, more than a colleague. Maybe a friend—a true friend. Maybe...more. When the storm of grief passed, she lay on her side, eyes closed, just breathing, existing only in the moment.

"Better now?" he asked.

"A little," she murmured. "I don't know that I'll ever be better again."

"You will, Meredeth. In time. What's that saying? Time heals all wounds?"

"Always thought that was a bunch of bullshit."

When he spoke, she could hear the shrug in his voice. "It hasn't been for me. When we lost Vanessa, I thought my life was over, that every good thing I thought I had had been nothing more than a lie. I stopped smiling—never felt the need. I no longer laughed, never saw the humor in anything. Time passed. I started to grin at things again, eventually laughing. The hole in my soul is still there, always will be, but it's not the only thing in there. I can see past it, now. Take it on faith. If you can't do that—and God knows cops see too many horrors to have faith in much of anything—take me at my word."

She nodded, rubbing her cheek against the comforter. "I'll do that." She rolled to her back, opening her eyes and staring up at the smooth hotel room ceiling. "Can you..." She shook her head, lips quivering.

"Yes, I can. Whatever it is."

She had to squeeze her eyes shut against the tears at that and spoke past the massive burning coal lodged in her throat. "Thanks, Kevin. I mean that."

"My honor, Meredeth, though I'll deny I ever said that in a court of law."

"Jerk," she murmured and was surprised to find a half-grin lingering on her lips.

"You don't know the half of it, FBI. But what did you want me to do?"

"Can you call my grand—Dawn for me? She won't see my number, so maybe she'll pick up. Can you do a three-way call to her and then stay on the line with me? Sort of act as my buffer? Tell me to go easy when I forget?" He was silent for a few moments, and she wondered what he was thinking. "It's a lot to ask, I know, and if you'd rather—"

"No," he said in a voice tight with iron control of his emotions. "No, I'm happy to do it. Give me her number."

Meredeth recited the phone number she'd known since childhood—their family landline, rather than Dawn's cell phone. Kevin placed the call and conferenced her in, and without speaking, they waited as the phone rang.

"Hello?" said Dawn.

"Mrs. Connelly? This is Kevin Saunders."

"Hello, Mr. Saunders. If you're calling to tell me I need to replace my roof, or that my computer has a cold, don't bother. I'm—"

"No, no. I'm a police chief in New York. A friend of Meredeth's."

"Oh." The sound of the word was small, the volume so low Meredeth almost missed it.

"I've got her here on the line with us. Say hello, FBI."

"Hello," said Meredeth, her voice as tiny as Dawn's had been.

"Hello, dear," said Dawn, resignation and pain evident in her voice.

"We're sorry to bother you with this, Ms. Connelly, but Meredeth has had some repressed memories surface in the form of dreams, flashbacks. She's shared them with me, and I've done a little investigating."

"Oh," Dawn repeated, her voice even smaller, even quieter, than before. "And what did you find?"

"Garry and Laura Reynolds."

"And Kenny," said Meredeth. "And *Mercy*."

"Oh," repeated Dawn, a waver in her voice. "I..." The woman in Georgia sniffled, and the rattle of a drawer opening carried across the line. "Damn," she whispered.

"You never have tissues when you need them," said Meredeth. "Me, neither. I guess I learned that from you."

"Maybe you did," said Dawn.

"Ms. Connelly, I—"

"Chief, since you're on this call, I know you're a good man. Meredeth wouldn't trust you otherwise, and she's an excellent judge of character. You may as well call me 'Granny' as does Mer—Mercy."

"No," said Meredeth in a quiet voice. "I'm Meredeth. Always Meredeth."

"Okay," said Dawn, and her voice brimmed with gratitude and hope. "If that's too personal, Mr. Saunders, you go right to calling me Dawn."

"Now, you can't stick to formalities and expect me to let them go," said Kevin. "I'm Kevin. It's what FBI, here, calls me, and you should, too."

"I seem to remember calling you 'jerk' most recently."

Kevin's chuckle rumbled across the line, warming Meredeth's heart. "Yeah, but you didn't mean it."

"I interrupted you a moment ago, Mister—Kevin. I apologize for that. What was it you were going to say?"

"After her dream last night—her nightmare—and after speaking to you this morning, Meredeth asked for my help in trying to find Kenny, and I was happy to do it. What we found is upsetting."

"It's horrible," said Dawn. "An ugly business. I tried to shield you from it, Meredeth. Everything I did, I did for you."

Meredeth didn't trust herself to speak; hot ire and ragged pain warring in her heart.

"What we found—and I'll tell you that we found a newspaper article which quoted you as an interviewee, then the 911 transcripts of Boudreaux Walker's call, and the police report filed by Deputy Markin. I read all three to Meredeth."

"I asked him to."

"Then you know," said Dawn in a voice that dripped with anguish and, at the same time, held an undercurrent of relief.

"Yes," croaked Meredeth.

"And you want to know why we lied to you."

"Yes," Meredeth said again.

Dawn sniffed, and another clatter sounded on her end of the call.

"Use a paper towel, Granny," said Meredeth in a soft voice. "It's scratchy, but you'll live."

"You know me too well, dear," said Dawn, a smile sounding in her voice.

"And you know me."

"Yes," said Dawn. "I do. Kjetl and I went round and round about it, Little Merry. He argued we should keep your birth name, let you have a tie to your family, but I thought it'd be better if you didn't have that baggage to lug around the rest of your life. That the lies would give you the best chance at happiness." She sighed. "I look back, now, at how you've kept yourself locked away, and I think I was wrong."

"You think?" snapped Meredeth in a surge of heat.

"I understand the impulse," Kevin said into the silence. "I'm a parent, and I've made costly mistakes by telling the truth and told lies that weren't mistakes. But..."

"I know," said Dawn, misery leaching the life from her tone. "I know it was a mistake to bury everything, but your psychiatrist said—"

"*Psychiatrist?*" barked Meredeth. "I went to a headshrinker?"

"Of course, dear, after what you'd been put through. Dr. Erikson was your psychiatrist, and Dr. Rice was your psychologist. Don't you remember?"

"No," said Meredeth in a small voice. "There's so much I..."

"The mind is a wonderful thing," said Dawn. "It protects us however it best can."

"How long did you have me in therapy? What did you tell me it was for?"

"At that time, you remembered everything quite vividly. Many a night I sat up with you after a screaming night terror. We'd talk and talk and talk. You were..."

"Say it!" ordered Meredeth, her voice like a hammer on hot iron, her left eye pulsing with agony.

"Easy, FBI," said Kevin.

"You were so devastated, Meredeth. Broken, really, on a fundamental level. One night, one in which no nightmares of that bastard troubled you, you got up to use the restroom, and Kjetl happened to be coming out for a glass of water. You looked at him and screamed bloody murder, then turned and ran from the house. You hustled off into the woods and hid from us for three hours. The old sun was peeking at us over the horizon when we finally found you and coaxed you out." She paused for a beat. "Kjetl felt horrible. He *cried*, dear. Cried like that day in the hospital when I lost our baby."

"What..." Meredeth shook her head. "Why did he freak me out?"

"You never did tell us. We guessed that, in the dark like that, you mistook him for Garry Reynolds."

"My father," Meredeth said in a flat voice.

"No, dear."

"What? Another lie?" Acid dripped in her tone, and though she expected him to tell her to go easy, Kevin said nothing.

"If it was, we didn't tell it. Your mother...Laura Reynolds nee MacGregor...was a troubled girl, even before she met Reynolds." Every time Dawn said that name, her voice grew as cold as the space between the stars. "She got herself in trouble at the end of her junior year at Rockford High. That's when I first met her. She was referred to me at DFCS to manage her pregnancy. Her parents... Well, she needed the help."

"Who is my father?"

"All Laura ever said was that he was a loser. I gather he was a pothead and a dropout. I asked her many times, but she'd never tell me his name. I believe she thought her father would kill the boy if his name became public."

"And Reynolds?"

"He came along about eighteen months later. And he wasn't a 'head, though it turned out he was a secret drunk. At first, things looked good. He had a good job cutting trees—he was three years ahead of your..."

"Call her Laura," said Meredeth. She didn't say it aloud, but in her mind, Dawn was her mother and always would be.

"Okay. The first year or so was good for Laura. Garry seemed to have his drinking under control at that time. Or maybe it was a living hell, and she just hid it from everyone."

"And Kenny?"

"Kenny was born a year and two months after their wedding. It was as if his birth was Garry's excuse for giving in to his demons. After Kenny came along, your mother started turning up in my office covered in bruises. Oh, she gave me the standard song and dance. 'Accident,' she would say. 'Stupid me. I wasn't watching where I was going and walked right off the deck!' I knew it was a load of stinking horse manure, but I couldn't get her to speak against Garry."

"One of the early flashbacks was when I was five or so. Garry came home drunk, and for whatever reason, decided I'd been bad. Laura went and tried to calm him down. He..." Meredeth took a deep breath. "He beat her down, and I ran and hid like a little coward."

"Hey, now, FBI. You were *five*."

"And he still found me—if I can believe what I saw."

"That was the first incident," said Dawn. "It was what placed you in my caseload. The way we met, dear...you covered in bruises, so scared you wouldn't speak, even with Laura right there."

"I...I don't remember. Sorry."

"There's nothing for you to apologize for," said Dawn in a stern voice. "Like your friend said, you were five. I don't remember anything from when I was five."

"Me neither," said Kevin.

"Anyway, I tried to convince Laura to go to a shelter. I warned her that once Garry started beating the two of you, it was unlikely he would find his self-control again. Unfortunately, I was right."

"We call people like him 'family annihilators.' Garry sounds like a self-righteous archetype. So, maybe you did convince Laura to leave him in time."

Dawn sighed and sniffed.

"He doesn't really fit the profile, though does he, Meredeth? He doesn't sound like a financial success, and if he was beating his wife and children, he was no doubt known by the local cops. There had to have been calls. DV reports."

"It was a different time, Kevin," said Dawn. "Especially in rural Georgia. People were becoming aware of the significance of the problem, but many people—people who occupied the same economic strata as Garry Reynolds—

viewed what happened in the home as a private matter. Worse still, they believed a husband had the right to 'discipline' his wife."

"I've been a cop all my adult life, Dawn, and we always know. We might not be able to prove it, might not be able to convince the Lauras of the world to file a report, but we know. I'll bet you a steak dinner someone in Rockford, some local cop, knew all about Garry Reynolds and was looking for something—anything—he could use to jam the man up."

"You might be right, Kevin. *I* was certainly aware of his activities, and that was without Laura being willing to tell me the truth."

"Of course," said Meredeth. "It's obvious."

"Yes, I suppose it is to a woman with your skills. Your knowledge of the evil that men do."

"And women," said Meredeth. "But enough of my evil stepfather. Tell me about Kenny. Why didn't you adopt him, too?"

Dawn drew a deep breath but said nothing for a long time. "You were very broken by that night, dear, but Garry didn't shoot you. You got away. Kenny..." She sighed. "Kenny tried to protect your—to protect Laura. She was already dead by the time he came to her rescue, but he *tried*, and Garry shot him for it, then left him for dead."

Ravaging guilt struck Meredeth then, overwhelming her with the suddenness and strength of the attack, and she groaned.

"Oh, don't you feel guilty, dear," said Dawn. "*You* tried, too, and while she was still alive. If anything, Kenny's late arrival probably saved your life. Garry had knocked you down, then told you to watch what happens to little B-I-T-C-Hes who get in a man's way. He turned the gun on Laura and shot her. He was turning back to you when Kenny charged into the room and started kicking and punching at him. You got up, but Garry struck your brother with the butt of that damn deer gun, then shot him. You turned and ran for your life, and the world is a better place for it."

"If you say so," murmured Meredeth.

"None of that, now," said Dawn in a stern voice. "Look at the work you've done! The women you've protected, found justice for. And the kids when you started. The poor, blameless children. I've often wondered if some part of you remembered your past, though your conscious mind seemed oblivious and directed your choices, your interest in forensic psychology, your attraction to law enforcement."

"She's got a point, FBI. You've done a lot of good in this world. Saved countless lives by nabbing serial killers and putting them away."

Meredeth said nothing, knowing they were right but unable to dispense with the niggling doubts circling in her mind like sharks around a shipwreck.

"Anyway, Kenny was in intensive care for weeks and weeks, and by the time he was ready to leave, it was apparent to everyone that he needed psychiatric care. He'd grown... He had outbursts. Anger, directed at the nurses. Cursing. He... He *hit* them at times."

"He was *seven*."

"I know he was, dear, and allowances were made for his age, but his behavior went beyond that. It wasn't safe to bring him into our home—and he only got worse over time. If we hadn't been caring for you, maybe we could have risked it, but we did have you. We owed you the best we could give."

"Then what happened to Kenny?"

"He was placed in a short-term psychiatric facility first, but instead of making him better, like I said, he seemed to get worse. To decompensate. After four months, a judge ordered him placed up to Milledgeville."

"Central State Hospital?"

"Yes," said Dawn.

"For how long?"

"No time limit was set in the order—well, evaluations every twelve months, but we all know that means an unlimited stay. I followed him for a few years, but his evaluations were...ugly."

"Ugly how?" asked Meredeth.

"His anger burned like a wildfire. His behavior got worse and worse, regardless of what antipsychotic they tried him on. His violence escalated, and he tore through that hospital like a fire running rampant. There were beatings—using anything to hand: a chair, a lamp, even a trash can. He choked a male nurse—would've killed him if the orderlies hadn't dogpiled him. He...he fashioned what they call a shank out of a plastic cup and stabbed a *doctor*, Meredeth. We couldn't trust him not to hurt you. You were so precious to Kjetl and me... We couldn't..." She blew out a long breath. "It was a mess. He was classified as an extreme risk to the male staff of the hospital."

"Just the men?" asked Kevin.

"Yes. He grew very attached to the females. Overly so. He became protective of them to the point he attacked anyone he thought was threatening or insulting them. It was very sad."

"You think he started acting that way because he was abandoned into the system?" Meredeth asked with a hint of heat.

"I..." Dawn drew a deep breath.

"Meredeth," said Kevin. "Your grandparents did the best they could with what information they had. Hindsight is always twenty-twenty."

A massive throb of pain lanced through Meredeth's brow. "You don't think I know that?"

"Meredeth Lynne Connelly! Stop snapping at everyone! But especially stop snapping at your friend who is only here to help you."

Meredeth drew a shaky breath. "I know, Granny. Sorry, Kevin. It's this damn headache."

"Well, Darren did say stress would make it worse. I think this counts."

Her phone beeped, and Meredeth glanced down at it, frowning at 'Bobby' in the caller ID popup. She ignored it and put the phone back to her ear. "I don't mean to be a jerk," she said. "My only memories of Kenny are steeped in blood. I don't even know him—didn't even *remember* him until this morning. What kind of sister am I?"

"The kind that experienced a huge trauma at a very young age. Someone who's dealt with PTSD her entire life, without knowing it, without knowing why." Kevin's voice rumbled across the line, warm and filled with empathy.

"The kind whose grandmother made a terrible mistake," Dawn said. "I'm so sorry, Meredeth. I thought it would be best if you could forget, and Dr. Erikson agreed."

Her phone beeped in her ear again, and Meredeth looked at it crossly. This time, it was a text from Bobby that read, "Turn on channel 27. IMPORTANT! The 'lying prick' got a letter." She glanced at the television, then looked around for the remote. "Bobby says I'm to turn on channel 27."

"What for?" asked Kevin.

"I don't know, but he says it's important. Goode got a letter."

"Better do as he says, then," said Dawn, but Meredeth was already fishing for the remote.

She snapped on the television, frowned at it, then turned the volume up a little. "CNN," she said. "The 'New Day' show. And guess who the guest is?"

"Jeremy Goode," said Kevin in a cold voice.

"Yep."

"—tell us about the letter?" the pretty blonde asked. The camera lingered on a tight close-up, but they put Goode in a small picture on the upper right side of the screen.

"I'd be happy to, Brianna," said Goode in an obsequious tone. "I found it under the wipers of my car around four this morning. I was up early, eager to track the progress of the investigation."

"Commendable," said the dark-haired man sitting next to Brianna Keilar.

"Thank you, John. I'm very motivated to keep my viewers in the loop. This case, the Dollhouse Killer case, stays in the forefront of the minds of everyone in the region—whether they live in a trailer park or not."

"Uh, yes. The letter?"

"Sure thing, Brianna." Goode glanced down and read: "'Dear Mr. Goode...or perhaps I should say 'Bad.' You persist in your efforts to demean and enrage me, but you are so far beneath me that I find your weak attempts at shaming me a little amusing. Perhaps stick to someone in your weight class, as you are punching far above your ability.'" Goode lifted his eyes to the camera. "He's referring to my nickname for him. I felt 'the .40 Caliber Killer' romanticized what this man is doing—which, frankly, amounts to terrorizing an entire region—so I dubbed him the Dollhouse Killer. He seems not to like it—despite his protestations to the contrary."

"And that's it?" asked Berman, one eyebrow quirked.

"No, John. Sorry. I'll continue. 'Since you are running your stupid gab about me every day anyway, I thought I'd write you instead of those stuffed suits at the Times.' He's referring—"

"Yes. Yesterday's letter. We're all aware of it."

"Oh, right. 'At least this way, you'll have something to report without *making stuff up* about the FBI agents tracking me.' The emphasis is his. 'And about that, I consider Agent Connelly *a friend*, Goode, so a smart guy would lay off the character assassination. But let me—'"

"What is that in reference to?" asked John.

"I have no idea, John," said Goode, turning a doe-eyed gaze on the camera. "I do my best to report the *facts*, as I'm sure the two of you do. I don't embellish them or use them to mislead the public. Just the facts."

"Oh, I'm sure," said John in a mild voice.

"Asshole," muttered Kevin. "If I weren't a cop, I'd..."

"Nah. Let him do his worst," said Meredeth. "What goes around, comes around."

"Continuing: 'But let me get to *the point*, and you'll note I underlined the point so *you don't miss it*, you cretin. I've left a little *something* in the home of the family I freed last night—"

"Oh, no," murmured Meredeth.

"—and someone as *smart* as Agent Connelly will have no trouble finding it. Think of it as a *greeting card*, but I'm not going to *spoil the surprise* by telling you what it is or what message is contained therein. For that, Goode, you'll have to convince Agent Connelly to give you an interview, and after your hatchet job last night, I consider the chances she'd tell you if you were *on fire* to be slim and none. I wish you *luck*, imbecile. You're going to need it.'"

"He seems to be quite a fan of yours, Jeremy," said Brianna.

Goode shrugged and flashed a boyish smile at the camera—as unlikely to appear on his mug as the humility he pretended at was to appear off-camera. "Everyone's a critic. Don't you find? And I've been quite stern with the Dollhouse Killer. Quite critical. He doesn't scare me."

"Is that man as stupid as he seems?" asked Dawn.

"Even more so," said Kevin. "He seems to think he's untouchable."

"You're very brave," said John. "I'm not sure taunting a serial killer is a good idea, though."

"He's a bully, John. Like any bully, if you stand up to him, he'll back down."

"Uh, I'm not sure serial killers can be classified as bullies," said Brianna, frowning a little at the camera. "Perhaps caution is the better part of journalistic valor in this case."

Jeremy shrugged again and flashed another jejune smile. "I'll take it under advisement. The letter goes on: 'Perhaps she will give an interview to *someone else*, though, and you can find out what my message is from *their* broadcast. Or you could just make it up—*like everything else you've reported in this case*. A man like you should be careful, Goode. Remember the old adage, *karma's a BEEP*. If you're smart, which everyone realizes *you are not*, there's still time to mend your ways. *Apologize* to Agent Connelly. To her partner. To the chief. And most of all, *to me*, bubba. A little humility will serve you better than all the bravado in the world. And speaking of *your braggadocio*, it's clear to everyone who's seen your ridiculous statements that *I do scare you*. In fact, I think you are *scared BEEP-less*, you *vile little piece of gutter trash*. Or you *should be*.' He signed it with this ridiculous word, 'Ankou,' whatever that means. It seems important to him, however. He signed the first letter the same way."

"If I remember my mythology, Ankou is a Celtic deity. He is the canonical representation of Death—skeletal, black robe, scythe, the works," said Brianna.

"Sounds grim," said John with a quirky smile.

"Yes," said Brianna without a hint of a grin. "It does at that, John. Mr. Goode, is there more? A postscript, perhaps?"

"No, that's it," said Goode. "But I think it's important—"

"Sorry to cut you off, Mr. Goode, but my producer's in my ear saying we need to cut away for a moment. Thank you for sharing the letter with us."

"But I—" Goode's image disappeared from the right-hand corner, and the shot changed to include both hosts.

John leaned forward and looked at the camera. "There you have it, in this Ankou's own words as read by Jeremy Goode, a local reporter with WUTV in Western New York."

"I think he's a stringer, John."

"Oh?"

Brianna nodded. "But it's no matter." She faced the camera, and it zoomed in tight. "I'm told high-ranking officials from New York State Police are about to give a news conference on the .40 Caliber Killer case, and we'll take you there live."

The view switched to a shot containing three men wearing the gray-green uniforms of the New York State Police and one man, standing to the side, wearing a black suit and a subdued maroon tie. The trooper standing behind the lectern set up in the center of the room, right under the NYSP logo stenciled on the wall in black, wore a cream-colored hat in contrast to the tan hats of his fellow troopers, and the two troopers flanking him stood with their hands crossed over their utility belt buckles. The trooper behind the lectern bore the golden oak leaf of a major, and his two pals both wore the double bars of captains.

"Good morning. I'm Major Kamphaus. To my left stands Captain Morgan, commander of Troop A, and Captain Morse, commander of Troop E. We have an ugly bit of news to share with you this morning. Early this morning, a grim crime scene attributed to the .40 Caliber Killer was discovered on the border of Wyoming and Livingston counties, which also happens to be the border between the coverage zones of Troop A and Troop E." He dropped his gaze and cleared his throat. "These most recent slayings mark the seventh such family the perpetrator has stolen away. The superintendent has decided it is time we assert jurisdiction over all eight cases. We will coordinate our investigation with those on the local county and city levels, as well as coordinating the efforts of the Federal Bureau of Investigation as related to the case within the boundaries of this great state." He lifted his eyes to stare into the camera. "All that sounds ominous and hoity-toity, but I assure you, this is routine, and all actors in the case are not only familiar with this development but expected it at some point. Members of the public may continue to liaise with their local departments, who will, in turn, make inquiries and notify us if the information merits it. I want to take a moment to assure the citizens of the Southern Tier and the rest of Western New York that the investigation will proceed with all possible speed, and that claiming jurisdiction is only done to bring the full resources of the State of New York to bear on the cases. Along with the resources on loan from the FBI, and that of local jurisdictions, our involvement represents a major increase in investigative power. The Bureau of Criminal Investigation has been tasked with overseeing the current efforts and bringing the perpetrator to justice. This case has been escalated to our top priority as of this morning, and I assure you, this means a swift resolution is likely. Now, if there are any questions, I will answer them as best I can."

Meredeth thumbed the off switch on the remote. "We'll have to cut this short," she said. "I'm about to get real busy."

"Yes, I understand," said Dawn. "But...am I forgiven?"

The line fell silent for the space of a few breaths. "Not yet," said Meredeth at last, "but you will be. In time. I have more questions. And I want to meet Kenny."

"I'm afraid I can't help you with that last one. On his twenty-first birthday, the State of Georgia released him from his commitment to Central. He..." Dawn sighed. "He never tried to contact me. Us."

"Would he have even known who you are?" asked Meredeth.

"Yes. I was listed as his local social worker. His local contact with the community. I have never understood why the hospital didn't notify me of his release. I have no idea where he is."

"We can handle that part—now that we know who to look for," said Kevin. "Kenneth Reynolds?"

"That's correct. Kenneth Robert Reynolds."

Meredeth's phone beeped, and she saw Bobby's name in the caller ID. "Okay," she said. "I've really got to go."

"Go get him, FBI," said Kevin.

"I'll call when I have the details."

Meredeth switched over to Bobby's call. "What do we have?"

"Nothing much—just an invitation from the NYSP to come to the crime scene between Perry and Mount Morris. But there is something new."

"Yeah?"

"No trailer park. This scene is in an old farmhouse."

"But it's definitely our guy? No copycat?"

"I can't say for sure, obviously, but the New York State Police believes it's an authentic crime scene."

"Dammit," Meredeth muttered. "He's picking victims of convenience, breaking his pattern to send us messages."

"Maybe. Or he's bored with the trailer parks."

"No, he's talking to us, and he's killing these families to do it."

CHAPTER 23

GREETING CARDS

Wyoming County, NY

MARKED AND UNMARKED New York State Police cars filled the dooryard of the old farmhouse, along with a coroner's van and a crime scene truck squeezed in for good measure. The troopers had cordoned off the gravel drive, but the Press had arrived on the scene in force—vans with transmitter dishes on their roofs parked up and down Water Road for an eighth of a mile in either direction. As Bobby turned into the drive, a trooper held up his hand, then walked over to the car, and Van Zandt held up his ID and badge. The trooper examined the credentials closely, then lifted the tape for them to drive under and waved them on. Van Zandt squeezed in between the CSI van and an unmarked cruiser and killed the engine. "Too many of them for me to corral," he said.

"Yeah," she said with a sigh. "I know. They're not going to give me the scene anyway. We're destined for hours of cooling our jets with the brass. Get ready to nod a lot."

"Joy of joys," said Bobby, but he plastered one of his patented grins on his face as the kitchen door of the farmhouse banged open. A large man in a trooper uniform bearing the chevrons of a sergeant stepped out onto the porch. At more than six foot five, the trooper must have weighed close to three-fifty, his wide frame layered with slabs of muscle—though he looked more like a hard-working farmer than a bodybuilder. His nametag read: "Schweighart." His gaze flicked to Bobby, then jumped to Meredeth.

"You Connelly?" he asked in a gruff voice.

"I am. Meredeth Connelly, FBI." She reached for her ID wallet.

The man scoffed and slashed his hand through the air. "Yeah, I got that part. Get in here." He stepped back and hooked his thumb toward the kitchen. "The captain has some questions for you."

"Is there a problem?" asked Bobby, still grinning, and again the trooper gave him a dismissive glance, then turned and walked back inside. "Well, at least he has a winning personality."

"It's a crime scene, and their seventh in less than six weeks. We can cut him a bit of slack." Meredeth couldn't help peeking over her shoulder, looking for a WUTV van or Jeremy Goode. Or both.

Bobby cut his gaze her way, one eyebrow raised. "Who are you, and what have you done with Agent Connelly?"

"Agent Connelly is getting a letter of censure for acting like an asshole." She held her hands out to her sides. "This is the new me. The one who is understanding and kind."

Bobby grinned. "The world will never be the same." They climbed the four weather-beaten steps to the porch, then Bobby extended his arm and said, "After you, Ambassador Connelly."

Meredeth rolled her eyes and walked past him. "I'm being nice to people I don't know, Bobby. I'll still kick your ass if you step out of line."

"Of course you will, Meredeth."

She pushed through the door, her gaze flicking around the room, noting the dour expressions, the men who cut their gazes away as soon as she glanced in their direction. She spotted the twin bars on the captain's uniform and strode over to him, her hand extended. "Hello, Captain Morgan. I'm Meredeth Connelly."

He looked at her a moment, his head cocked a little to the side, eyelids at half-mast.

"I recognize you from the Press conference."

"Yeah? I recognize you from your performance the other day."

Meredeth grimaced. "I had a bad day."

"You don't get to have bad days on this investigation, Connelly." The man's face settled into hard lines for a moment, then he sighed and relaxed his grimace.

"Noted. Sergeant Schweighart said you had questions for me? I can provide you with a written profile if you give me your email address."

Captain Morgan patted the air between them. "We'll get to that. Right now, there are more important questions you need to answer."

She quirked an eyebrow and couldn't resist sending her gaze bouncing around the room, watching the troopers shuffle their feet and find interesting things on the floor to look at. "Oh, yeah? Like what?"

"Like who the .40 Caliber Killer is," rumbled Schweighart.

Meredeth cracked a lazy smile. "I'm good, Sarge, but I'm not that good. ESP is beyond my current skillset." No one smiled, and the sergeant went so far as to narrow his eyes and clench his teeth, jaw muscles bunching. Her grin died a painful death. "Look, you all obviously have something on your minds...a bone to pick. Let's get on with it, shall we? Is it all about Jeremy Goode?" Her face settled into the cold, hard lines of her "FBI grimace," and she stared Captain Morgan in the eye. When no one spoke, she grunted and said, "I play guessing games with unsubs, not my colleagues."

Morgan scoffed but flicked his fingers at the sergeant. The big man withdrew an evidence bag from his pocket. A dog-eared business card rested inside. Flecks of red dotted the vellum surface of the age-yellowed card, and it appeared someone had dunked it into a clear liquid not long before she'd arrived. "Explain this." He held the evidence bag out to her, and Meredeth took it.

She frowned down at it. The card had been white and pristine the last time she'd seen one like it. The Bureau's seal was on the left, and the phrases "U.S. Department of Justice" and "Federal Bureau of Investigation" took up the space on the right. Beneath them read, "Meredeth Connelly, Special Agent, Crimes Against Children," and then listed the address and phone number of the office she'd shared twenty years before. She looked up at the sergeant for a heartbeat, then dismissed him and pinned Morgan with a hard glare. "This was found where?"

"Inside the mouth of an eight-year-old," growled Schweighart. "A *dead* kid upstairs, if you're having another of your bad days...if the subtleties of the situation escape you."

Meredeth shook her head. "All of you know how many cards we give out. This one's twenty years out of date or so." She raised her eyes to glare at the sergeant. "How many cards like this have *you* left on a door or under a wiper blade?" None of the troopers spoke, and none of their hard expressions softened.

"Come on, guys," said Bobby. "What's this really about?"

"Flip it over," said Morgan in a soft voice.

Meredeth turned the card over, and what she saw sent a chill down her spine and a spike of brutal pain lancing through her brows. Scrawled in blue ink across the back of the card were her Bureau cell phone number and "Call me when you get down to DC—if I'm in town, dinner's on me." She looked Morgan in the eye. "So?"

"The goddamn killer left that for you. Obviously, you know this guy."

"He said as much in that letter to Jeremy Goode," said the sergeant.

Meredeth sighed and couldn't stop herself from raising her hand to rub her eyes. "That he did. And he had this card, but neither of those prove it's true. He could have stolen this card or found it in the trash."

"Who did you give it to?"

"Twenty years ago? I have no idea. I gave away hundreds of cards with this message on the back. Maybe thousands."

"Right," rumbled Sergeant Schweighart. "A message like that? That's not for a whit. That's not something you left on someone's car window."

Meredeth shrugged. "No, it isn't. It's more like something I'd give a colleague—which I routinely did. If someone expressed an interest in the National Academy, I offered what advice I had and—"

"Strictly professional, right," said Schweighart with a twist to his lips.

Meredeth's hackles rose, and more than one snappy comeback flashed into her mind, but she buried those feelings, that defensiveness. "*And* I offered to take them out to dinner in DC. This was no kind of offer, no date. What

Jeremy Goode's been reporting..." She shrugged. "It's all lies."

"You sure?" asked the sergeant, but Captain Morgan said nothing, only watched her closely.

She thought she had it figured out. She pointed at Morgan. "Good cop." She swiveled and pointed at the sergeant. "Bad cop. This routine work for you two? It's a bit obvious."

The sergeant continued to glower at her, but then his eyes flicked to the captain standing behind her, and his shoulders relaxed. He wagged his head from side to side. "Most of the time. We didn't get to the good part."

A small smile twitched into existence on Meredeth's lips. "I see. You could've skipped the theatrics."

The sergeant shrugged.

"Butch likes them—the theatrics," said Morgan in a voice that had lost its hard edges. "And after that show we saw in the HVPD station house..."

Meredeth nodded. "Not my best day, like I said." She looked down at the dog-eared and creased card. "I'd like to know where he got this."

"Maybe you did give it to him twenty years ago," said Bobby into the silence that followed. "Maybe he chatted you up, expressed an interest in the National Academy. Maybe he was a part of the kidnapping investigation as well."

"As well?" asked Butch, arching a thick eyebrow at Bobby. "You two know something we don't?"

Meredeth shook her head. "My partner is concerned that a local cop is involved in the current series."

"You don't agree?" asked Morgan as he glanced at Bobby.

Meredeth twitched her shoulders. "I don't know. The unsub does seem to know things only people working on the case would know, but then again, so does Jeremy Goode. And he's as good a suspect as anyone."

Morgan quirked one eyebrow.

"No, it's not just sour grapes. He's a classic Machiavellian personality type."

Butch rolled his massive shoulders. "Yeah, the man's an ass all right. But a serial killer? I don't know."

"I'm only saying that there's a leak in a department somewhere. If Goode's able to access the information, then anyone can."

"That doesn't necessarily follow," said Bobby. "Goode, for all his faults, is a member of the Press."

Footsteps sounded on the porch steps, and Meredeth glanced toward the door in time to see Kevin Saunders step through it. She pursed her lips and threw a quick glance at Bobby, but Van Zandt wasn't looking her way—he was staring at Chief Saunders with that look in his eye—his "I'm onto you" look.

"About time, Kev," said Captain Morgan.

"I was helping a friend in need," said Kevin, not even glancing Meredeth's way.

"You two know each other?" asked Bobby, glancing at the NYSP captain. "You sure get around, Saunders."

It couldn't have been more obvious that Bobby found it suspicious, and Morgan rolled his eyes. "Yeah. We worked in the same unit together for twelve years. Kev's got skills I need, even if he retired. That okay with you, or should we all pretend we've never met?"

"I was BCI, remember?" said Kevin.

"And the Besson murders put him right smack in the middle of this," said Captain Morgan.

Bobby's glance at the captain was a stony one, but he said nothing and didn't even glance at Saunders.

"I asked him to come up," said Morgan. "He's the best guy I know at reading crime scenes."

Bobby jerked his chin at Meredeth. "She's better—and I think Kevin will back me up on that—yet you've got her stuck in here, playing twenty questions."

"Back off, jarhead," grumbled Butch. When Bobby glanced at him and arched an eyebrow, the big trooper nodded. "Takes one to know one."

"They're only following the leads, Bobby. Calling in people they know and trust," said Meredeth in a calm voice. "We'd do the same thing in their place."

"Would we?" he asked. "I doubt that." His gaze slipped from hers and locked on Kevin Saunders.

"Something you want to say out loud?" asked Butch with a wink at Kevin. "I think he likes you, Kev."

"I like him fine," said Bobby. "But there are certain questions that should be answered."

"Like what?" asked Kevin.

"Like nothing," said Meredeth. "There's no need—"

"It's okay, FBI. Your partner's just doing his job. Following his gut, his leads." He shrugged. "I'm not offended, and I'm an open book."

Bobby nodded once. If he noticed the escalating tension in the room, he gave no indication. "Let's start with this: were you affiliated with the kidnapping cases my partner worked two decades ago?"

Kevin's gaze flicked to hers. "No. At least, not directly. I was a rookie patrol cop in Buffalo back then—three years away from joining the state police."

"What was your indirect involvement?"

"Like every cop in the state, I was looking for those kids. Not actively, mind, but checking every car I stopped, watching the runaway hangouts, that kind of thing."

"Did you meet Meredeth?"

Kevin's gaze swam to meet hers. "I didn't meet Agent Connelly until she pissed me off by calling in the Troop A CSI team for the Besson murders."

"And you never had her business card?"

"Business card?" Saunders looked a question at Morgan.

"We found one of Connelly's cards inside the mouth of one of the kids," said the captain.

Kevin grinned a little as he shook his head at Bobby. "No. In fact, I don't have one now. I've never had one."

Van Zandt cut his gaze toward Meredeth but didn't meet her eye. "Why are you getting so involved in this? You retired from the BCI because you wanted a simpler life, right?"

"I did," said Kevin, "but you don't always get what you want."

"Yeah," said Butch. "Sometimes you get what you need, and sometimes you don't get either. Sometimes, you get a second helping of shit-sandwiches without even a smile from your waitress." Bobby shot a quizzical look his way, and Butch shrugged. "I'm a muscle-bound cop, not a poet."

"I didn't ask for the .40 Caliber Killer to come to Hanable's Valley, Bobby," Kevin said in a quiet voice. "And I'd be happier if he'd passed us by, but I'd still probably be standing in this kitchen, and Jackstral still would've called me in to the Eider crime scene. It's the nature of the beast."

Morgan sucked his teeth. "That's what you get for being so damn good, Kev."

"Heh." Saunders shrugged his shoulders. "But Bobby's right. Meredeth is better. Turn her loose."

Captain Morgan gave her a long, slow look. "Kev doesn't hand out compliments like they're candy. If you've impressed him..."

"Look," said Meredeth, "as much as I appreciate everyone singing my praises, you don't need me to—"

"I'll use every resource at my disposal," said Morgan. "If letting you do your thing in there will hasten this mad dog's capture, you can spend the damn night in there."

With a sudden swell of pain behind her left eye, Meredeth nodded. "Okay, then."

Morgan jerked his chin toward the door that led to the house's interior. "Knock yourself out."

"My partner needs the scene to herself. It helps her—"

"Yeah, we got that message from Goode's report," said Morgan with a nod toward Schweighart. "Round 'em up, Butch."

With another roll of his shoulders, the sergeant turned and walked through the door, bellowing, "Everyone out for a few minutes. The *F-B-I* is here, and she wants it quiet, so the cap says, 'Get Out!'"

Morgan glanced at her, a small smile on his lips as if to say, "See what I have to put up with?"

A smile—even a small one—in return felt impossible, so Meredeth settled on a curt nod. "The unsub watched us in Hanable's Valley," she said. "Probably at the Eider scene, too."

The state police captain nodded. "We've got cameras up. If he shows himself, we'll get him on video."

She couldn't think of anything else to say, anything else to keep her in the clean kitchen rather than the bloody bedrooms, so she nodded once more, then turned and stepped through the dining room and into the great room.

The house smelled old and sweet—as if someone had smoked sweet tobacco sitting there by the big stone fireplace, but she knew that scent would fade as she climbed the steps, and a sour, metallic scent would take its place. She pinched the bridge of her nose, pain forking through her left eye, brow, and brain. Too late, she thought of the sumatriptan and Excedrin bottles in her purse locked in the car outside. The room was furnished well but frugally—comfortable furniture but wrapped in fabrics rather than leather or other materials. The carpet, also, was middle tier, but she'd bet her last donut that the family's tractors were shiny and well-maintained. Butch came thundering down the stairs, and she winced at the noise.

"All yours," he said.

"Thanks, Butch."

"Sure, Meredeth." He paused, looking at her with bright, penetrating eyes. "Are you all right? You look..."

"A little green in the gills?" She flashed a tired smile. "I'm okay, Butch. I get headaches at crime scenes involving children."

"Can't blame you there. I get the GERD for days from scenes like this. If you want, I've got ibuprofen in the car."

"Thanks. I've got stuff with me."

"Okay. Offer's open, though."

He strode past her, and Meredeth watched him go, then stood staring at the dining room door for a few moments after he disappeared through it. After a few fruitless minutes, she turned and trudged up the stairs and into the stink, her head screaming louder and louder with each step. She found herself sighing, then taking a few steps, then sucking in a breath to kick off the whole process, again and again. *I really need a break from this*, she thought, then immediately felt guilty—as if Goode was right and she was personally responsible for every dead body that dropped from the moment she caught a case until they could close it.

A dark, paneled hallway awaited her at the top of the stairs. Photographs of the family lined its walls—Mom, Dad, and five kids between five or six and sixteen or seventeen from the look of them. Their smiling faces beamed at her as she walked by, and she tried to keep herself from imagining them with gaping black holes where their left eyes should be.

An image flashed through her mind—an image of a dark-haired woman, almost half Meredeth's age, lying in a red puddle, a dark gaping wound taking the place of her left eye. Meredeth gasped as a searing pain ripped through her own left eye, recognition rolling in with it, thunder and lightning, a hurricane and its storm surge. *That's Laura. Laura Reynolds. My biological mother.* The calm, professional voice that spoke within her seemed so cold, so distant, and she realized that must be how she sounded as she delivered her profiles, her reports about murder, debauchery, death, and mayhem.

She shook her head to clear it, to rid herself of the unwanted distraction, to banish that image. *Or is it a memory?* she asked herself. *Is that what all these things are? Memories of life with my fath—with my stepfather? Life and death with Garry Reynolds?* Nothing within answered, no nightmare images swept her up, no screams, no gunshots, no grand epiphanies.

She continued down the happy-photo-lined hallway, eyes down but still catching glimpses of joyful family holidays, of harvests, cultivation of both crops and love, of state fair days and afternoons at the local swimming hole. Smiles blurred in her vision, sun-weathered faces seemed to melt into blotches of flesh tones and hair colors, and Meredeth realized she was crying, soft snorts of sobs escaping her iron control as tears slid freely down her cheeks.

Halting, she swept her palms across her cheeks, angry with herself for losing control. *I don't even* know *these people,* she chided herself. But even as she thought it, she knew it for a lie, knew the source of her turmoil, and knew it wasn't grief for—or even *about*—the murdered family she was about to examine. No, it was grief for her own murdered family, her own shattered childhood, for happy family outings with Dawn and Kjetl but without Meredeth's—Mercy's—family; for afternoons spent swimming; for game nights, but only for the *three* of them; for vacations to Florida; for skiing trips to Colorado, for summer days at the beach with friends—all while Kenny suffered alone, uncared for, abandoned, left to rot; and no matter what she tried, she couldn't stop the deluge of tears, the sniffles, the soft grunt-sobs that coincided with her insides tearing themselves apart.

She grabbed at the closest doorframe, feeling the world closing down around her, the darkness squeezing inward. All color leeched out of her vision, leaving her trapped in a silver and white toned world shrouded in haughty silence as though she were not worthy of recriminations, of arguments, of accusations of neglect and apathy.

The tendons in her hands creaked as she squeezed and squeezed and squeezed the doorframe, her knuckles—as white as the paint covering the wood she gripped for dear life—standing out from her wind-reddened hands. Pain roiled in her chest, cold lumps of diamond-hard nothingness snagged at her breath in her throat, hot lances of pain slamming through her brain and soul. She stood there, frozen by a pain too big to ignore, too powerful to banish to the back of her mind. She stood there and fought to regain control, her whole attention dedicated to the task. She lost track of time, lost track of the muffled sounds drifting up from the kitchen, lost track of the clock *tick-tick-ticking* away on the mantle.

A light footstep sounded behind her, a stealthy tread on the stairs, and she held out her hand, fighting for control of her voice, of her emotions. "Not now, Bobby," she said. She expected some kind of repartee but was met only with silence. "I'm fine. Go back down." She knew her shaking voice wouldn't fool him, he was too good of an observer of human behavior to be fooled by such empty words, but she tried anyway. After another silent moment, she swiped her cheeks as clear of tears as she could, despite the fresh flood of grief replacing what she'd wiped away the moment she'd finished, then glanced over her shoulder.

There was no one behind her. No one on the stairs, no one in the shadowy hall. No one. Fear tickled her belly, but she clamped down on the emotion, commanding it to retreat, to get the hell down, and put its hands over its head. Instead of dying away, the panic in her heart swelled, ran rampant, bulls in Pamplona, free at last, free at last, and before she knew it, she was on her butt, her knees up in front of her, her arms wrapped around her legs, strangling them tight, fear and panic and grief and rage and sorrow ruling her in turns, ravaging her of her coping mechanisms, of her ability to stuff those emotions down, down, down within herself, of her iron-clad control.

Footsteps sounded on the oak steps, and Kevin called out, "Hey, FBI, I know you like this whole solitude and silence bit, but it's been a while, and Morgan wants—" He stopped speaking as his eyes cleared the top step, and he stood there a moment, too stunned to say or do anything.

And then he was moving, coming up the stairs at speed, his face a study in worry, in concern, in empathy, and he slid to her side, catching her up, holding her tight, hugging her to him in the way of fathers everywhere, shielding her from threats—but the threats were within her, in her past, in her mind and memory. "Shh," he crooned. "Easy now, Meredeth. Be easy. Just breathe."

She turned toward him, burying her face in his chest, grabbing him around the neck, latching on to him the way a drowning woman might latch onto a life ring, tears hot and heavy on her cheeks, throat filled with cold fire, heart heavy, broken, barren. Soft grunts were the only noises she made, though she wanted to be silent, to be in control.

He held her tight, rocking her a little as she dissolved into jelly, as her iron will rusted and gave way, as she disintegrated back, back, back through time, becoming that ten-year-old version of herself, the girl who stood next to Boudreaux Walker and told Junior Martin her name and address and that her daddy had a problem with whisky and getting mad about nothing.

Time drifted by around her, but she had no idea how much of it passed. Eventually, the pain receded—not all of it, but enough that she could breathe as Kevin told her to do. Enough that she could regain control, reassert herself, snap her mask back into place; enough that she could relax the hooked claws her hands had become; enough that she could stop the orangutan grunting deep in her chest; enough that she could sense Kevin's worry, his compassion, his warmth. She patted him on the shoulder but didn't let go of his neck. She wasn't ready to face it alone yet.

"Better now?" he murmured.

She nodded against his chest but wondered if she would ever be better again, if the pain would ever recede to the background, to the mists of time. "The pictures..." she whispered. She felt Kevin moving, craning his neck to see the photographs lining the walls.

"Yeah. Rough," he said.

"Kenny..." she whispered, and he stroked her hair.

"Shh, FBI. Time's a real bastard. Won't let us travel back and fix things. We can only move forward."

"He must've felt so alone, so—"

"Yes," said Kevin. "And none of it—*none of it, FBI*—is your fault."

She sighed, enervated and wrung out, and slumped back against the wall, letting her arm slide out from behind his neck with more than a little reluctance. She scrubbed her cheeks, probably making a smeary mess of her face, then giggled a little at the thought of suffering through a complete emotional breakdown at a crime scene, then worrying about her damn makeup.

"Better now?" asked Kevin again.

"Yeah," she said. "This has never happened to me before."

"You've never discovered your past before today, either."

"True." She leaned her head back against the wall and looked at the ceiling. "I don't know if I want to do this anymore, Kevin."

He shrugged. "You don't have to decide today. And either way, you'll make your way. You're tough, FBI. Nothing's going to hold you back."

"Are you sure about that?" Her voice shook a little—a little girl's voice.

He nodded once, treating her to a slow smile. "I am."

"I don't want to..."

"Let's walk this one together," he said.

She gave him a sideways look. "If *you* need *me* to walk with you, I will."

"I do," he said with a solemn expression. "I need the company."

"I'll be your white knight, young damsel. Help a girl up."

With a small, grave grin, Kevin rose smoothly to his feet and extended his hand. When she took it, he pulled her up, but when he relaxed his grip, she held his hand tight. He glanced at her, but she kept her eyes locked straight ahead, so he said nothing.

He led her to the first bedroom door and rested his hand on the doorknob. "Ready, FBI?" When she nodded, he turned the knob and pushed the door open.

Joyful, powder-blue walls with crisp white trim greeted them. The floors were heart pine, finished with a lovely amber glow. The body of the child lying in the powder blue swathed bed had been nine or ten years old—a blond boy looking peaceful in his eternal rest. Toy tractors and action figures and puzzle pieces and baseball gear littered the wood floors, and posters from video games she'd played as a teenager—Super Mario Kart, The Legend of Zelda, Sonic the Hedgehog, F-Zero, and Lemmings—adorned the walls. He had a small television setup on his desk, with one of those console emulators positioned in front of it. Old school game cartridges littered the desk, leaving no room for the schoolbooks heaped in haphazard stacks on the floor.

She glanced at Kevin, then followed his gaze to the bed, to the face of the blond boy, to his missing left eye. She squeezed her eyes shut and shuddered. When she opened them, Kevin was staring at her, a question in his eyes. She nodded and said, "I'm okay." Then, Meredeth stepped closer to the bed—but kept her tight grip on Kevin's hand—noting the powder burns stippling the boy's cheek, his carefree position, the gore-splattered stuffed bear nestled to his cheek. "He felt nothing," she whispered.

"Nothing," Kevin agreed. "The unsub did it while he slept. He never knew a moment's fear."

"Nothing new here," she whispered. "Or I should say, more of the same."

"Ready to move on?"

She turned her slow regard on the rest of the room, gazing at the boy's things in silence. When she nodded, Kevin returned the gesture, then led her across the hall. This room had the same warm heart pine floors but shone a light yellow that made Meredeth recall Easter eggs and early morning sunrises. The room was tidier than the boy's across the hall, with everything in its place and a place for everything. No video game posters adorned the walls, and no video game console took up the entirety of the desk space. A half-height bookshelf lined the wall across from the bed, filled with books from the Wimpy Kid series, the Magic Tree House series, the Chronicles of Narnia, and the Little House on the Prairie books. On the desk, open and held that way with a paperweight, was Anne of Green Gables. Meredeth steeled herself, then glanced at the beatific face of the blonde girl lying in the bed, wrapped as she was in soft pink sheets and a bright yellow comforter. Her face had the same distortions as her brother, and she'd also died without waking.

They continued down the hall, making stops in the bedrooms of a seventeen-year-old—a football star from the photos and trophies on his shelves—and the youngest, another blond boy. Neither had awoken, and both had died in their sleep. Across from the youngest boy, they found the bedroom of the eight-year-old girl.

Her room was as neat as a pin, like her sister's, but the bedclothes had been thrown to the floor, and her desk chair was overturned and shoved away from the desk. Her body was back in the bed, but it was obvious to both of them that she'd been shot while hiding in the kneehole of her desk, blood and other matter splattered the wall there.

"He shot her, then pulled her out and put her in the bed," said Kevin.

"Yes," said Meredeth. "Why?"

Kevin shook his head. "He had to touch her anyway. He put the card in her mouth."

Meredeth shook her head once. "Still. Why not leave her where he shot her? He made no attempt to clean up, to hide what he did here."

"You're the profiler, FBI. I'm just the hired help."

She shook her head again, then looked at the girl's wounds. A single gunshot had ruined the side of her head—no doubt as she'd huddled under the desk, squeezing her eyes shut, looking away—and once in the left eye—obviously postmortem. "And why the last shot? She was already dead."

"Compulsion?" Kevin said.

Meredeth looked at him sharply, his voice containing a note of speculation. "What?"

"It's nothing."

"Like hell. Give."

"They're all shot in the left eye."

"Right..."

He ducked his head. "So was Laura Reynolds."

"So were a lot of people, Kevin," she said in an emotionless voice. Inside, though, she was going to pieces—the chief's implication so obvious she didn't know why she hadn't seen it herself.

"And the unsub said he knows you, that the two of you know each other."

"He meant the card. That we met on the kidnapping case."

"Did he?" Kevin asked in a still, quiet voice.

Meredeth turned away. "Yes. There's no other answer." But there was, and she knew what it was. *Kenny.* Though he said nothing, she could almost feel his disagreement floating in the air. "It doesn't mean anything anyway," she said after a moment of silence. "Except that the unsub is right-handed. He shoots them in their left eyes because it feels natural to do so."

"Is that all it is?"

"Yes. That's all it is. Come on, let's go look at the master bedroom and then get the hell out of here."

CHAPTER 24

GOODE FOR YOU
Wyoming County, NY

AS MEREDETH AND Kevin approached the kitchen, she could hear Bobby's rolling voice, in the middle of some joke, then the uproar of all the troopers in the room breaking into laughter. The laughter had the typical desperate quality common to horrific crime scenes. Gallows humor—a grim coping mechanism, a blow-off valve that helped keep law enforcement officers from losing it in the face of grisly, inhuman acts.

She pulled Kevin to a stop and stood for a moment, then turned to him and said, "I'm not ready to deal with your...theory of the crime. Can you sit on it for a while?" Her left eye throbbed with each word, and as she waited for his reply, the pain in her brows mounted.

Kevin puffed out his cheeks and dropped his gaze away from hers. "For a little while, I guess." He shook his head. "I don't know how I feel about blocking off an avenue of investigation that might yield fruit."

She shook her head, disregarding the dizziness that came with it, and moved a step closer to him. "I don't think it will. It doesn't make temporal sense, for one thing. If it is...my brother, and he knew me twenty years ago, why wait until now to"—she glanced around the farmhouse—"all this? Why not make all this happen years ago? Why wait to take his revenge or teach me a lesson or whatever?"

"I don't know, Meredeth. Why do any of it? Why not contact your family when he was released? Why not write to you from his confinement? There are too many whys and why nots, too much we don't know."

"You're right. Of course, you are—about the questions and about telling the state police, but it's..." She shook her head again. "It's too much for me today. Too much all at once. Can you wait until after Bobby and I leave, at least?"

"Yeah," he said, nodding. "Yeah, I can do that."

"Thanks, Kevin...for everything." The pain behind her eye retreated a little.

He gave her a quick shrug. "I did what anyone would do."

"No, you did more than that, and I appreciate it."

"Well...you're welcome, then."

She gave him a tight grin, and then, as the laughter in the kitchen died down, she stepped through the doorway. She glanced around at the faces decorated with mirthful smiles and forlorn eyes, then approached Captain Morgan. "There's not a lot I can add to the profile from this," she said by way of a greeting. "He's breaking his pattern, using these recent murders as a way of justifying his communications through the Press, of proving he is who he says he is."

"And taunting you," said Morgan.

"Maybe, maybe not. But he is sending messages at these poor folks' expense." She shrugged. "I don't want this to continue." She waved her hand to encompass the farmhouse.

"I don't either. What do you have in mind?"

"Maybe we can open the lines of communication."

He arched an eyebrow at her, then looked at Kevin. "How?"

She turned and looked at Butch Schweighart. "Is Goode out front?"

The big trooper knotted his brows and shot a glance at his captain. "I think so."

"Let's give him what he wants," Meredeth said with a frown. "Bring him up to the dooryard with his cameraman. I'll give him the interview of his life."

"Meredeth, are you sure?" asked Kevin.

"It will ensure we get on the air," she said with a dour shrug. "It will ensure we get broad enough coverage that the unsub will see it, no matter where he is. If we pick another reporter..." She let it trail away, punctuated with a quick shrug.

"But Goode? He's already gunning for you."

"Yeah, I'm counting on that. And the unsub has already used him as a line of communication," she said. "Let's use that."

Butch looked at Morgan and arched his eyebrows.

"If you're sure, Agent Connelly, I'll go along," said Morgan.

It took fifteen minutes to find Goode in the throng of reporters and camera operators, get them inside the perimeter, then find a spot they deemed suitable while not being too creepy, and then set up their equipment. All the while, though he shot her speculative looks, Goode didn't say a word to Meredeth, and she didn't say anything to him.

"Okay," he said as the camera operator nodded. "We'll be live in a few minutes. You'll know because I'll say hello to whoever is doing the break-in." As he spoke, Goode's gaze crawled over the troopers, over Kevin, over Bobby, but he never once looked at Meredeth. "It's imperative you are quiet. Any noises, any talking, whatever, will trigger the producers to cut away. Am I clear?"

"Let's get on with it," said Meredeth. "We've all done this before."

He stabbed her with a dagger-sharp glare for half a heartbeat, then faced the camera. "Hair?"

"Check," said the cameraman.

"Face?"

"Ugly, but yeah, you have one."

"Background?"

"Check."

"Okay, then," said Goode. "We're ready."

They waited a few minutes in silence, while the crew back in Buffalo broke into the morning's scheduled programming, then set up the report. Goode's perpetual plastic smile creeped Meredeth out as it didn't come close to his eyes—something that couldn't be seen on television. He stood stock-still, microphone held to his chest, arm bent at the elbow and pressed tight to his ribs. "Yes. Hello, Melanie. It's good to speak with you again."

Meredeth waited, standing just to the side but out of the frame.

"And it continues this morning," said Goode. "I've been invited inside the perimeter of the most recent scene by Sergeant Schweighart of the New York State Police for an in-person update with so-called superprofiler Special Agent Meredeth Connelly." He paused, that creepy smile stuck to his face like a sticker, and then he tilted his head to the side. "Yes, Melanie, you did hear me correctly. Agent Connelly is standing right here, ready to give me a few minutes. And I agree, the interview is likely to strike sparks, but that's what I'm here for—to get the news and share it with all of you." He turned to face Meredeth, and she saw the camera swing her way in her peripheral vision. "Special Agent Connelly, good morning."

"Hello, Mr. Goode."

"My viewers are—"

"I beg your pardon, Mr. Goode, but before we continue, I owe you an apology for yesterday. I was suffering from a horrible stress headache, and I'm afraid that wore me down."

Goode quirked an eyebrow at her, unable to stop the subtle tilt of his head, hesitating, clearly not expecting the interview to be civil. "It's fine," he said.

"No, it really isn't okay," Meredeth went on. "My behavior was totally out-of-line. You didn't deserve to be treated that way." *No, you deserved much worse, you lying prick. Much worse.*

With a half-smile, Jeremy nodded. "Thanks. I appreciate your candor. I—we understand." His eyes sparkled, however, and she knew she wasn't forgiven.

"I have an update for you and your loyal viewers, Mr. Goode, and a special message for the .40 Caliber Killer."

"The Dollhouse Killer, you mean," he all but snapped.

"No, I said what I meant," she said, pinning him with her sharpest glare, and he smiled a little, catching on to her real meaning—that she meant everything she'd said the day before. "It's silly to antagonize serial murderers, Mr. Goode."

"I'm not scared—"

"That much is clear, but you really should be. Serial killers are like wild animals—unpredictable, dangerous to the extreme."

Goode scoffed. "Bullies are often—"

"That's another thing, Mr. Goode. I've heard you compare the unsub to a bully numerous times, and while his actions may seem like that of a bully to the uninformed, I can assure you that they are as different as night and day, and any comparison you might be harboring of the two types of behavior is in error and should be abandoned."

Goode nodded, a spark of emotion in his eyes. "Well, thanks for your concern," he said, his tone edging toward nasty. He glanced at the farmhouse. "What happened in there?"

Meredeth shook her head. "I can't give you specifics about an ongoing investigation, but I can tell you a little about our unsub, if you'd like."

"Agent Connelly, that's exactly what my viewers *need*."

"Excellent. He is a man, probably in his late forties, which is a little older than we'd typically expect. He's also a little different in that his crimes tend more toward an assassin personality rather than, say a sexual sadist like Ted Bundy. In many ways, our unsub mirrors David Berkowitz in more than just nickname—he's what we call a 'collector.' Given the nature of his crimes, he grew up in the lower economic strata and possibly in an abusive home. He definitely believes he was abused or bullied extensively, most likely by his mother's boyfriend or his stepfather."

"Excuse me, Agent Connelly, but I have a question."

"By all means," Meredeth said and rocked forward onto her toes, the perfect picture of attention and interest.

"You said he's a collector. What is he collecting?"

Meredeth smiled a little. "He's after perfection, Mr. Goode. He considers his real family a failure and is out to 'collect' examples of families he feels would be perfect if not for their economic difficulties, and the choices of the mother, which he characterizes as bad choices."

"Ah. In his letter to the New York Times, he mentioned 'freeing' families. Is that what he meant?"

"Well, I'm no mind-reader, but that's what my years of experience and formal education point to. More specifically, he's freeing the youngest child while punishing the mother a little before freeing her. He also punishes the middle child a little—with the knowledge that her mother and younger sibling have been murdered. In essence, he's telling her she should have done a better job protecting her younger brother, that she had the opportunity to fight for him, yet failed to do so."

Goode quirked his head to the side. "You say 'she and her' and likewise indicate the younger child is male. I was under the impression no patterns like that existed."

Meredeth nodded once. "You are correct. I misspoke. I've spent a lot of time thinking about the Hanable's Valley murder. It...it struck a chord." She turned a little and glanced back at the farmhouse. "Of course, all of that is in flux, given the shift in targeting the unsub has displayed with his last few murders."

"Hmm," said Goode, glancing at the farmhouse himself. "What do you make of it?"

She tilted her head to the side a moment, staring at Goode with an uncomfortable intensity. "Are you asking me as a journalist covering this case or a citizen interested in serial killers and their motivations?"

A small smile tweaked Jeremy's lips. "Are you asking me as a profiler or an interviewee?"

"Touché," she said with a wry grin. "I'm afraid I can't separate one from the other."

"My answer is the same."

"My take is that the unsub wants lines of communication with law enforcement. These last two killings are crimes of opportunity that allow him to feed his addiction and, at the same time, prove he's the man writing the letters."

"Addiction?"

Meredeth nodded. "Yes. Research—*interviews* with serial killers who have been captured—indicate that these men are compelled to repeat their crimes in much the same way that a drug addict is compelled to take more drugs despite any knowledge that what they are doing is wrong or unhealthy in the long run. The need to get a fix consumes them, compels them until they give in and feed their dark passengers."

"I see," said Goode with a speculative air. "You say he wants to establish open communications with law enforcement, yet not a single letter has gone to law enforcement agencies—unless that's something you've kept under wraps?"

"No, you are correct."

"Then isn't it more likely he wants to open communication with the press?"

Meredeth pumped her shoulders up and down as though the question bored her. "The press is often used as a middleman in these kinds of things. Some unsubs want a certain distance between themselves and those hunting them. They offer many avenues of obfuscation, many different hands touch those letters before we get them, muddying any forensic investigations we may undertake."

Jeremy nodded. "That makes sense. It seems like a good strategy."

Meredeth considered him a moment, a small smile on her lips. "What many people do not understand is that while some serial killers *are* undone by forensics, most often the techniques used are ones the public isn't as familiar with. Not DNA or fingerprints, in other words. Often—"

"A moment, please. I can't let that pass. What kinds of forensics do you mean?" Goode leaned toward her a little, his burning gaze drilling into hers.

"I'm obviously not going to give specifics about our techniques, except where the information is already public knowledge. Take the Rader case—"

"The so-called BTK Killer," said Goode, and Meredeth nodded.

"In that case, while Rader left certain fluids that did lead to a genetic match with a member of his family, it was computer metadata on a disk he sent to a television reporter that initially led authorities to run those genetic comparisons and perform a handwriting analysis. Handwriting was likewise used to convict Albert Fish. Many serial killers study forensic techniques and become experts at *not* leaving any—which is why I must be careful about what techniques I discuss here today. Joseph DeAngelo was one such, who used his experience as a police officer to extend his reign of terror to more than forty years. If not for the advance in open-source genealogy, he might still be out there. But none of these criminals can mask their own behavior, their addiction to murder, and the motivational and personality traits that drive them. *Those* are the things that lead us to knock on their doors, to run their familial genetic records against fluids from crime scenes, et cetera."

Goode frowned. "Then you're saying these letters to the press serve no real purpose in protecting the identity of the unsub?"

"From a forensic sense—outside of the hassle of elimination testing for the people at the press outlet—they don't offer us much in the way of evidence. But psychologically? It's still a buffer. To the unsub, it is less threatening to send a journalist his letters than to send them to the police or FBI. *You*"—she paused and gave Goode a significant look—"with your desire to report the contents of the letter, rather than me, with my drive to dissect the writing for behavioral clues."

"I see. And have you found any?"

"Behavioral clues?" Meredeth grinned. "That would be telling, wouldn't it?"

Goode's frown deepened. "Sure, but that's the point of giving this interview. Telling."

"Is it?"

His eyes narrowed. "What other motivation could you have?"

"None, I'm sure."

Jeremy considered that a moment, then, with a slight shake of his head, he moved on. "You mentioned a message for the Dollhouse Killer?"

Meredeth shook her head. "I really wish you'd stop doing that, Mr. Goode. Poking sleeping bears is stupid, and you're anything but a stupid man. And it's dangerous—as I said before."

"You'd prefer I catered to this man? To call him Ankou, his self-styled moniker?"

"Personally, I treat these men with respect—the way I would a timber rattler or a crocodile. I wish you'd take my example—in that at least."

"I'll take it under advisement," said Goode with a sour twist to his lips.

"Do as you like, but..."

"But?"

Meredeth thought his tone had grown a touch aggressive, which was fine by her. Time for a taste of his own medicine, and no one could manipulate a conversation like a student of human behavior. "It's nothing," she said at last. "Do as you like. I'm sure you know best."

"I think I do," he said in an even tone. "I think I know how to do my own job."

"And mine," she said with a quirky grin.

Goode looked away for a hair's breadth. "It's not that I understand how to do your *job*, Agent Connelly. How could I? I'm not a profiler by any stretch of the imagination, but I do understand your *responsibilities*...something I think you spend too little time reflecting on."

Meredeth suppressed a grin. "Ah. Armchair quarterbacks always say something like that." She shrugged. "Do you have other questions about the case?"

"*Armchair quarterbacks?* Lady, let me tell you something—" Goode stopped, and for a mere moment, Meredeth saw the real Jeremy Goode looking out at her, but then his control snapped back into place, and he grinned. "Interview tricks? Very good, Agent Connelly."

"Only one of the things you need to understand in order to do my job, Mr. Goode."

"Point taken." He looked at her for a moment, a peculiar expression on his face. "Ah, we have a question from Melanie back in Buffalo," he said.

"Sure, if you'd prefer some time to gather your thoughts." She let her eyes shine with challenge, thinking he'd surge forward like a lion after a gazelle, but he only smiled.

"I'm afraid we all must serve our masters," he said. "Melanie would like to know what you think the Doll"—he closed his mouth, a small smile appearing there for a moment—"what the *unsub* will do next."

Meredeth smiled and inclined her head. "He will go on killing until we catch him. It's the one thing in his life he truly enjoys."

"Yes, yes, but *who? Where?*"

"I'm not a psychic, Mr. Goode, but I can say that if the unsub is driven by the motivations I see in his crimes, he will return to the trailer parks of the Southern Tier sooner, rather than later."

"More children, then?"

"Unfortunately. His need to 'save' that youngest child drives him like nothing else in his life."

"And—this is my question—what are you and your colleagues going to do to stop him?"

"Everything within our collective powers, up to the extent the law allows."

"A pat answer, Agent. I expected more candor."

"Perhaps, Mr. Goode, but that answer is both accurate and true."

"Let's get down to it, then, shall we? What *exactly* is your plan for stopping this madman?"

"Oh, he's not mad—at least in the legal definition. Far from it. He knows what he's doing is wrong. That's why he takes steps to avoid capture. A true visionary killer wouldn't necessarily make that distinction—doing God's will, for instance, requires true believers to put everything in His hands. No, this unsub understands exactly what he's doing and what society at large feels about his 'work'"—she made air quotes with her fingers—"and though he claims he wants us to understand, all of that is window dressing. Much as your questions in the story you ran last night."

"I—"

"Was that petty?" she asked with a grin. "My mouth ran away with me."

His eyes narrowed a moment, but then he returned her grin. "I won't be provoked, Agent Connelly."

"Farthest thing from my mind, Mr. Goode."

"I notice you've evaded my question with all this 'bear poking' as you styled it."

"Have I? You know I can't answer that question. You understand my responsibilities, after all."

"Yes," he grated. "Tell me, Agent Connelly... My research indicates you've never married. Is that true?"

Meredeth nodded. "It is. Does that bother you?"

"And do you still deny your romantic interest in Chief Kevin Saunders of the Hanable's Valley Police Department?"

"None of this seems relevant to my responsibilities."

"Come, Agent Connelly. Let's dispense with the wordplay." His face hardened. "Isn't it true you've never married because, in fact, you are a lesbian?"

Meredeth chuckled and saw the rage grow in his eyes. "Mr. Goode, even if I was, what possible relevance would that have on this case?"

"You're not married. You have no children."

"Neither is a Bureau requirement." She put on a speculative expression as though the thought had just occurred to her. "Almost the opposite, as a matter of fact, though I'm sure my bosses will deny that. If I'd married, the Bureau would have moved me out the field long ago."

"And what is the FBI's stance on homosexuality?"

"We have Pride Summits now. We're inclusive."

"Would admitting you are a homosexual incur *another* letter of censure?"

Meredeth treated him to a one-sided smile and a shake of her head. "No, though your assertion is vacuous on its face, as I think you know. I, too, Mr. Goode, will not be provoked."

"Then your tirade yesterday did *not* earn you a letter of censure?"

"I have no letters of censure in my file," she said—after all, A.D. Brenton had not yet written her letter.

Goode frowned, a severe line furrowing the skin between his brows. "But I was told—"

"By whom, Mr. Goode?" she asked quietly. "You were told by whom?"

He tilted his head back and gazed down at her. "Why does my investigation into your career scare you so much? What do you have to hide?"

"Nothing, Mr. Goode, and you don't scare me. Not in the least. I *understand* you, you see."

"You understand me." Goode's voice had taken on a sterile, lifeless quality.

"Yes. Profiling isn't limited to serial killers. The concepts apply equally well to journalists and FBI agents." She wasn't sure, but she thought she saw a heartbeat of fear in his eyes. "A true student of human behavior can see through most shielding behaviors, Mr. Goode—even those the individual being studied doesn't know exist."

"Such as?"

"Such as the editing job you did on last night's story." She stared up at him, her face a mask of cold apathy. "I think many of your viewers probably saw through it, as well. Your motivations were clear from the outset of the piece."

"If they were so obvious, perhaps you'd like to share them?"

Meredeth shrugged. "I can if you'd like." Her voice was firm, competent, self-assured.

"This should be good. Go on, please." He put his finger to his ear, then looked directly at the camera. "No, Melanie, I think this is quite telling behavior from Agent Connelly, and we should allow her to continue." He glared at Meredeth. "To get it on *the record.*"

Arching one eyebrow, Meredeth said, "If your producers want it, I can provide my analysis in writing, and we can resume this interview after they've had a chance to review it."

Goode turned a hot-eyed glare on her. "No. Go on. *Educate* us."

With another bump of her shoulders, Meredeth nodded and said, "Sure. Your intentions were to advance your own brand at the expense of my professional and personal lives, regardless of what happened to the credibility of WUTV's news services. You saw an opportunity, and like a great white shark circling an injured seal, you couldn't stop yourself. You leaped at the opportunity. You intentionally goaded me, knowing I was suffering, then, when you had enough to splice together a damning video, you smiled and left to re-record your questions, taking care to look professional—as contrary to your actual questioning style as you could get." She twitched her shoulders again. "Of course, all of this serves your ego—your ambition, your self-interest, your lust for power."

"All of that, eh?"

Goode's face was impassive, but she thought there was a slight tremor to his voice, and Meredeth nodded solemnly.

"So, let me recap the relevant parts of this interview for my viewers. You don't know who the Dollhouse Killer is. You don't know *where* he is. You'd rather spend time analyzing *me* and *casting dispersions* on my professionalism than working out how to stop him. Is that accurate? Is that fair?" His words came rapid-fire, hot and intense,

Scoffing, she shook her head. "Hardly, Mr. Goode, and you know it."

"Oh, do I?"

Meredeth only looked at him, then turned a slow look directly into the camera and nodded.

"Isn't it true that most serial killers—most *bullies*—are cowards?"

"Mr. Goode, these kinds of stereotypes—"

"That most *profilers* show, in fact, at least as much cowardice as their so-called unsubs?"

Wearing a small grin, Meredeth shook her head. "Where do you get this stuff? Does it occur to you naturally or have you spent time developing a notebook of these smears to trot out when you're on your back foot?"

Goode scoffed. "You are not capable of making me uneasy, Connelly." Even so, his gaze darted toward the camera before he could stop it.

"There are quite a few serial killers imprisoned who probably thought the same thing. But before this disintegrates, I would like to give my message to the .40 Caliber Killer." With a glance at the camera, she squared her shoulders and looked straight into Goode's blazing eyes. "You have the power, the strength, to stop this. I can help you stop. I can help you understand yourself, your behavior...to give context to your life. I understand what motivates you, and I can share that with you. Many of the men I've caught felt relief, knowing the things I can share with you. I want you to dispense with these letters to the press. You can call me directly, and we can talk like two rational adults—no press, no judgments. You can have a productive life in what time you have left. You don't have to live in the service of your addictions."

"That's it?" Goode asked in a flat tone.

Meredeth nodded without taking her eyes from his. "I hope he hears this."

Goode rolled his eyes and sighed. "Agent Connelly, before today I thought you merely incompetent. I thought you were a dullard, a slacker, more interested in sex than in doing your job. I now see that I was wrong."

"I accept your apology."

Goode snorted. "I was wrong. You are not incompetent. You are not a slut. *You are a coward.* You and the Dollhouse Killer, both. The two of you deserve one another."

"I wasn't wrong, Mr. Goode," she said, turning her calm gaze to the camera lens again. "About any of it."

"I'm afraid we've wasted our viewer's time, Melanie. My apologies. After yesterday, I shouldn't have expected Agent Connelly to deal squarely with me. Back to you." When the camera operator signaled they were clear, Goode dropped his microphone to the ground and turned away.

"That last part was overkill, Goode," Meredeth said. "You hurt yourself there. You should have played it better."

"Yeah?" he asked without turning back or slowing.

"Yeah," she said. "Jeremy!"

He stopped walking but didn't turn. "What now?"

"Let me put a detail on you. On your home."

He laughed. "Do I scare you that much? Better people than you have tried to silence me. The network...that bastard Postwaite. I'm still here, Connelly, and I always will be."

"You have been goading the unsub for a week, whether you believe it or not. At least get out of town. Take a vacation. Pack up the wife and kids and go to Disney World. Go tonight." She knew he wouldn't go but wondered what excuse he would use. She wondered if he knew it was an excuse. "Think of your kids, Jeremy."

He scoffed. "Your scare tactics won't work on me. Every time you turn around, expect to see my face, because I'll be there, hounding you, exposing you for what you are. And I'm not limiting that promise to this case. You made an enemy, Connelly, and I'm a bastard to have for an enemy."

"That's a two-way street, Goode," she said. "Who do you think wins such match-ups? The journalist or the FBI agent?"

"I guess we'll find out."

"Guess so," she said. She didn't know whether it was the sumatriptan and Excedrin finally kicking in or not, but she barely felt her headache.

CHAPTER 25

GOT YOU GOODE

Buffalo, NY

THE CALL CAME in what felt like only moments after Meredeth had finally gotten to sleep, but when she looked at the clock on her phone, it was nearly five-thirty, and the sky beyond the sheer curtains had lightened from midnight blues and purples to brighter colors—orange, yellow, and pale blue-gray. Her head throbbed once as she rolled over—perhaps a warning of what was to come, perhaps not.

Bobby's name and picture appeared in the caller ID field—which meant there was another houseful of bodies for her to go look at—a thought which elicited a groan and another throb behind her eyes. She thumbed the accept button and put the phone to her ear. "Where this time?"

Bobby sniffed, but when he spoke, there was no trace of sleepiness in his voice. "Right here in Buffalo."

"Trailer park?"

"Uh, no. Not this time."

"Well?"

"The scene is in Orchard Park."

"Why do I get the feeling I'm not going to like this?"

"It's... The house belongs to Jeremy and Sandy Goode."

Meredeth pursed her lips and blinked at the ceiling for a few heartbeats. "And the victims?"

"All four of them. It sounds as if the unsub took particular care with Jeremy Goode."

"Shit," she breathed.

"You tried to tell him. Several times."

"I should have put someone on him whether he wanted the detail or not."

"You did ask for increased patrols, and Morgan had troopers in the area all night in case something kicked off. But Butch said it was a quiet night by all reports. Not so much as a car alarm."

"Shit," she said again. "I should have insisted. I should have—"

"You tried, boss. Goode refused. You told him to take a powder, and he laughed. You can lead a horse to water and all that."

"Right. Give me ten minutes to get dressed."

She climbed out of bed and went straight to the coffee machine, primed it, then took the prevention meds Dr. Taber had prescribed. Her head felt heavy, hot, and she hesitated while looking at the bottle of sumatriptan and the Excedrin. He'd told her to take it before the pain rolled in, and she decided to give it a try, figuring the coming day was going to be an ugly bastard.

Meredeth pulled on a fresh pair of slacks and a navy-blue Bureau polo shirt, then slipped on her shoes as the coffee pot perked and bubbled merrily. When the machine beeped, she was ready to go, save for pouring herself a to-go cup.

Bobby had the car running, waiting in the portico attached to the lobby of the hotel, and she slid into the passenger seat. He drove them south to Orchard Park, and neither of them spoke.

What was there to say? She'd used Goode *knowing* he might provoke the unsub, *knowing* the .40 Caliber Killer might go after the man, and while Jeremy Goode was a Machiavellian snake, his family was a different story—innocents, undeserving of what Goode brought into their home. They idled down Boardwalk Boulevard, looking out at the affluent houses on their sleepy half-acre lots. Warm yellow light glowed from most of the houses—families up and at 'em, getting ready for school, for a day at the office, none of them knowing how close death had come—but that wouldn't last long.

Bobby pulled to the curb in front of a seafoam-green Cape Cod with black trim. NYSP and Orchard Park patrol cars filled the tree-lined asphalt driveway with the coroner's van nestled up next to the garage—hardly visible from the street, but the grim word of the family's demise *would* get out. Sooner rather than later. Meredeth imagined that the story would run on the local morning news programs, and then the public outcry would begin in earnest.

She put her hand on the door handle but hesitated, looking across the prim lawn at the black front door of the Goode family house. "You said he paid special attention to Goode?"

"Yeah," said Bobby.

"How bad?"

Bobby shook his head. "Butch said it was 'grotesque and appalling.'"

Meredeth grimaced.

"He also said the unsub left us a message."

"Did he say what?"

Bobby shook his head again. "He said we'd have to see it to get 'the full effect.'"

"Great," she muttered.

"How's your head?"

She looked at him, searching his face a moment, then said, "I took the sumatriptan and Excedrin before we left. Taber said taking it before the pain hit would be most effective."

Bobby nodded. "Want to give me an extra dose or two? I know you don't like taking your bag into a scene."

"No, I can come out to the car. It'll be better that way." Her gaze went back to the quiet little Cape Cod, and her frown deepened. "Why did he have to go after the kids?"

"It's what he does, boss. Families."

"How can he justify this one, though? In his 'I'm freeing them' fantasy?"

"You knew Goode as well as I did. Can you imagine he was a different person here at home?"

"I guess I can't, at that."

"There you go. It even fits with the psychopathology of an abused child. Free the little ones from the terror named Daddy." In her peripheral vision, Meredeth saw him flinch, then throw a quick glance her way. "Meredeth, I—"

"You heard it from Kevin, then. It's fine, Bobby," she said. "It is what it is, and I get your point." She opened her door. "Let's go get this over with." She got out and entered via the front door. Inside, a trooper stood with the scene log, and the two FBI agents produced their credentials and signed the log. "Where's Butch?" she asked him.

"Kitchen, where else?" He pointed to his right, through the formal living room filled with uncomfortable-looking antiques and fancy doilies. A small, immaculate dining room stood between the formal living room and the kitchen.

Butch waited for them in the kitchen, arms akimbo, expression austere but not sour. "We've got to stop meeting like this."

Meredeth grunted. "Then let's hope he left something that helps."

"I suppose you want to take your tour."

Grimacing, Meredeth shook her head. "I'd rather not, in fact...but I'd better."

"He made a mess this time," said the big trooper. "A mess of Jeremy Goode, a mess of the office. The wife and kids, he put down quick but..." He shook his head. "And there's a message. It's for you, I think."

Meredeth nodded. "Are your people out?"

Butch nodded. "I may look big and dumb, but I'm only the first part."

Without another word, Meredeth turned and stepped into a small den, a large television hanging over the fireplace, recliners and a comfortable leather couch squatting over oak floors. She glanced at the magazines on the coffee table as she passed it—Cosmo, Allure, Glamour, Self, Oxygen—the standard fare as far as Meredeth knew. Her gaze snagged on several newspapers, all open to her picture, all marked and defaced with red Sharpie. She glanced back at the kitchen door, but though she could hear the soft murmur of Butch and Bobby's voices, they weren't visible.

She bent over the papers—all evening editions from the previous day, all covering the live interview she'd given Goode. Someone had used the red marker to edit the articles, to "correct" them, twisting them from pieces that questioned Goode's ethics, that cast a stark light on his career, into ones that lambasted Meredeth. Jeremy, no doubt. She could imagine him sitting there, making his changes, a grin of childish delight on his face. She straightened, shaking her head, then moved on, climbing the stairs and walking down the hall toward the bedrooms, steeling herself against the killing room smell.

She placed a hand on the closed door of Jeremy's five-year-old son, but then moved on, leaving the door closed. *That ain't what he wants me to see. He wants me to see Goode, to see the horror the unsub made of him*. Her mental voice twanged as though she'd never stepped foot outside rural Georgia, and her eye gave a single, vicious throb.

She found the master bedroom at the end of the hall, a large space painted a soft gray, a plush, square rug centered with the bed anchoring its north side. Sandy Goode lay sideways at the headboard, her head on Jeremy's pillow, a single bullet wound taking the place of her left eye. Another magazine lay in her lap, her limp hand lying across it as if to ensure she kept her place. Of Jeremy Goode, there was no sign.

Meredeth turned and entered the master bath—one of those remodeled monstrosities filled with expensive stone and gilt fixtures. Goode wasn't in there, either. She crossed back to the hall door, sparing Sandy Goode one last look, then turned away and went looking for Jeremy's home office.

She found it across the hall from the five-year-old's room, its door closed until she twisted the knob. She pushed the door open and froze, staring into the room of Jeremy Goode's final confessions.

Butch hadn't lied. The unsub had foregone using his gun with Jeremy, utilizing an edged tool of some kind—probably a knife with a wide blade—perhaps a Bowie—by the looks of the wounds. He'd slashed at the man, chopped away bits of flesh—no doubt an effort to win Goode's cooperation with the apologies scrawled on the walls. Her gaze crawled across the walls—words of contrition written in Goode's own blood decorated them—penitent phrases she couldn't imagine ever passing the man's lips.

I, Jeremy Goode, am a bad man, a lousy father, a horrible journalist, and ultimately, a weak man without the stones to resist Ankou's demands.

She shook her head with sadness. She'd warned Goode. She *had*. He hadn't believed her, and maybe she hadn't tried quite hard enough to make him. Her gaze twitched to the man's corpse, her eyes flirting with the horrible wounds and disfigurements, then slid away like a thief slinking into the night and caught on her name on the wall to her left.

Meredeth Connelly is none of the things I said. She's a— The space after it was smeared as though Goode had collapsed against the wall, perhaps swooning from blood loss, but the sentiment continued on the other side of the smear. *She has served Western NY, the Southern Tier, and ME for over two decades, giving up a normal life to hunt serial killers and kidnappers for us. I am a louse for attacking her, and I hope she can forgive me.*

Meredeth blew out her cheeks. She hadn't liked the man—not one itsy bitsy bit—but he hadn't deserved this.

And forced contrition wasn't really contrition at all. The unsub hadn't done this for her. It was only his *excuse*, his rationale for torturing Goode to death.

I am a base and weak man, Jeremy wrote—no doubt taking dictation from the unsub—the final leg of the N a streak that went most of the way to the floor. On the other wall, *In my weakness, I attack others who intimidate and scare me. People like Agent Connelly and Ankou. People who are my betters, both intellectually, morally, and ethically*. On the wall behind the desk, *Print my words. Put these confessions in the New York Times. Report them on television*. Next to the door, beside the light switch, *Spread my confessions far and wide*. Bloody letters and words filled the walls, including a number of short phrases: *Forgive me, I am sorry*, and *Learn from my example*.

Meredeth's guts roiled. It wasn't the most gruesome scene she'd ever worked, but it ranked up there, that was for certain. She tore her gaze from the scrawled words—more an expression of the unsub's psychology than Goode's regret.

On the desk, placed before Jeremy's body like some kind of display, sat eleven sheets of paper. Ignoring the corpse for the moment, she walked behind his desk and gazed down at the papers.

It was a printed transcription of the interview. Her words were left clear, but Goode's sentences had been heavily redacted, and as she scanned the transcription, she realized the unsub had scratched out every insult, every insinuation, every unfound accusation Goode had leveled at her that day. Also, every instance of Goode's pet name for the unsub—the Dollhouse Killer—had been blotted out, but in those cases, the unsub hadn't used ink. He'd used Goode's own blood.

He had savaged Jeremy Goode after he'd gotten what he wanted—hacking, slashing, chopping, cutting at the man until he'd expired. Blood splatter on the ceiling and the most distant walls spoke to the unsub's rage...and while Meredeth had expected that, she hadn't expected his anger would include Goode's nastiness toward her.

Maybe it is— She clamped down on the thought, squeezing her eyes shut.

Meredeth backed into the corner farthest from the door, her gaze zipping from blood splatter to bloody apology to chunks of amputated flesh to the blood-smeared transcripts to the puddles of urine and blood beneath the desk. It was a level of rage she hadn't seen before, a level of violence that the unsub had avoided in his previous murders—even against the men he'd killed.

She hoped it wasn't an evolution in his signature.

She looked around again, examining the scene closely, but none of it made sense to her. The unsub believed they had a relationship of some kind, and that wasn't a new concept for her as it had happened before, but never had she heard of anything like what she was looking at. And all from a man she didn't know—or, at least, didn't know she knew. His reaction had been extreme. Goode hadn't done her much damage in the live interview—he'd done more to his own credibility and career than he had hers. That the unsub saw it differently was telling.

Through her examination of the room, she'd kept Kenny's name out of her head, kept herself from thinking of her brother at all, in fact. Her eyes went to the acts of penitence the killer had forced on Jeremy, the brutality of his "punishment," and she could no longer keep the thoughts at bay.

Kenny... She tried to imagine him as the cold assassin creeping through the halls and rooms of decrepit mobile homes, silent as Death himself, putting bullets through the eyes of sleeping children and women, and couldn't do it. Perhaps that was because her only memories of him came from the dreams—the dreams in which Kenny's father raged and turned savage. Garry Reynolds hadn't employed cold-blooded punishments—his acts came from hot rage, much like what the unsub had done to Jeremy Goode, and she *could* imagine Kenny's hand holding that knife, his twisted face demanding Jeremy's confession, his repentance.

But the rest of it? The rest of the cold crimes? She shook her head. And what Dawn had described—Kenny's decompensation into violence in the Central State Hospital. Those acts had come from a place of repressed fury—at Dawn, at Meredeth, at their father, whoever—and Kenny had expressed himself as fire running rampant.

And if he was driven by rage, her profiling experience suggested *she* was probably its target, that Kenny would revel in Jeremy Goode's attacks, viewing them as just desserts for a lifetime of ignoring Kenny. She shook her head again, her gaze crawling across the scene one last time, then she left Jeremy to his rest and went back downstairs.

"I asked what you're doing here," said Bobby, his voice raised above his aw-shucks regular crime scene voice.

There was a murmur of a reply, a familiar timbre, a familiar cadence. *Kevin*, she thought. She entered the kitchen, her face a careful neutral.

Bobby glanced at her, then snapped his gaze back to Kevin's. "You don't have 'every right to be here,' Chief," said Bobby. "This isn't your jurisdiction. You weren't called here by the sheriff or troop commander. So, tell me. Why are you here?"

Kevin's gaze swam to hers, his face devoid of emotion, only a slight crook in one corner of his mouth hinting at his thoughts, then even that faded into a blank mask, and he turned his gaze back on Bobby. "I'm part of this, Bobby. As more than just the chief of Hanable's Valley PD.

"I know you *think* that Kevin, but—"

"Tell him, FBI. Tell him I have every right to be at this scene."

Meredeth tilted her head to the side and pursed her lips. "You've been at all the scenes since the unsub picked your town."

Bobby lifted an eyebrow at her, and she nodded. "And that's part of my question, Kevin. The question is: *why?* Why have you needed to be at all the crime scenes? What is it about this case that drives you to insert yourself into all of its aspects?"

Kevin's gaze rested on Meredeth, his eyes hardening as she kept silent. "You answered your own question already, kid. I was *asked* to take a deeper interest in this case—by Sheriff Jackstral and by Captain Morgan. So, I'm here. I'm part of this. Understand?" As he said the last word, his gaze snapped to Bobby, and his eyes blazed. "Does that meet with your approval?"

"Woah, there," said Butch. "No reason to get heated."

"No?" demanded Kevin with a hot glance at Meredeth.

"No. Bobby's just asking you what you'd be asking him if the roles were reversed. You know that, Kev," said Butch.

"Maybe," said Kevin, "but that doesn't mean I have to like it. These...insinuations. It's bad enough when an asshole like Goode casts dispersions on my entire career, but to have one of my own do it..." He shook his head, an expression of disgust on his face.

"He didn't mean it that way," said Meredeth, and from the tail of her eye, she saw Bobby turn toward her, a surprised expression on his face.

"No, FBI? Then how did he mean it?"

"Come on, Kevin," she said, her tone going silky and warm. "You know how it is. You're on a case and a question keeps coming up in your mind. You have to answer it or it won't go away. You have to get it out the way, so you can move on to more productive avenues." Bobby's expression darkened.

"He doesn't know better ways to scratch that investigative itch?"

Meredeth shrugged, caught between her partner's suspicion and feelings of betrayal and Kevin's hot rage. "Help him out. Put it to bed."

"So he can trot out his suspicions again tomorrow?" Kevin asked.

"No, so he can move past them."

He looked at her for a moment, his eyes narrowed a little, and then, all at once, he relaxed, a faint smile surfacing on his lips. "Yeah, okay. If I'm completely honest, I'm here for two reasons, Bobby. The first is what I've already said. I've been asked by two men—two friends—at the top of the heap to take a more active role. And, second"—his gaze came back to rest on Meredeth's—"because Meredeth needs my help."

"I do?" she asked, a soft grin on her lips.

"You do. You've got Mr. Sunshine here to ride herd on everyone else, but you need someone to help ride herd on you."

She chuckled. "On me?"

"Yeah, on you. You know it, FBI. You need me standing next to you, helping you look where you don't want to look, to see what you don't want to admit you see."

Butch cleared his throat and looked at his feet.

She lifted her chin a little, her grin fading a touch. "Maybe."

"Maybe? Where would you be right now if I hadn't taken an interest? Those..." He glanced at Butch Schweighart. "You'd never have met Darren, for one thing. You'd never have found that Celtic symbol up in the tree."

"All that's true enough," she said, glancing at Bobby.

He jerked his chin at the ceiling. "Then tell me what you saw up there."

She tilted her head to the side again, and a worry-line appeared between her brows. "How'd you know the scene was upstairs?"

Kevin froze, then forced his muscles to relax. "A house like this? Where else would it be?" He grinned at her. "Besides, I heard your heels on the stairs as you came down."

"Ah," she said. "That makes sense, I guess." Again, she saw Bobby shooting an incredulous look her direction. "Let's put it to bed, then, shall we? Kevin Saunders, are you the .40 Caliber Killer?" She grinned as she asked the question, but his expression tightened.

"No. Categorically, no." His voice was cold, but his eyes blazed at her, his expression knotted with anger. "I can't believe you'd ask me that."

A spike of ice sank into her guts, and she had to stop herself from shuffling back a step. "Come on, I didn't mean it like that."

He turned his glare at Bobby. "Huh. Neither one of you mean it the way it sounds. Maybe it's just me. What about you, Butch? Did it sound like my so-called friends from the Bureau were trying me on as a suspect, or am I just off in left field smelling the goddamn daisies?"

Butch looked at Meredeth, one eyebrow raised a mite. "I don't know, Kevin," he said.

"This is getting out of hand," she said. "I was joking, Kevin. Of course, I don't suspect you. Neither does Bobby—not really. Tell him, Bobby." She made a shooing gesture at her partner, who looked at her as though she'd grown a third eye between her nose and lips. An uncomfortable silence descended around them.

"Well, screw this," said Kevin. He turned and walked out of the kitchen, slamming the door behind him.

Meredeth watched him go, part of her wanting to run after him, to apologize, to smooth it over, the other part of her relieved he was going, that the confrontation was over. Behind her left eye, a coal of white-hot fire sizzled.

"That went well," said Butch in a droll tone. "You always treat your friends this good?"

Meredeth winced, but Bobby said, "Friend or foe, we're here to catch the .40 Caliber Killer. Is that a problem for you, Butch?"

The sergeant held up two thick hands in surrender. "No, not at all."

"Then do you have a better method of ruling Saunders out?"

"Better than all but accusing him outright? Sure. Choose just about anything else."

Meredeth felt heat crawling up her neck and into her cheeks and turned toward the door to hide her flush. "I'm going to the car for a minute. You two work this out. Arm wrestle or something."

She stepped onto the porch just as Kevin closed the door of his cruiser. She raised her hand to ask him to wait, but he didn't even look her direction. As he pulled away, he seemed calm already as if he'd let go of the anger he'd showed in the kitchen. *Or maybe he dropped the act without an audience.* Her brows knitted at that thought, and she stared after the HVPD car for a long time before heading to their car to take more sumatriptan and Excedrin.

CHAPTER 26

PUZZLE PIECES

Buffalo, NY

BUTCH AND BOBBY reentered the kitchen grinning at one another as Meredeth came back inside. *Leave it to Bobby to turn the tables so completely in half a minute.* "Take a peek upstairs?" When Bobby nodded, she glanced at Butch and said, "What joke did he use?"

Butch chuckled. "The one about the FBI, the CIA, and NYPD tracking the rabbit."

Meredeth raised her eyebrows at Bobby. "You haven't even told me that one."

Bobby shrugged with one shoulder. "The FBI, the CIA, and the NYPD get into a pissing contest about who's better at tracking down fugitives. They agree to a competition: tracking a white rabbit in Rockefeller State Park. The FBI organizes a complex system including dogs, the Forestry service, the Hostage Rescue Team, and a thousand agents, including three ex-Green Berets. The CIA uses a spy satellite to take fourteen thousand photos of the preserve, then sends in twelve undercover rabbits while preparing an extraction team in blacked-out helicopters. But before either agency can get a bead on the poor rabbit, the NYPD SWAT team comes rolling out of the forest. They're dragging a hogtied bear behind them, and it's clear NYPD beat the poor brown bear to within an inch of his life. The bear yells, 'Okay! Okay, I'm a rabbit! I'm a white rabbit!'"

Meredeth grinned. "What police department do you use when we're in New York City?"

Bobby's lips twitched in a one-sided grin. "The LAPD, of course."

"And in Langley?"

"The Marshal's Service or the DEA."

"Do you sit around in your hotel room late at night working all this out?"

"Nah," said Bobby. "It's a gift."

"I've got one for you," said Butch.

"Shoot."

"Out of the FBI, the CIA, and the DEA, who is better at finding people?"

"That's an old one," said Meredeth. "The IRS, of course."

Butch grinned and nodded. He sobered after a few moments, however. "Kevin Saunders aside, do you have any suspects?"

"Only about nineteen and a half million or so."

"The entire population of the state, eh?"

"I've been thinking about that, boss," said Bobby. "I think the unsub used your CAC business card for a reason. I think the comments on the walls upstairs underscore that reason."

"Another message?"

"Yes, but a far more *subtle* one. He wants you to know the two cases are related."

Meredeth shook her head and shrugged. "But why? You know as well as I do that the whole 'serial killers want to be caught' thing is a myth."

"Yeah, I know. But why else use that card? If he just wanted to prove he can get close, he'd use your current card. Why else use one twenty years out of date? Why force Goode to write you've spent twenty years protecting New York?"

"Who knows why these guys do anything? Like I told Kevin: deviant behavior doesn't have to make sense."

"But what's he been doing for the last twenty years?" asked Butch.

"Prison, maybe," said Bobby. "It doesn't matter. Not at all."

"Why's that?"

"Because we don't need to know or care what he's been doing for the last two decades. We have what we need to whittle that suspect pool down significantly from that nineteen and a half million souls."

"The geographic profiling?" asked Meredeth, a twinge of excitement dancing in her belly. "Use the last three murders as confidence zones?"

"Yes."

"And these last three crimes—they were opportunistic, right? That means he wouldn't necessarily have stuck to his hunting pattern."

"And, like you said, they would show the most confidence from the unsub."

"Small towns and trailer parks in the previous cases. What kind of threats are there in small towns?"

"Right," said Meredeth. "Neighborhood preference."

"You two mind breaking this down for the big dumb guy?" asked Butch.

"Crime Pattern Theory," said Meredeth. "None of these sites are 'random,' that's another myth. There is a relationship between the offender's mental map—his perceptions of his locality—and the target backcloth."

"What relationship?" asked Butch.

"In the beginning, the unsub's confidence in his ability to get away with his crimes is low." Bobby leaned against the oak cabinets. "He sticks closer to home for the initial hunts and criminal acts. As he commits more crimes, his confidence and level of comfort grow, as does the range he's willing to travel."

Meredeth nodded. "And he might make rational choices when he reaches that point. He might decide to stick close to home, with a buffer zone to divert attention, or he might range far afield, commuting to his hunts, if you will."

"But in either case," added Bobby, "the unsub and the victim have to cross paths somewhere. Maybe he's rambling around the Southern Tier, visiting small towns, stopping off at cafes and the like, scoping out the wait staff."

"Or grocery stores," added Butch. "Everyone has to shop."

"True."

"But if he got away with all those kidnappings," said Butch, "wouldn't his confidence be sky-high? Doesn't that mean this new series would be farther away from his home?"

"The kidnappings were likely his first serious offenses," mused Meredeth. "If that's true, at the beginning, he'd be less confident. He'd stick closer to home, and had he offended constantly for those two decades, his confidence would be high, and what you suggest is what I'd expect. But..."

"But if he didn't, if he was incarcerated, for instance, his confidence would reset?"

"Possibly. We'll see it when we merge the geographic profiles. We need to start mapping out crime scenes, checking for overlapping circles, identifying trailer parks that were skipped."

"I've got a zone map in the car," said Butch.

Meredeth smiled. "We can do better than that, Butch. We've got software for this. We're FBI, remember?" She jerked her chin at the door, and Bobby ran out to the car and fetched his laptop.

They spent the next hour and a half putting the addresses of the newest murders into their localization program and, using those new data points, they tweaked the probability map of where the killer lived tighter and tighter. When they merged the data from the kidnappings with the murders, the threat map drew a tight circle over the southwestern tip of Livingston County.

Butch frowned at the map. "It's so close to the farmhouse."

"That makes sense," said Bobby. "It was an opportunistic crime—the first that broke the trailer park pattern. He probably knew them or was at least acquainted with the family."

"What do we do now?"

Meredeth tapped the town in the exact center of the circle of highest jeopardy. "We start here. In Barkerville. We'll take my profile to the local police department. If we strike out there, we'll move on." She tapped Cooperstown, South Hill, Jonodot, and Yoagoh. "We keep moving through this circle until someone recognizes the profile."

"Simple," said Butch with a wry grin. "The only question is why you didn't do all this sooner."

"Because we couldn't be sure the two series were related. We suspected it, but..." Bobby shrugged.

"But you didn't want to influence anything with mere suspicions."

"Right," said Meredeth. "You'll ride with us?"

"Sure," said Butch. "I can twist an arm or two over there if need be." He glanced at Bobby. "Should I call Kevin?"

"No," said Bobby immediately.

Butch arched an eyebrow at Meredeth, who glanced at Bobby's impassive face and sighed. "He'll pout all afternoon if I override him. We'll go on our own. Kevin will understand after he's had a chance to cool off."

"If you say so," said Butch. "But I think you're wrong to exclude him."

"Will it be a problem?" asked Bobby.

Butch sighed and shook his head.

CHAPTER 27

CIRCLE OF JEOPARDY

Jonodot, NY

BOBBY TURNED LEFT off State Street and pulled into the small commercial parking lot that sat across from the police station and town hall that served both the town and village of Jonodot—a distinction Meredeth didn't quite understand but thought it had to do with historic districts. In addition to the city buildings, the small downtown area boasted a bar and grill with the interesting and imaginative name of Lightyears, a pizza parlor, a sign shop, a florist, pharmacy, a small chain bank, a hair place, a convenience store, and the ubiquitous VFW outpost. It was the fourth such small town they'd visited, and the last one they planned on before heading back to Buffalo for the night.

It was late—just after five—but they'd called ahead and arranged to meet the chief of police, Andrew Warton, and his second in command, Mark Delacey, at the town hall and police station. They crossed Mill Street and entered the red brick building, then made their way to the police department section. After presenting their credentials, they followed a uniformed civilian to the chief's office. Warton smiled at Meredeth and then offered his hand to Bobby and Butch. Mark Delacey slouched against the far wall of the office and nodded while looking bored with the lot of them.

"I think you must be in the wrong place," he said after they'd found their seats. "I can't imagine what business the FBI has in Jonodot."

Butch leaned forward. "Chief, we hope we don't have any business here, for the sake of your community, but these two have done some magic I don't really understand, and as a result of that magic, we think the man we're looking for is in this area. We're hitting all the towns around."

"You're talking about this .40 Caliber guy, right?" Meredeth nodded and opened her mouth to speak, but Warton shook his head. "No, you've got to be wrong. We're a small community. We know each other here, not like in the big cities."

Meredeth smiled across his wide desk. "Chief, that's exactly why we're here. Most often, in cases like this, we are in desperate need of narrowing our field of inquiry, and the .40 Caliber Killer case is no exception. We use these fancy tech tools to help us do just that. In this case, we used a geographical profiling tool to generate a map of likely areas the unsub may reside in. We're here to get your community's help in *excluding* Jonodot. What we'd like to do is circulate our profile, perhaps in the local paper if they run an evening edition, and—"

Chief Warton sniffed. "No, I don't guess we'll be doing that. At least, not until *I've* heard it."

"Fine by me, Chief," said Meredeth. "You'll be more likely to give us an unbiased opinion anyway. The man we're looking for is single, white, and between forty-five and fifty-five. He drives an older vehicle, probably something with a high degree of utility. A Bronco, a panel van, something like that. It's a dark color—blue or black—and well maintained. He's probably outgoing. He's the type who can talk to anyone and put them at ease. He's charming, funny, and probably seems unflappable in most situations, but when he goes off, he *really* goes off. He doesn't share much about his past—probably adeptly turning the conversation back on the other parties involved—but he keeps an extensive journal and holds long-term grudges for things he considers slights. Now, to you and other members of the community, these slights might seem insignificant or in his head."

Warton frowned and glanced at Delacey, who'd straightened up while she spoke and had a telltale line between his brows.

"Something?" asked Meredeth.

"Let's hear the rest of it first," said Delacey.

Meredeth shrugged and went on. "His self-control seems total, except for one situation. He's got a white knight complex. He is overly protective of women and children and might have a few beefs as a result of stepping in and escalating a situation that might have resolved itself otherwise. This is the one thing that can shake his self-control. In fact, as I mentioned earlier, he will seem off the deep end in these situations. He is a phenomenal marksman and probably spends a lot of time at area shooting ranges. He may hunt, and he may poach. He considers himself above most laws, only sticking to them when someone's around to see his behavior. In the public eye, he appears to back you, to back your officers, but when there's no audience, he might sing a different verse. He's careful and meticulous. In fact, he's probably a perfectionist, and when he finishes a project, he expects it to be perfect—and to stay that way. His biggest gripes with others in the community may revolve around his perception that they've ruined, or contributed to the ruination, of one of his projects."

"That thing you said...about the slights and grudges. Talk more about that," said Delacey in a bright tenor.

"He lives with a deep-seated anger, a rage so deep he may not recognize it as such, and he won't have traditional ways of dealing with that anger. His perception of slights is part of his relief valve for that beast within him, and he may seek revenge for those slights, though his revenge will come in passive-aggressive forms. A fender-bender that seems a touch too perfect to be an accident. Chemicals sprayed on a lawn in the dead of night. He may use his charm and social skill to turn other community members against his enemies, or at least try to."

Delacey glanced at Warton and lifted his eyebrows.

"You know someone like I'm describing," she said.

Warton frowned at his desk, then said, "Maybe." He waved his hand. "That thing about the diary."

"Come on, Andy," said Delacey. "She just painted a picture of David Branch and you know it."

"Maybe," Warton repeated with a sour glance at Delacey. "But can you believe Dave is a killer?"

"Maybe not, but that sounds just like him. Remember all that mess with the Planning Committee? And when he busted Pete Rodgers's jaw in the supermarket that time?"

Bobby looked at Meredeth, and she could see his excitement. Trying to sound casual, she asked, "Does Mr. Branch live here in Jonodot?"

Delacey shook his head. "He lives on his farm on the other side of Yoagoh, a few miles south of here."

"Single?" asked Bobby. "Lives alone?"

"Yes," said Warton, "but that doesn't prove anything. Hell, I'm single. Besides, he's had people living with him in the past. He'd have kids—relatives from the City, he said—out to the farm, let 'em stay as long as they wanted or needed to. Sort of an unofficial foster situation."

"Kids?" asked Meredeth, leaning forward. "How old?"

"They'd all be grown by now." Warton turned and looked at his second. "Early twenties by now, most of them. Right, Mark?

Delacey nodded, his eyes glittering. "But that doesn't exclude him. I can tell by how you perked up."

Meredeth flashed him a grin. "No, it doesn't. You and he are of an age?"

Delacey nodded again. "Within a couple of years, I'd guess."

"Guess?" asked Bobby. "You didn't grow up here in Jonodot?"

"No, I did. *He* didn't." Delacey gazed at the ceiling for a moment. "He inherited that farm...what, Andy? Twenty-five years back?"

"About that. His aunt and uncle died in that bad crash out on I-390 in the late nineties. He came a few months after that, took over the farm." He turned and looked at Meredeth. "Though he never so much as started one of those John Deeres. Left the fields fallow, he did, and auctioned off all the equipment. Made quite a stink with the local farmers until he started leasing the land."

"Did he have dealings with the Lancasters over in Wyoming County?" asked Butch.

Warton narrowed his eyes. "Why do you ask that?"

"Did he?" asked Bobby.

"Well, yeah. They've been farming most of his land the past few years. There was some gruff between them last fall, and I don't think Dave extended the lease to them this spring."

"What kind of beef?" asked Meredeth.

"Oh, I don't know. I kind of tune Dave out when he gets on a rant. Something about fair price for the crops. Or maybe crop insurance. All I know is Dave wasn't very complimentary about Jon Lancaster's style of farming—he ran him down pretty good." He grimaced and shook his head. "But it was typical Dave. All words. All vitriol. Now, you want me to believe he trucked over to their place across the state park and murdered them all? Even the babies?" He shook his head again. "That doesn't fit with the man I know. He's all talk. All bluster and hard words."

"Except for Pete Rodgers," added Delacey. "And I bet there are others we don't know about. Other things he did that no one ever caught on to."

"You believe Dave Branch is a serial killer?" asked Warton, his face a study in disbelief. "I'd have thought better of you, Mark."

"I'm not saying it's him," Delacey said with a frown. "I'm saying we need to help them, one way or another. It's our duty." He pumped his shoulders up and down. "And you know what? If Dave is innocent, he'll think this is funny."

Warton puffed out his cheeks and stared down at his blotter. "Yeah. Maybe." He lifted his gaze and met Meredeth's. "We'll take you out to Branch's place. I need to take care of something first, though."

Meredeth nodded and got to her feet. "Thanks, Chief. We'll wait outside."

Fifteen minutes later, Chief Warton came out of his office and locked the door behind him. "We'll take my vehicle," he said. "It's an Expedition—plenty of room if you three don't mind getting cozy."

"We'll follow you," said Bobby. "That way we can move on from there if we can clear Branch."

Warton shrugged and turned away, pulling his keys out of his pocket. "Suit yourselves. You're out front? I'll swing around. Come on, Mark." The two Jonodot cops turned and threaded their way deeper into the building.

Butch, Bobby, and Meredeth left by the front door and crossed over to their car. After they slid into the car, Butch said, "I don't think Warton is playing us straight."

"Why not?"

"Gut. He's...I don't know. I don't think he's exactly lying, but..."

"He's holding things back. Things he knows about David Branch," said Meredeth. "He's friendly with the man. He can't bring himself to believe Branch is dangerous, a serial killer. He doesn't *want* to believe it."

"You believe it?" asked Butch.

With a wry grin, Meredeth said, "He's our best suspect."

"He's the *only* suspect."

"You catch on quick for a big, dumb cop," she said, and Bobby chuckled.

"You think the chief warned Branch?" asked Bobby with an air of speculation.

"Maybe."

"That's obstruction," said Butch.

"Yes, it is," said Meredeth. "Are you going to charge him?"

"Maybe I will," said Butch, gazing across the street at the red brick town building. "If it goes tits up. *If* he did warn the guy."

A large black Ford SUV swung around from State Street, with "JONODOT POLICE" emblazoned on the side over the town's seal. Warton glanced at them from the driver's seat and blipped his wailer once.

Bobby pulled out behind him and followed him south for ten minutes. Warton led them through the "town" of Yoagoh, which was more a collection of street signs, churches, and a few small agricultural support businesses than anything else. The largest building turned out to be the elementary school. Warton continued to the south, cruising another mile and a half before he put on his blinker and wheeled the big Ford onto a gravel lane that twisted back through the trees. Their tires crunched the gravel as they followed him down the road lined with red maples. They crossed a rickety wooden bridge over Yoagoh Creek, then plunged into the forest proper.

"I thought they said he lived on a farm," murmured Butch.

"They did say he let it go fallow."

"Trees like this..." Butch shrugged. "I guess they grow about a foot a year, so twenty years is twenty feet. Still. These woods seem...old."

"Car behind us," said Bobby. "Came in hot from the road."

Meredeth turned and squinted through the gravel-dust that hung in the still air. "Sedan," she said. "It's a..." She frowned. "I think that's Kevin Saunders."

"I thought we agreed—"

"We did," said Butch in a musing tone.

"Then how did he—"

"The chief," said Meredeth, still frowning. "The thing he had to do."

"But why? Why call Saunders?" asked Butch.

"We'll have to ask Warton when we stop." She cast one more glance back at Kevin's cruiser, then turned and looked out the front window. Warton's SUV led them around a tight bend, and they were out of the woods and into an idyllic meadow with fields stretching over the tops of the hills beyond. The meadow was dotted with farm buildings, including a massive barn and a magnificent farmhouse painted titanium white with a bright red door and black shutters. The sun was approaching the horizon behind the house, casting everything on their side of it into shadow.

A man stood on the porch—he seemed so ordinary that he almost blended into the furnishings on his porch—just inside the shadow cast by the porch roof as if he knew exactly where that line fell. He lifted his right hand, his left clasped behind his back. Warton blipped his horn, then slowed to a stop and killed his engine.

"I don't like this," murmured Butch. "Why's he got that hand behind his back?"

"Take it slow," said Meredeth, the calm of hundreds of felony arrests, thousands of confrontations, and twenty-three years of experience asserting itself in her voice. "Bobby, you know what to do."

"Yep." He pulled the car in slightly behind and to the right of the Jonodot SUV, then put the car in park and got out.

Meredeth got out with the two cars between her and the house and watched Kevin crunch up behind them and shut off his engine. She grinned at him, but he didn't even look at her. He got out and walked around the back of his car, his face a stony mask. "Hey, Kevin," she called, but he didn't even slow as he walked over to join the Jonodot officers. She glanced at Bobby and found his eyes tracking Saunders the way a young wolf might warily watch the pack's alpha. "Hang back, Bobby," she said. "Be ready to cover."

"Affirmative," he said without taking his gaze off Kevin.

Meredeth frowned and walked around the back of their car and the Expedition, plastering a smile on her face as she went. She strode up to stand between Butch and Kevin, slightly behind Warton and Delacey.

"Hey there, Andy. Mark," said the man on the porch, his voice a pleasant baritone. His gaze crawled over Kevin, then Butch, then lingered on Meredeth, his expression changing from neutral to one of recognition before ending in a soft smile as he turned his gaze back to Andy Warton. "What brings you out, Andy?"

"You mind showing us your left hand?" asked Butch, his voice an almost-growl.

David Branch cocked his head to the side and flashed a quizzical smile at Meredeth, then turned his gaze on Butch. "Certainly, Trooper. Here goes. Don't shoot me, okay?" His tone gave the lie to the semantics of what he said. He was amused, not scared. He pulled his left hand out from behind his back. It was empty.

"Thanks," muttered Butch.

"What's this about, Andy?"

"These folks have a few questions for you, Dave. To eliminate you from their investigation."

Dave quirked his eyebrow and again glanced at Meredeth. "You're that FBI agent, right? The one that bastard Goode is persecuting?"

"That's Special Agent Connelly," said Delacey.

"Goode was murdered last night, Dave," Warton said softly.

Dammit! Meredeth thought. She watched the man on the porch closely, assessing his reaction, trying to determine if he'd already known that. His face went smooth as he heard and processed the chief's words, but his eyes... *Did they dance for a split second?* she wondered.

"Oh, that's terrible," said Branch. His gaze settled on Meredeth again. "I bet you're relieved, though." He paused, just looking at her. "You are, right?"

Meredeth shook her head. "Mr. Goode was no threat to me, regardless of what he might have thought."

"Right, but still... You don't have to worry about him anymore. No more allegations, no more insults. No more character assassination."

Meredeth shrugged one shoulder. "Those are all true statements, but none of them are worth the lives of Goode and his family." For just a moment, the muscles and skin around Branch's eyes tightened, but then he smiled again and turned his gaze back on Warton.

"You said, 'eliminate you from their investigation.' Am I suspect in the Ankou murders?"

He didn't pronounce it the way the news slinger had been—he pronounced it "ancoo" rather than "ancow." Meredeth kept her face a careful blank, but excitement thrummed through her nervous system, and as she caught Kevin glancing at her from the corner of her eye, she knew he felt it, too. "Most people are still calling him the .40 Caliber Killer," she said with a casual air, "but, yes, that's the investigation Chief Warton is referring to."

David Branch smiled widely and looked at her with cold eyes. "How in the world did my name come up in that mess?"

"Mr. Branch, in my—"

"Call me Dave," said Branch.

"Okay. Dave, in my line of work, 'investigation' means whittling down the suspect pool from huge to as small as we can. We interview tens or hundreds of people just to exclude them. They are technically suspects until we can exclude them, but we don't actually *suspect* them of anything. Does that make sense?"

Again, she got the feeling he was more amused than anything else. "Oh, sure. I imagine your suspect pool is ginormous."

She forced a smile to her lips. "Only about nineteen and half million right now."

He returned her grin easily and nodded. "Then let's make it one less, shall we? Come on in." He broadened his gaze to include them all and waved them up to the porch. Then he turned and went back inside through the red front door.

Branch's home was decorated in a colonial style to match the exterior, but Meredeth didn't see much of the man in the decorations. She suspected he hadn't changed a thing since inheriting the place from his aunt and uncle. "You live here all alone?"

He smiled over his shoulder. "I do now. I'm a confirmed bachelor, though in the past I did host my nieces and nephews. In fact, several of them actually graduated from Jonodot High." He led them into a formal living room and waved them toward seats scattered around the massive fireplace. He stood next to the fieldstone edifice and rested his elbow on the solid slab of cottonwood that served as the fireplace's mantle.

"That was awfully nice of you," said Meredeth.

"They are the children of my brothers and sisters," he said, his eyes resting on hers. "Blood, you know?"

She nodded.

"I played the role of the 'cool uncle' out in the country for their kids when things got tight back home. Oh, nothing so dramatic as abuse or whatever. Standard teenager stuff." He flapped the hand resting on the mantle. "But I'm sure you're not here to hear about my family troubles."

Butch looked around, his gaze lingering on the built-in cabinets filled with Hummel figurines. "Chief Warton said you inherited this place a couple of decades ago?"

"My how times flies," mused Branch. "I suppose it has been twenty-seven years now."

"But you don't farm," said Kevin.

Branch quirked an eyebrow at him.

"No equipment. No tractors. No combine."

The man's unassuming gaze flicked over Kevin's uniform, resting on the stars on his collar. "You've a keen eye, Chief. But, uh, if you don't mind my asking... Why are you here? This is a little outside Hanable's Valley town limits."

"I've been asked to assist in the investigation." As Kevin said it, his gaze flicked toward Meredeth but didn't quite meet her own.

"Ah. To answer your question, no, I don't farm. I have no talent for growing things. Plus, the local farmers were keen to lease my land."

"You mean the Lancasters." Butch's voice was iron-hard.

"And others," said Branch with a shrug. "Jon Lancaster and I ended badly, I'm afraid. We didn't see *eye to eye.*"

Again, Meredeth found his gaze on hers. Again, she sensed amusement in his expressionless gaze. "Can you tell me about your confrontation with Pete Rodgers a few years ago?" she asked.

For a moment, something flickered in Dave's eyes, and he shot a look at Andy Warton. "It was nothing, really. The man is a lout. A drunkard. He was, in public mind you, jerking his poor little girl around like a ragdoll. When his wife said something to him, he gave her such a look." He turned his gaze back on Meredeth. "Anyone who has suffered through abuse would've recognized that look as I did: the promise of pain when the family returned home. I couldn't let that stand." He shrugged.

"You stepped in? Took the law into your own hands?" asked Butch.

Branch flicked a gaze at him that was half amusement, half rancor. "No laws had been broken, Trooper. Should I have called 911 and said Pete gave his wife a dirty look?"

"Yet you *knew* from that single look he was going to hit her?" asked Kevin.

"Like I said, when you've been on the receiving end of a look like that you know." He turned to Meredeth. "Don't you agree, Agent Connelly?"

"I wouldn't know," she said. "But if we can get back to the confrontation itself for a moment... Chief Warton told us you broke the man's jaw."

Branch shrugged. "I told him to cool his jets. He didn't like it."

"And you hit him?" asked Butch.

"Really, Andy, if you were going to blab about that, you could've at least told them the *whole* story."

Warton's face reddened.

"I told them," said Delacey. "The chief had nothing to do with it."

"Well, you, then, Mark." Branch sighed and shook his head. "No, Trooper, I didn't hit him then. We exchanged neighborly pleasantries—the kind I don't want to repeat in the presence of a lady. He took a swing at me, and I told him to cool out, told him I wasn't a kid, I wasn't his wife, I wouldn't stand for his bull—" He cast a quick glance at Meredeth. "His nonsense. He kept coming, kept swinging for the fences." He pumped his shoulders. "I had to put him down to stop it. I guess I hit him a little too hard."

"It takes around a hundred and twenty-five pounds per square inch of force to break a jaw," said Kevin. "That's more than a little too hard for the confrontation you describe."

"My mistake," said Branch. "I paid my fines. Paid Rodgers medical bills, too, though he probably drank that money up the first week he had it. I was angry," he said with a shrug. "And I have PTSD from my own abusive upbringing. Sometimes I just react."

Kevin shrugged.

Butch stood up and peered through the window behind Branch. "You said you live alone?"

"I do. Why?" Branch turned and looked. A twenty-something man stood in the shadows near the big red barn, the Bowie-knife in his fist reflecting house lights back at them. "Oh, my..."

"Who's that?" asked Kevin.

"Is that..." murmured Mark Delacey. His gaze snapped to Dave. "You know him? One of your nephews?"

"No, I've never seen him before. Do you think..."

"We'll check it out. Stay here." Kevin flashed a glance at Butch, then made for the door. As the two left, the young man with the knife turned and disappeared into the gloaming. Bobby flashed a look her way, and Meredeth nodded. He followed them out.

"So much excitement," murmured Branch. "Years of nothing, now the FBI, the NYSP, two police chiefs, and an intruder, all in one afternoon." He glanced at his watch, and as if on cue, Warton's radio squawked.

The chief glanced at Delacey and jerked his chin toward the door. "See what they want, eh, Mark? Unless it's an emergency, have Nancy send Bob out."

Delacey grunted and made for the door.

Meredeth watched Kevin and Butch enter the barnyard, but whoever the young man was, he'd hadn't reappeared. The two cops moved slowly, hands on their holstered sidearms. They stopped about halfway to the barn and exchanged a few words.

"You should go help them, Andy," said Branch. "That ruffian has disappeared into my barn."

"They are armed, Dave, and experienced officers. They can handle it."

"Still... Better safe than sorry, right, Agent Connelly?"

Meredeth tore her gaze from the window, eyes narrowing a little at the man's insistent tone.

The man stared at her, and a slow grin spread across his face. "Well, maybe not then," he said. With a quick grab, he took up the fireplace poker and swung it hard at Warton, bouncing it off the side of the man's head and laying him out sideways on the couch. He turned a predatory grin on Meredeth and slid a step toward her, the poker clenched in his hand. "There now," said Branch. "Alone at last. You shouldn't have brought all these people, Meredeth."

She leaped up, pulling her pistol from its holster with one smooth, automatic motion, bringing it up, but Branch was faster. He darted forward like a master fencer, swung the poker, grinning at the solid thwack it made against her Glock's nylon frame, squashing her fingers between the two, then turned and fled deeper into the farmhouse.

Meredeth's vision was red with agony. She thought he'd broken the bones or knuckles of her middle two fingers, and she could barely keep her fingers wrapped around the pistol's grip. "Bobby!" she shouted. She moved to the couch, keeping her eyes on the hallway Branch had disappeared down, and checked Warton's pulse. Blood ran freely down the man's head, but his pulse was strong.

She grabbed her phone from her back pocket and hit the emergency call button.

"Livingston County 911. What's the address of your emergency?"

"Meredeth Connelly, FBI badge number HS98 84586. I'm at 9517 Old State Road, south of Yoagoh. Officer down, blunt force trauma to the head. Roll medical, roll NYSP SORT. Do it now!"

"Come on, Mercy," called Branch from somewhere in the back of the house. "Hang up the phone or I'll kill someone else. Someone like Bobby or that big bastard from the State Police."

Meredeth grimaced.

"I mean it. I'm as good a shot with a rifle as this pistol. I can take them out easily from here."

"Got to go. Hostage situation." She thumbed the disconnect button praying it was enough, praying backup would come quickly, praying the ambulance would arrive soon enough to save Andy Warton.

"Very good, Mercy. Now, let's play!"

Then the lights went out, plunging her into darkness.

CHAPTER 28

MIND HUNT

Yoagoh, NY

MEREDETH FROZE WHERE she stood, the screen of her phone the only light source, shadows dancing, looming, skittering along the walls. "Bobby!" she shouted.

Deeper in the house, Branch laughed. "I had these walls packed with sound-deadening insulation. He's not coming, Mercy."

"That's not my name!"

"Yes, it is." Branch's voice was flat, devoid of emotion.

She turned on the flashlight built into her phone and then shifted her Glock to her left hand, her phone in her mangled right. She pointed the flash at the window and waved it around, hoping the men outside would see it and—

"Chief?" called Delacey. "Nancy says—"

A spitting sound—the *pfft!* of a silencer—came from the other side of the house, and Delacey grunted and went down.

"Anyway, you'd better hope your buddy doesn't come through that door next," said Branch in a low growl. "You know how good I am with this pistol."

"What do you want?"

"Want?" He chuckled. "Mercy, you crack me up. I have everything I want. *Now.*"

She turned in the direction of the voice, shining her puny light and peering into the shadows, the Glock up in her left hand, ready to fire. She wasn't as good with her left as her right, but she was better than most. "My name is Meredeth Connelly—"

"*Mercy Reynolds,*" he said, talking over her.

She froze, a war on her face. "Kuh... Kenny?" she asked, a quaver in her voice.

When his voice came again, he'd moved...or at least sounded like he'd moved. "Are you going to shoot me, Mercy?" he asked in a singsong voice.

"If you make me. I can shoot left-handed."

"I know that," he said. "Your shooting competitions. I've followed your career for years." He chuckled. "I even did my best to help you."

"To help me? How?"

"I gave you clues. Tips."

She moved away from the couch, putting distance between her and the unconscious chief of police, trying to keep him out of the line of fire. "Tips? Clues? Why..." She shook her head.

"No, go on," said David's voice, sounding impossibly close, but when he spoke next, it sounded far away again. "Ask me anything."

"Who are you?"

"I'm Ankou," he said. "I've already told the world that."

"I mean, what's your name? Kenny? Kenny Reynolds?"

He chuckled, again sounding right next to her. "No, Mercy. Ankou. Just Ankou."

She put her back into the corner where she could glance out into the dark barnyard. Shadows moved there, but whether they belonged to men, she couldn't say. "Are you going to 'free' me like you did those other women?" she asked.

"Maybe. Should I? Do you want me to?" He laughed, and it echoed from the hall. "No, don't answer that. Not yet. I have plans, and they include you, so don't tempt me."

"Plans? What plans?"

"That would ruin the surprise." A door opened somewhere in the house, and a floorboard squeaked. "Do you like surprises, Mercy?"

"Stop calling me that!"

"Why? It's your *name*. Don't you remember?"

She slid along the wall, approaching the hall from an oblique angle, maximizing the cover it afforded her while giving her the best firing line into its dark depths. "I...I didn't know about you, Kenny. I didn't know about Central State.

Dawn didn't tell, worked to make me forget about Laura and Garry, about that night."

A dark chuckle rattled through the house. "Did she now?"

"She thought it would be best. She said you were insane. Violent." Silence greeted that, and she stepped lightly around the corner and into the hall. "Is that why you've done all this? The kidnappings? The murders? To get back at me?"

Again, he didn't answer her.

"Talk to me, Kenny... Help me understand."

"Such an ego," he mused. "Does the sun revolve around you, Mercy, or is it the other way around?"

"Then why?" The darkness around her seemed to breathe, to pulsate with malignancy, but the unsub said and did nothing. She moved forward, sliding one foot in front of her, then moving her weight atop it, her meager flashlight stabbing at the black monster surrounding her. "Kenny, I—"

"Kenny, Kenny, *Kenny*," he sneered.

"What—"

"I thought you were smarter than this, Mercy. Where's that vaunted superpower? Where's the superprofiler gone off to? Or have the drugs dulled your wits?"

A doorway yawned to her left, and she darted a glance into the room, moving her gun hand and head as one unit. It was the kitchen, and it was empty.

"How long have you been watching me?"

"A long time, Mercy. A long time." Something clunked in the darkness. "Whoops. Who put that there?" he asked with a chuckle. "Oh, well. I know everything there is to know about you, Mercy. Things you don't even know. I've made you my life's work."

"I don't understand."

"You will, Mercy. You will, soon enough."

She approached a pair of doorways, one on each side, both open, stygian darkness leering out at her. She flashed her light into the one on the left—a mudroom with a washer and dryer, heaps of old boots, and worn work clothes hanging from pegs. She flipped the phone to the right, and something—*someone*—lunged deeper into the shadows. She tensed and tracked the movement with the business end of her gun but checked herself. Firing blind was stupid—something FBI agents did in movies, not real life. "Is that you, Kenny?"

"Were you born this stupid, or did you have to practice at it?" The voice sounded far away—maybe upstairs.

She slipped her finger over the LED in her phone, blocking the light. She moved into the room on the right—a home office with a rolltop desk, an old wooden chair, and pocket doors leading to the den on one side and the dining room on the other. Meredeth stared at the spot in the darkness where she'd seen movement but could see nothing, *sense* nothing. She held the phone out to her side and moved her finger, washing the corner with light. A coatrack stood in the corner, a trench coat hanging from one of its hooks and waving back and forth, either in the path of a fan or the air conditioner...or as a reaction to someone disturbing it as they passed.

"This is my favorite game. Isn't it a blast?" asked the unsub, sounding as if he were on the other side of the house, in the mudroom or the kitchen.

"Not really," she said.

"Oh, Mercy," he said with a sigh. "You're no fun at all."

"Tell me who you are, and I'll play along. Are you Kuh—"

"Obviously, I'm not David Branch," he said with a chuckle. "He was a loser I met in Virginia. A lucky jerk who was going to sell this place and drink the money away."

She moved into the dining room. A floorboard squeaked, and she froze.

"I know where you are," Ankou sang.

She didn't know how he was throwing his voice around the house, but she was mostly sure he was still on the ground floor. "How did you fake the will of the people who lived here?"

"Fake it? Mercy, I didn't have to. They really did make Branch their sole heir—something he let slip when he was in his cups. I made him disappear, took over his life, then made Aunt Maggie and Uncle Rod go bye-bye. It was easy. These rubes out here never batted an eyelash."

"How many have you killed?"

"A lot. Not enough. From the looks of Delacey when he fell, one more than at the beginning of the evening."

"He said you were friends." She bit her lip, hoping the barb was set.

"Don't be ridiculous. I have only one friend."

Every nerve within her sang with tension, every muscle quivered with a barely restrained urge to run headlong into the darkness. "Who? Me?" He burst into unrestrained laughter, and she moved toward the sound, fast steps, a shark following the scent of blood in the water. The soles of her shoes drummed on the hardwood floors, and the laughing stopped, cut off dead.

"Tricky girl," he said in a low voice. "Tricky, tricky." His thudding footsteps hammered over hers, moving away, moving *around* her, taking doors and passages she knew nothing about. A door snapped open. "Come on down, Mercy. I've got someone down here you're dying to meet."

She stopped short, heart in her throat. "Who?"

"You know who. Come down to the basement."

"Bobby? Kevin?"

"Come to the basement or I'll kill him."

She lunged into the darkness, moving back through the office, back out into the hall, back toward the living room, slowing only as she approached the kitchen. She stepped away from the wall, creeping up on the corner wide, left hand—*pistol*—held straight out in front of her, moving it as she moved her eyes, always in the frame, the Trijicon night sights always in her field of view, snapping from one dark man-shape to the next, pausing only long enough to identify it as an ethereal shadow or a corporeal man.

A door swung on its hinges, squeaking a little, the barest brush of wind on her face, and she stepped into the kitchen, gaze intent on the swinging door. "Kenny?" she whispered.

"I'm not Kenny," said a voice behind her, and she felt the cold cylinder of steel press against the back of her neck and even colder spot in its center. The silencer of his gun. "Dumb move, Mercy." The cold metal pressed into her neck, harder and harder. "I should free you," he snarled. "I should free you right here, right now!"

Meredeth squeezed her eyes shut, wondering if she'd feel the bullet when he squeezed the trigger.

But he didn't. Instead, he sighed and the pressure on the back of Meredeth's neck eased. "What a letdown. I expected better."

"So did I," said Kevin Saunders.

There was a thud, the sound of a butcher's maul striking a cow's forehead, and as the silencer fell away from her neck, Meredeth lunged forward, spinning as she did, bringing her gun to bear, her flashlight dancing, splashing the kitchen with light as she dropped it to the floor.

Kevin held up his hands, his pistol loose in one of them. "Go easy, FBI." He looked down.

The unsub—Ankou, the .40 Caliber Killer, the false David Branch—lay at his feet, blood trickling to the floor from a cut on the back of his head, his eyes rolled up, closed for the season.

Now that it was over, fear exploded through Meredeth, adrenaline fueling its charge, and she lunged across the kitchen and into Kevin's arms. At first, he stood there stiffly, but after a moment, he softened and put his free hand around her. He chuckled, a soft rumble in Meredeth's ear. "Thanks for not shooting me in the office." Her emotions boiled over, and hot tears fell on Kevin's uniform shirt. "Hey. Easy, Meredeth. It's over. We got him."

She nodded against his chest. "We got him," she croaked.

CHAPTER 29

QUESTIONS LEFT UNANSWERED

Buffalo, NY

MEREDETH SAT AND stared across the table at John Doe, formerly known as David Branch, Ankou, the .40 Caliber Killer, and who knew how many other names. Irritation ragged at her nerves, and her head throbbed in response. Her knuckles itched, and she longed to scratch the scars she expected to find underneath the cast. It had taken surgery to correct the damage he'd done to her with the fireplace poker.

Still, it was better than the fractured skull Andy Warton had gotten...better than the pine box Mark Delacey had received. A pang of dark emotion rolled through her, but she forced herself away from those thoughts, forced herself to focus on the man sitting across the table.

"You might as well tell us," Bobby said, his buddy-buddy tone turning Meredeth's stomach and making her head throb. "They'll try and convict you either way. John Doe is good enough for the courts."

"It had better be," said the man in the orange jumpsuit, "because you'll never know my real name."

"What did you do with the kids?" Meredeth demanded, leaning forward.

"I shot them. You saw their bodies."

"Not those kids. The ones from twenty years ago. The ones we never found."

A small smile twisted his lips. "Took you long enough to get around to that, Mercy."

"Stop calling me that. It's not my name."

He treated her to a dismissive shrug. "Yes, it is."

"No, it's Meredeth. Now and forever." Her lip curled, and he smiled. "Don't you want me to know? Are you ashamed?"

"Not at all." He grinned wider. "It's just that you want to know so very badly." He pressed his lips together and mimed turning a key.

Meredeth shrugged. "Did you really know my brother?"

John mimicked her shrug. "I know Kenny. I've known him since Central State Hospital."

"You were a patient there?" she asked casually.

"That's for me to know, and you to find out."

"Where is he?"

"I'm not going to tell you that. When he wants you to know, he'll tell you himself."

"But he's alive? Is he..." She glanced up at the camera watching them. "Is he like you?"

John smiled and spread his hands.

Meredeth puffed out a breath. "This is a waste of time, Bobby." The cell phone in her pocket vibrated, notifying her of a new text, and she repressed a smile. It was a new phone, a *private* phone, and only one person had the number—Kevin Saunders. She *hadn't* written the number on the back of her business card.

"I don't think so," said Bobby, making eye contact with John Doe. "I think he wants to tell us something. He asked for this meeting after all. Am I right, John?"

John's shoulders pistoned up and down. "Could be, *Bobby*. Then again, it could be I like pulling Mercy's—I mean *Meredeth's*—strings."

Meredeth shook her head. "I'm done with this," she said, scooting back her chair and getting to her feet. "Let's get out of here. We can still make the 3:30 to Dulles."

"Oh, don't go," said John Doe, chuckling. "We're just getting started."

"No, we're done," she said and turned toward the door.

"Wait. I've got a lot to tell you."

She shrugged without turning. "You had your chance to tell me face to face. Have your lawyer write me a letter."

"I'm going *pro se*."

"Then you're an idiot. *You* write me the letter. Maybe I'll even open it."

"Maybe I'll send you another special email..." John smiled. "What I have to say, you'll find very interesting."

"Nah. That's the thing. Since Douglass's book, all of you think all of us are enthralled by your *intellects*, by your *mystery*." She waved the four fingers she could. "You think we all find you oh-so-interesting."

"And you don't?" he asked with a smug smile.

"No. I think you're on the level of pond scum intellectually and about as interesting. You're no different to me than any other scumbag skulking around in the darkness, taking potshots at innocent people. And Douglass and Ressler already talked to all the *interesting* people. You're nothing special."

Doe leaned back in his chair and smiled. "Wrong again, Meredeth. I'm something new. No one's ever talked to someone like me."

"Sure, sure," she said and rapped on the door with her left hand.

"You shouldn't be so nasty, Mare. You don't mind if I call you 'Mare' do you? I mean, you shouldn't. Not with those teeth and that horsey way you walk."

She glanced back at him, smiling. "Oh, you cut me." She rolled her eyes.

John sniffed. "Anyway, when you come back, I might not be inclined to talk to you."

"Didn't you hear me? *I'm not interested in what you have to say.*"

"Oh, I heard you, Mare. But I know something you don't."

With a sigh and a roll of her eyes, Meredeth turned back and lifted her hand. "What? Last chance."

He narrowed his eyes at her, a small grin playing on his lips. "No, that's no fun. That would ruin the surprise."

"Then..." Meredeth made it halfway around.

"I know you'll be back because I know what's about to happen out there, Mare. And it's all for you. I know who's going to be doing what, and where. And I should, after all. I've taught them everything they know."

"Who? You've taught who?"

"My children, of course."

"Your what?" Bobby asked in a cold tone.

John smiled at him. "My kids." He turned a piercing gaze on Meredeth. "I really did have kids living on that farm. They just didn't belong to my fictional siblings. They belonged to me. Ever since I took them."

Strength drained out of Meredeth's legs, making her long for a chair to collapse into. "The kidnappings," she whispered. "All those children."

John smiled. "I made the perfect family. I was a good father. I taught them how to make their way in the world. I *prepared* them for what's coming. I helped them make their first kills."

Meredeth closed her eyes. "They were just kids."

"Sure, when I freed them from their miseries. But I helped them grow. I helped them learn their own dark depths."

"All that shit in the barn," Bobby said breathlessly. "Those boxes with the padlocks.

John shrugged. "They needed to learn to be quiet before they could learn to shout their barbaric yawps over the roofs of the world."

"You..." Meredeth shook her head. "You twisted them to be like you."

"No, Mare. I *freed* them from being like you. It's a better way of life. You'll see." He grinned and winked at her. "You'll see very soon." He looked up at the camera. "I'm ready to go back to my cell now." He turned his gaze back on Meredeth, pinning her where she stood. Fire danced in his gaze—hot and hateful. "I'll see you real soon, Mare." His face devolved in a mass of twitches into a grimacing snarl. "*Real soon!*" he rasped, spittle flying.

I HOPE YOU'VE enjoyed *Mercy Forsaken* and would kill to get your hands on the next installment. The second book in the series is titled *Her Last Sunset*, and you can find it on Amazon: https://ehv4.us/4herlastsunset.

To be among the first to know what I'm up to and when the newest book I write goes live, please subscribe to my newsletter at https://ehv4.us/vvjoinehv or join my online community at https://ehv4.us/discord. You can also support me on Patreon at https://ehv4.us/patreon.

You can find my complete thriller bibliography at https://ehv4.us/booksehv. I also write supernatural fiction, and you can find my bibliography under the name Erik Henry Vick at https://ehv4.us/books.

Books these days succeed or fail based on the strength of their reviews. I hope you will consider leaving a review—as an independent author, I could use your help. It's easy (I promise). You can leave your review by clicking on this link: https://ehv4.us/2revmf

AUTHOR'S NOTE
5/11/22

WHEN I RETURNED to writing fiction, supernatural fiction and horror were my passions as a reader, so naturally I started my fulltime writing journey there, and it was a blast. I met a ton of new friends and found a wealth of readers who are suffering from the same or similar conditions as my own Personal Monsters™—Petunia, my name for my Rheumatoid Arthritis nonsense, and Frangipani, my name for my Fibromyalgia. I still love all things supernatural, but last year, I decided to try a story without any demons, any errant gods, and where the ugliness is all human, all the time.

If you've read my earlier work (see https://ehv4.us/books for my horror, DF, and UF bibliography), you' know I almost always include a law enforcement character on the side of the "good guys" and a serial killer or two in league with the "bad guys" (demons, in other words). Writing a book about an FBI superprofiler who is suffering through a new medical condition as she hunts a serial killer was a natural and easy next step I did go back and forth on whether to try this pen name in traditional publishing circles, but in the end, didn't have the patience for that.

When I'm on the trail of a hot and exciting story, it's all I want to write, at least for the first little while, which is good news for you if you loved Meredeth Connelly and Bobby Van Zandt. There is a lot more to come—John Doe's malignant plan for Meredeth and society at large is a huge, complicated scheme, and it will take Meredeth thousands of pages to unravel it,...if she can.

I have a lot of stories to share with you. I hope you'll stick around. I also want to personally invite you to join my online community, Vick's Vikings, at: https://ehv4.us/discord—it's free. I'm also on Patreon with a ton of benefits. Check it out at https://ehv4.us/patreon. I appreciate every subscription, but it isn't required for anything but the addition benefit at each tier.

PATRON RECOGNITION

A BIG VIKING hug to all of my patrons!

    Special thanks to Dawn Bogue and an anonymous patron for being the first of hopefully many patrons of the upper tiers.

ABOUT THE AUTHOR

E.H. VICK IS THE pen name for critically acclaimed, bestselling, and award-winning horror author Erik Henry Vick. He specializes in pulse-pounding stories filled with nail-biting tension—usually involving serial killers as villains and psychologically-flawed protagonists. As an author disabled by autoimmune diseases (also known as his

Personal Monsters™), Vick writes to hang on to the few remaining shreds of his sanity. He lives with his wife, Supergirl; their son; a Rottweiler named after a god of thunder; and two extremely psychotic cats. He fights his Personal Monster™ daily with humor, pain medicine, and funny T-shirts.

With a B.A. in Psychology, an M.S.C.S., and a Ph.D. in Artificial Intelligence, Vick has worked as a criminal investigator for a state agency, a college professor, a C.T.O. for an international software company, and a video game developer.

He loves talking to his readers, so please email him at berserkerik@ehvick.com--he tries to respond to everyone.

He'd love to hear from you on social media:
Website: https://ehvick.com
Facebook: https://fb.me/ehvick
Amazon author page: https://ehv4.us/amaehv
Goodreads Author Page: https://ehv4.us/grehv
BookBub Author Profile: http://ehv4.us/bbehv

Made in the USA
Columbia, SC
19 December 2023

28957546R00222